Italian Rules

Or

The Three Endings of Toni Fausto

Tom Benjamin

CONSTABLE

CONSTABLE

First published in Great Britain in 2022 by Constable

1 3 5 7 9 10 8 6 4 2

A CIP catalogue record for this book
is available from the British Library.

ISBN: 978-1-40871-549-9

Typeset in Adobe Garamond by Initial Typesetting Services, Edinburgh
Printed and bound in Great Britain by Clays Ltd, Elcograf S.p.A.

Papers used by Constable are from well-managed forests
and other responsible sources.

MIX
Paper from
responsible sources
FSC® C104740

Constable
An imprint of
Little, Brown Book Group
Carmelite House
50 Victoria Embankment
London EC4Y 0DZ

An Hachette UK Company
www.hachette.co.uk

www.littlebrown.co.uk

For Russell

Chapter 1

The finale, the final twist: the private snoop keeps pace with Ursula through the red city while fresh-faced company clerk Maurizio fusses over the lunch table set for two.

The camera tracks Ursula along the portico, that pulsing synthesiser accompaniment and her blond feathered hair very much dating the film to the mid-1980s.

A BACK SHOT down the seemingly endless portico of Bologna's Via Saragozza, stretching ahead like a target. FRONT SHOT: in her low-cut blue dress and white heels, Ursula is swallowed by the shadows, bleached by shards of light.

CLOSE UP of the chopping knife Maurizio is using to slice the tomatoes.

It is the denouement of wrought (some critics say over-wrought) *giallo*-cum-melodrama *Amore su una lama di rasoio*, literally, *Love on a Razorblade*, which would be retitled *Bad Blood* for its English language release: austere, widowed factory boss Vittorio, played by American star Ron Manchester, dubbed in Italian, goes to pieces over his sexually voracious new wife, who in his jealousy he pushes into the arms of another man. But which man?

Maurizio starts at the sound of the buzzer, slicing his finger. As he goes to the door, the shot lingers on the track of blood along the knife edge.

Sucking his injured digit, the young man awkwardly opens the door with his left hand, and in steps . . .

Deborah, the boss's young secretary.

'What happened?' She takes his hand away from his mouth.

'Accident.' Deborah, who until now has been depicted as a paragon of virtue and Catholic morality, takes Maurizio's finger and – CLOSE UP – slides it into her mouth.

CUT to a shadow falling across an editing block. Franco, played by smouldering George Malouf, also dubbed in Italian, looks up, a strip of film in one hand, razorblade in the other. Ursula, Italian actress Vanessa Tramonte, begins to say something but Franco already has hold of her, is pressing his mouth against hers. He pushes her backwards, grips hold of her thighs, pulls her dress up to expose her lime panties, props her against the edge of a desk and wrenches her bare thighs apart.

Ursula shoves him away. He stumbles back, a hand – nice detail this, considering this is one of the twentieth-century's great heartthrobs we're talking about – still inside his unbuttoned flies.

'It's over,' she says.

'What are you talking about?'

'That's why I came – to tell you.'

'Are you crazy?'

'Yes, I'm crazy – and that's why it has to end.'

'You know you want me,' says Franco. 'You know this will never end.'

'I mean it.' But this time she doesn't resist. Does she want him too much? Or is she thinking: *one last time, then I'll go.* What hasn't been explicit until this moment is what her unspoken interactions with her husband in the last third of the movie have amounted to: that even as Vittorio's obsessive jealousy has secretly grown – to the extent that he has put a tail on his wife – Ursula has come to appreciate how much she loves him following an attempt on his life by communist terrorists. She has finally decided to commit herself to her husband.

Only her husband is standing at the open editing room door.

It is a powerful and excruciatingly uncomfortable scene because it does not end there. The lovers continue to make love. Ursula gasps, wrapping her arms, her long legs around Franco's back.

WIDE SHOT framing a tableau of three, the camera moving leisurely forward across the gloomy editing suite with its pools of artificial light, passing the rutting couple, until it finally ZOOMS IN on Vittorio's – Ron Manchester's – weathered face, those bloodshot eyes. EXTREME CLOSE UP. The reflection of the couple, an ingenious effect, captured in his pupils.

The couple climax. Are frozen in their embrace in those black orbs.

The shot begins to withdraw as they do. Vittorio remains the motionless spectator while Ursula lowers her legs, releases Franco's neck from her grasp. They begin to rearrange themselves, and only then do they see him, and see the revolver in Vittorio's hand. And now Franco says it, the word that makes this betrayal far, far worse than with any vigorous office clerk:

'Brother.'

Chapter 2

It smelled of olden times, of past places and things – of those celluloid spools hung along metal racks, loose film curling downwards like monkey tails.

It was the dusty, vinegary odour of dangerous, potentially flammable substances that evoked memories of a pre-digital age when everyone smoked and had plenty of excuses for not knowing better. I felt nostalgic for about as long as it took it to trouble my sinuses, then I wanted out.

'Can you show us precisely where the film should have been?' I tried to keep the irritation from my voice, but Italians would insist on their lengthy preambles. I usually went along with them, but I usually wasn't cooped up in an airless ante-room. Through a Perspex window running the length of the wall, I could guess where the next door led: a bright, sterile contrast with this gloomy past – a properly airtight lab peopled by workers kitted out in hooded white boiler suits as they painstakingly restored frame after precious movie frame on high-tech machines.

'I was explaining how the Moviola machine worked . . .' The chief archivist stood before a green metal beast with four legs, pedals, and between a pair of chunky, shoulder-like canisters, a viewfinder sprouting toward us.

I turned to Dolores: 'I think we've got it, haven't we?'

'I was interested in what the signora was saying about sound. I've always wondered why our old movies appeared dubbed even when all the actors were Italian, and they were clearly speaking Italian . . .'

'But I don't see how that relates to the missing negatives,' I said testily. 'Unless you have any suggestions, signora?'

'I couldn't say – I mean, *you're* the detectives.' She fingered the chunky wooden beads of her necklace like a rosary. It had probably been picked up on holiday in Africa or South America with the kind of tour group that specialised in detail-hungry teacher and librarian types on a modest budget. She was wearing a similarly bazaar-bought, densely patterned silk shawl above a loose-fitting, dark cotton dress, along with sandals made out of recycled materials. Her grey hair was tied back with a burnt orange elephant-print band.

'It's the atmosphere in here,' I said. 'Would you mind if we stepped outside?'

'That would be the cellulose nitrate,' she said loftily. She nodded to her assistant, a skinny young woman dressed head to foot in black with matching oversize glasses. 'We're currently restoring a print of Buster Keaton's *The Electric House*, a full length feature from 1923. We were sent it by Yale Film Labs . . .'

We followed the assistant through a side exit onto a platform overlooking a brick walled former factory space, now the CineBo library, Signora Varese rattling on about the technical challenges that had defeated even the Americans.

CineBo was the pre-eminent film lab in Italy and one of the best in the world, holding tens of thousands of films in its archive in a former tobacco factory situated only five minutes across the road from our office in Via Marconi. It was a huge presence in Bologna – a 'film city' inside the walls, comprising not only of the archive and restoration wing but also, across the scrappy Parco Settembre 11, a cinema complex on the site of a former slaughterhouse, plus a giant screen every summer in the main square, Piazza Maggiore, which featured a range of films, from recent restorations to popular movies and classics, often accompanied by a live orchestra, free to the public. Projected against the backdrop of those Renaissance arcades and the looming, copper green dome of Santa Maria della Vita, it was *Cinema Paradiso* on steroids.

So in a sense, and certainly in a very Italian sense where municipal trumped national pride, we all had a stake in keeping news about the missing movie quiet, especially with the pending arrival of legendary American director Indigo Adler to film a remake of *Amore su una lama di rasoio* – which he had decided to re-christen *Love on a Razorblade* – and the much heralded screening of a fresh print of the original at CineBo, which was scheduled to be introduced by the renowned director.

Only when the time had come to book the negatives out, they were nowhere to be found.

In contrast to the library, where through the arched windows the spring sky was painted an unmistakably Italian azure, the windowless archive could have been anywhere in the world. This was where those thousands of films were stored, neatly stacked in flat grey boxes on metal racks, their titles written in thick black felt-tip.

The entire history of Italian cinema was represented, beginning at the 1890s and encompassing early talkies, Fascist propaganda, prints by neorealist greats like De Sica and Rossellini, plus a comprehensive range of *gialli* – exploitation thrillers – and westerns, alongside additional bequests from non-Italian cinema greats like David Lean, Charlie Chaplin and Buster Keaton.

It was air-conditioning cool, presumably to preserve the film stock, and although a stale, dusty smell dominated, there remained that tang of acetate.

A crashing sound came from the far end, followed by the timpani of colliding metal canisters. They settled with a shiver upon the concrete floor.

We followed Signora Varese's rapid progress along the outer lane, clearly about to give some benighted fool a bollock-ing, only to find CineBo's director, *dottore* Rocco Domori, sitting with a curly haired young woman, the pair of them surrounded by open boxes. Seemingly random spools of film topped precarious-looking towers of metal canisters.

'Dottore.'

The director held up his hands. 'Forgive me, Donatella, but, well, you see, I had this idea . . . I couldn't resist . . .'

'I told you, *dottore*, I went through the entire rack person-ally, very thoroughly. Very thoroughly, indeed.'

'I know, it was just . . .' The director pulled himself up by one of the shelves. I noticed the chief archivist wince. 'I didn't think it would do any harm.'

'Director,' she said, 'I don't know how they did things in

London, but here we have different standards. The spools! They shouldn't be exposed like this. Gloria,' she meant her assistant, 'help Valeria sort this out.'

The director, now on his feet, could clearly see this was not a battle worth fighting. He turned to us.

Despite having been sitting cross-legged on the floor, *dottore* Rocco Domori was dapper in a natty navy-blue suit with a silver silk tie. With his square-cut grey goatee and what was left of matching hair shorn neatly around the sides, he looked as if he only lacked a carnation for his wedding. I was pleased I'd made the effort to wear a suit, and asked Dolores to dress accordingly, albeit she had gone with her habitual 'vintage' look: in this case a black seventies trouser suit, although beneath those bell bottoms I knew lurked a pair of trainers.

'Daniel? A pleasure to finally meet you.' He held out a manicured hand. A few years ago I might have taken umbrage at being addressed in English – as a sign, perhaps, that I hadn't yet mastered Italian – but now I took it for what it usually was, an opportunity for my interlocutor to practise, or show off, their language skills. 'The Comandante mentioned you at one of our burraco evenings: Bologna's very own English detective! It sounds like the plot to a film – you haven't thought of writing a script, I presume?'

'I haven't had the time.'

'I expect Giovanni keeps you busy!'

I found it hard to imagine my father-in-law, and boss, the Comandante, chatting airily about me at his weekly card sessions, but then I found it equally difficult to picture the slick *direttore* here, participating in them.

Rocco Domori had been an assistant director at the British

Film Institute, and previously at Munich's cinema museum before being recruited to head up CineBo. I had always considered those weekly burraco nights held at the exclusive members-only club Cisalpina exclusively for old folk, but apparently they were a hot ticket.

'I guess you're now satisfied these negatives aren't where they're supposed to be,' I said in Italian. I took in the vastness of the room. 'And you say you've checked the rest of the archive?'

'Thoroughly,' said the chief archivist. She glanced at her new boss. 'We have an extremely strict policy in place, maintained by our qualified professionals, to ensure this kind of thing does not happen. This is not a public lending library.' Signora Varese seemed part offended, part relieved by our presence – *only* something that merited the involvement of private investigators could begin to explain this phenomenon.

'And who has access?'

'Exclusively members of the archive department.'

'You. Gloria, here,' I looked at the woman on the floor. 'Valeria, I think you said?'

'Oh no, Valeria is the director's secretary.'

'I have the access code,' said the director. 'I asked Valeria to help me.'

'But obviously you, *direttore* . . .'

'Please, Daniel – Rocco.'

'Rocco. But you've never actually put anything here.'

'*Oh no.*' Another gesture of surrender to Signora Varese.

'And the film was donated by . . . ?'

'The estate of Toni Fausto,' said the director. 'It had been held in a vault together with his papers. The masters to *Amore su una lama di rasoio* were bequeathed to us, but we had to bid for the papers, a joint bid, in fact, along with the National Museum of Cinema in Turin. However, these were purchased by signor Adler.'

'The American director,' I said. 'He must be a real fan.'

'You could say that,' he nodded. 'Look,' he took me aside. 'The Comandante said you might be able to . . . *turbo charge* our investigation here because, well, time is pressing, and the *reputational damage* of this loss being discovered . . .'

Behind him, I noticed Valeria pass some kind of over-sized video cassette to Gloria but in doing so brush against one of those stacks. It began to sway as if in slow motion. Gloria yelped and Valeria turned to grab it, but too late: it exploded, scattering another stack of films across the floor.

In the accompanying hullabaloo, Dolores and I took the opportunity to take our leave.

'What are you thinking, Dan?' she asked as we headed back up the outer lane.

'Whatever the chief archivist might say about her highly trained professionals, it's possible someone simply screwed up. Maybe one of the young ones lent them out and forgot to book it into the system and now it's set off this shit show they're too terrified to fess up. See if you can get pally with the assistant archivist, maybe she'll let her guard down.'

We walked the lanes, Dolores starting at one end, me the other. I crouched, peering beneath the shelves for a tell-tale sliver of film, but apart from dust, a ballpoint pen and some loose change, found nothing.

I met Dolores mid-way. 'Anything?'

She shook her head. 'Well . . .'

'What?'

Between the tips of her fingers she produced an empty condom wrapper. 'It was underneath.'

'And what does that tell us?' She looked at me like I was mad.

'That people are having sex?'

'Somewhere they're not meant to. Unless Signora Varese is more liberal than we thought.'

'No CCTV in here,' said Dolores.

'A condom – young folk.'

'Why do you say that?'

'They're more careful, and more reckless. In *here*? Either they can't keep their hands off each other or they live with their parents. And I can't exactly see Donatella at it with Rocco.' Dolores pulled a face.

'It also tells us that the chief's rules exist solely for her,' I continued. 'Her staff definitely break them. Shame the used condom's not inside, we could have run a DNA check.' Dolores's look of disgust became total. 'But I guess there's CCTV on the outside . . . and only one way in and one way out . . .'

'There's an emergency exit at the far end of "XYZ",' said Dolores. 'But it's alarmed.'

We went to take a look. The standard double doors with a pair of push bars, above them – lurid yellow warnings that the exit was, indeed, alarmed.

'Judging by where it's situated,' I said, 'I'd guess this leads onto the park.'

'We could check outside.'

'Or we could . . .' I placed my hands on the bars.

'Dan!'

I pushed, readying myself for bells or sirens. Nothing.

'Maybe it's a silent alarm?' said Dolores.

We stepped onto a concrete stoop which sloped onto one of the sandy paths cutting through Parco Settembre 11. I looked up. There was no CCTV above the exit. No CCTV back here at all.

'There's that, though.' Dolores pointed to the set of cameras crowning a lamppost by the children's play area.

Beyond them, the flat park ended at another set of old industrial buildings constituting more of CineBo, plus a university hall of residence and the communications faculty.

'I can't hear the fire brigade, yet,' I said.

'Perhaps they've got silent sirens,' said Dolores.

We stepped back inside. 'Is the alarm broken, switched off, or simply a fake? Check that.'

I began to close the doors, but noticed a sliver of card wedged just beneath a bottom hinge. I pulled it out: a torn piece of a CineBo programme. Shaped like a ragged archipelago it fit into the palm of my hand. Still, I could clearly make out part of what appeared to be a name in capitals AWA, a slippered foot, and few words like an especially obscure haiku.

> *the for*
> *ronin come*
> *villagers hop*
> *defeat for us, but a*

'You picked up a programme earlier, didn't you?' I said. Dolores pulled it out.

'Look for Kurosawa's *The Seven Samurai*.'

'How do you know that?'

'Isn't it obvious, *dottoressa* "I studied Latin and Ancient Greek"? Remember when you took the mickey out of my degree "watching films all day"?'

Dolores opened the programme but couldn't find anything that resembled our piece of card. 'All right,' I said. 'Let's find out when they last screened *The Seven Samurai*, and if we can match the entry to a specific programme. That should enable us to date it back to when the door was opened – and kept ajar. What?'

'You look like the cat that got the cream,' said Dolores.

'I admit,' I smiled, 'I never considered it a particularly practical degree, but neither was your Latin and Greek, and that's not done us any harm.'

'*Eia igitur, age, et portas clauderent.*'

'Oh, and what peculiar morsel of Roman wisdom is that?'

'Close the doors and get a move on – it's lunchtime.'

Chapter 3

CLOSE UP of the revolver, the length of its barrel, the lead-grey domes of the bullets in the chamber.

CLOSE UP of Franco's face, George Malouf looking at once defiant and resigned. It is a quarter of a century since the Franco-Lebanese actor made his Hollywood debut, but the actor still brims with the sensual power that his 'brother' Vittorio, the then seventy-four-year-old Ron Manchester playing a man perhaps ten years younger, plainly lacks. But what Vittorio misses in potency, he makes up for with power, and isn't this the theme of the film? The tension between the powerful and powerless, young and old – in this case during 'boom years' Italy, whether it is the communist students attempting to assassinate stolid factory owner Vittorio, or his little brother sleeping with his wife. In this context Ursula might be seen to represent Italy herself, given what transpires next.

With a shouted 'No!' she steps in front of Franco to shield him from her husband at the very moment Vittorio pulls the trigger.

The bullet hits her square in the chest, the violence of the act portrayed with brutal realism, the force slamming her against her lover, who stumbles back, reaching out to grab hold of her but failing as she falls through his arms.

He looks down, horrified.

The closing shot from above as bright red blood spills from the corner of Ursula's mouth.

CREDITS.

'So, what do you think?'

'It's fun watching films at work,' said Jacopo. 'Even old ones. I can see why you did it for your degree.'

'I always hated that ending,' said Dolores. 'Such an Italian cliché. The men do the dirty and the woman pays the price.'

'Well,' I said. 'It was of its time and, as I was explaining, it's symbolic.'

'If you believe any of that,' said the Comandante.

'*Et tu, Giovanni?* Cut me some slack.' The Comandante, who was two years older than Ron Manchester when he shot *Amore su una lama di rasoio*, shrugged.

We were in the boardroom of Faidate Investigations: myself and Dolores, who had recently been promoted from trainee to fully-fledged 'Investigator', Jacopo – Giovanni's son and our tech guy – the Comandante himself, fresh from his weekly trip to the barber's to have his grey beard trimmed, a manicure and a few air snips around his thinning hair, and Alba, his niece and our company administrator, who was heavily pregnant and perfectly asleep, sitting at the far end of the polished oak table, snoring lightly.

I had enjoyed learning more about director Toni Fausto, who began his career in neorealist cinema before helming innumerable *gialli* – basically garish crime dramas – and westerns, while outside the studio becoming a high-profile champion of the radical left, including paramilitary factions like *Lotta Continua* which had, presumably, sealed his fate: gunned down by fascist terrorists on the set of *Love on a Razorblade* before its completion in a grim parallel with the shooting of Ursula.

It was this, I think, that provided Fausto with the aura that had fascinated generations of film buffs, American celebrity director Indigo Adler among them. His 'manifesto to produce cinema for the masses' had given lovers of trashy films the kind of intellectual cover it provided the director himself for what remained an extremely lucrative enterprise, his subsequent on-set martyrdom cementing his place in the nerd pantheon of fallen film greats.

'I guess his assassin is out of gaol now,' I said.

'Assassin.' The Comandante half pulled out a cigarette but, stilled by Dolores's scowl directing him towards Alba, slid it back in. 'A number of people were implicated in the crime and convicted of being accessories to his murder, along with an equally large number of other, related offences, but no single individual was ever convicted for pulling the trigger, as such.' The Comandante, who back then had belonged to the Carabinieri's Special Operations Group, would know.

'But despite the . . . vagaries of the justice system,' I said, 'you must have had a pretty good idea who actually did it.'

'On this occasion, no. It could have been any number of individuals, or none of them. Certainly, we found no forensic or material evidence pointing to a single individual. It could just as likely have been someone from outside brought in. In fact, that was the theory – a gunman from Rome, possibly. Or sub-contracted to organised crime. We were lucky to get the convictions we did, although naturally as a result, the Left claimed we were in cahoots with the killers.' Another shrug, the cigarette pulled half out, pushed back in again.

I looked at Jacopo. 'Perhaps now it's time to . . .'

'Oh, right.' He nudged Alba, who woke with a start. There was an *attimo* – less than a second, more than a moment – when I considered teasing her, but decided against it. Although it was all family here – well, Dolores excepted – Alba wasn't having the easiest pregnancy, yet had insisted on coming in.

'We've been so busy following up leads,' I said. 'I thought it might be a good idea to actually watch the film. You never know – the answer might be staring us in the face.'

I was greeted by my team staring me in the face – blankly. I pressed on: 'Why *this* film? Why *these* negatives? Was there anything you saw that sparked any ideas? How about the cast?'

'I don't believe Mr Manchester and Mr Malouf are any longer available for comment,' the Comandante said dryly.

'But the younger actors probably still are,' said Alba. 'We could ask them.'

'This Pierluigi Affronto,' Dolores looked up from her phone. 'Who wrote the soundtrack. Isn't he quite famous now?'

'A good point,' I said. 'We can check the other credits.'

'Surely, Daniel,' said the Comandante, 'we have higher priorities.' He pulled the cigarette full out of the pack and began tapping the tip against the table.

I had hoped that showing the film might prompt that most Anglo-Saxon phenomenon – a brainstorm – but thinking out of the box was anathema to the Comandante's generation of Italians. To them, boxes generally served one purpose – to put things in.

All right, I would have another go when he was out of the way because, two days on from our visit to CineBo, while we were apparently edging closer to understanding *what* had happened to the negatives of *Love on a Razorblade*, we were still some way off from understanding *why*.

Alba had managed to wangle access to the CCTV in the playground. Although the camera did not point directly to the exit of the archive, it did reach up to the part of the path that ended at the concrete stoop. As for the alarm system – it turned out it should have been working but wasn't. After they had got the contractors down it was discovered a fuse had blown. How long it had been that way was anyone's guess.

We had dated the torn CineBo programme to the previous year which had given Jacopo a starting point with the CCTV, and after a couple of days squinting at grainy footage, he seemed to have come up with something pretty strong:

'You see this guy.' He paused the bleached image. 'I've tried to blow it up, used all kinds of software to enhance it, but the cameras are focused on the play area, so everything beyond is unfocused, fuzzy.'

'Jeans, jacket, baseball cap,' said Dolores. 'Well, it looks like a male, but it could be a woman.'

'Walks more like a man,' I said.

'And how does a man walk?' said Dolores.

'Well, less like a woman . . . you know, wiggly.'

'Do I walk "wiggly"?'

'No, Dolores, you do not walk wiggly.'

'Well then.'

'Can we have a consensus around the table – male or female?' The consensus among the men was male.

'It's obviously a bloke,' said Alba. 'He walks like Dolores.' She seemed to find this hilarious.

Jacopo pressed Play again. The video had been taken at three o'clock in the morning. Beyond the swings, a man, and let's call him a man, walked along the path toward the rear of CineBo, disappearing in and out of the lamplight glare.

He slowed as he neared the section where the path forked around the park toward the exit of CineBo. Stopped, took a careful look around, before striding forwards, and out of shot.

'He's gone for four minutes, thirty seconds.' Jacopo fast-forwarded four minutes. The film began running again. Thirty seconds later he was walking quickly back in the direction he had come, this time carrying a large, CONAD-branded re-usable shopping bag, bulked out.

Jacopo paused again, magnified the image. The shapes inside the bag were indistinct but certainly could have been the material in question.

'There would be sixteen reels in total,' I said. 'Eight film, eight sound.' Alba gave me a questioning look:

'But I thought . . .'

'When we were talking about "a film", we meant one big canister?' I shook my head. 'In the old days, which would be,' I said for the sake of the millennials, 'before around 1990, a movie would be mixed down onto a print from separate film and sound reels, known as negatives. A "director's cut" or "restored" version of a movie ideally begins with them, and they're what's missing.'

'So you *were* paying attention to the signora's lecture,' said Dolores.

'Did you ever doubt me? Anyway,' I turned back to Jacopo. 'You were talking about our guy . . .'

'Well, we can follow him across the park,' he said. 'After that . . .'

'You've checked other CCTV?'

'The only one was outside a pizzeria a few streets along. I asked them for a look but there was nothing.'

'It's enough. More than enough, I would say, to re-interview the archivists, apply some pressure. One of them must have wedged the door ajar so it could have been opened during the night . . .'

'Or perhaps it occurred when they were undertaking work, Daniel,' said the Comandante. 'Transporting something inside from the rear.'

'We've checked. There wasn't anything going on, and because of the temperature controls they are under strict instructions to keep the doors closed.'

'Still, a cleaner . . .'

'Cleaners are only permitted under supervision, although I take your point – there's always a random possibility. But what that doesn't do is explain what this guy – if he is a guy – was doing there at three in the morning. You know what I'm wondering? If the missing Toni Fausto negatives aren't just the tip of the iceberg.' I turned to Dolores. 'Best case scenario, kids are borrowing CineBo films by the back door, and simply forgot to put this one back.

'Worst case, this chap in the baseball cap isn't a film buff, but a thief, and they're quietly emptying the archive.'

'Films to order?' said Dolores. 'Are you going to tell Signora Varese or shall I?'

'You can tell her – I'll watch from a distance.'

The Comandante's phone pinged a message. Those freshly curated eyebrows arched.

'News?'

'It's from Alberto Fausto.' He nodded. 'The late director's older brother. It appears we are paired against him at this evening's burraco game.'

'We? What happened to your regular partner?'

'I'm sure Don Filippo will be content to sit this one out. You know how to play burraco, don't you, Daniel?'

'Sure,' I said. 'Although I suspect that's not the only game we'll be playing.'

Chapter 4

We locked up the office at seven thirty and, after supper at Da Luigi, one of the 'old men' *trattorie* the Comandante had on constant rotation, we headed along Via Ugo Bassi in the direction of the two towers. The pair – Asinelli as tall as a modern highrise but topped by Roman bricks, Garisenda leaning into her like a child around its mother's skirts – had marked the city centre, and provided its distant landmarks, for almost a thousand years. Backlit by the rose dusk, they saw everything and nothing, as was their custom.

The whole city seemed to be out – it was that *ponte* of perfect May weather. The tsunami of summer heat was yet to hit, the August escape still seemed distant.

We crossed Piazza Maggiore. The sheer vibrancy of a city energised by the thousands of students pulsing through its open spaces and arteries. People might complain about their high jinks; the noise and chaos, trail of graffiti from the innovative to idiotic, but we all fed off of it.

We plunged into *Il Quadrilatero*, the food market, past the crowded tables of the pricey *salumeria*; Osteria della Luna, my usual, unashamedly shabby watering hole; we continued further down, between the greengrocers' and fishmongers', until we arrived at the beginnings of Via Castiglione.

The Comandante spoke into the intercom and the spiked iron gate buzzed open. We walked along a gloomy internal portico, up a set of marble steps, and arrived at the entrance to Club Cisalpina.

If Bologna derived its potency from the young, then it was places like Cisalpina where its heart ticked over, beat by ante-diluvian beat.

There was certainly no shortage of members clubs 'inside the walls' (and, really, where else would they be?) to service the old – and new – wealth of the city, but Cisalpina had managed to maintain a certain edginess despite having recently celebrated its bicentenary.

Established in an expropriated bishop's palace during the height of Napoleon's rule by a group of profiteers who had embraced 'the Corsican's' iconoclastic tendencies, Cisalpina had become Bologna's deal-making centre as the decades, then centuries, had worn on. For a family whose fortunes were built on connections like the Faidate, it was a forum that could not be ignored, and what might have seemed like a rash decision by an ancestor to purchase membership 'in perpetuity' had gone on to enrich future generations.

The club's entrance may have lacked the grandeur of aristocratic establishments like Paradise over on the other side of Maggiore, but it made up for it in scale – room after modestly-sized room set up for eating, drinking, smoking, billiards and card playing. Yellowed flock wallpaper lined the walls while, above, frescoed ceilings depicted scenes from the ancient Greek republics that would have symbolised human-istic, anti-clerical modernity to Cisalpina's original 'Jacobin' patrons while scandalising visitors still loyal to the church (even today, only supposedly 'liberal' priests like the Comandante's friend Don Filippo dared enter). The gold-coloured bricks of its age-smoothed *Veneziana*-style floor, meanwhile, suggested the decadent *fin de siècle* background of Klimt.

The 'Card Room' did what it said on the bronze plaque – there were a dozen or so green baize tables with accom-panying cane-backed chairs. An art deco mahogany bar stood at the far end, where a black-bow-tied *cameriere* was setting out drinks.

Half the tables were already occupied. At the far end, a man raised his arm in greeting. He was about the same age as the Comandante, and dressed equally formally – in this case a brown double-breasted suit that could only have been tailored, with a crimson silk tie upon a white shirt. With his pomaded bouffant of silver hair and lantern jaw, he might have been cast as a mafia *consigliere* in an American movie, but here he was more likely to be a powerful politician or banker or, as I presumed, industrialist – Alberto Fausto.

As he stood to greet us, I couldn't help but notice he was with a young woman.

'Giovanni,' he said. 'May I present my granddaughter, Elettra.' She rose, tall like her grandfather, taller than the Comandante, almost as tall as me, and politely shook our hands. Apart from her height, she was fortunate not to have inherited any of her *nonno*'s other features: she was a classic Italian beauty with sharp, dark good looks that seemed oddly, almost unsettlingly, familiar.

'Yes, it's me,' she said.

'I'm sorry?'

Her grandfather, Alberto, chuckled. He explained to the Comandante: 'He's wondering where he's seen her.'

'You do seem familiar . . .'

'*Bewitching.*' She pronounced it in American-accented English. 'No?' She continued in perfect English: 'It's big on Netflix both sides of the Atlantic, although admittedly you're not exactly the typical audience. And they dub me for the Italian version, obviously. Ridiculously, really, if you think about it. I mean, I could dub myself.'

'Oh,' I said. 'You're *her.*'

She gave a little bow. 'Cassandra Sinistra.'

'My daughter and her friends are huge fans.'

'Admittedly, I'm the villain, not the blonde goody – they gave that to an American, of course.'

'You seem pretty American to me.'

'You know what I mean. How old is your daughter?'

'Sixteen.'

'Come.' She beckoned me to stand beside her. 'You've got your phone? Go on then.' She placed an arm around me and struck a suitably devilish pose. I took a couple of selfies. 'You might not think to ask, but she'd be pretty annoyed if she found out you'd met me and hadn't.'

'Thanks.'

'You're welcome.' Elettra Fausto might not have formally been American but we could have been standing in a Californian coffee shop.

Alberto had called over the *cameriere*. 'I'll have a Crodino,' he said.

'Aperol Spritz for me,' said Elettra.

I requested a Montenegro, with ice.

Alberto and the Comandante cut the pack. Alberto won and was about to deal when he looked at me gravely: 'Italian rules.'

'Of course,' I said. 'What else?' He gave me a thin smile, and we began.

Actually, *only* the Italians had formally codified burraco, thereby setting the official tournament standard, although it had its origins in Argentina and was played widely throughout the world. Less pompous than bridge, simpler than canasta, deceptively simple to the novice, who was likely to swiftly find themself tumbling down the 'hole', or *burraco*, the game had grown popular in Italy during the 1980s – many-time prime minister Giulio Andreotti and opera icon Luciano Pavarotti were both *burrachisti*.

'So.' Alberto began to deal. 'I hear our film has gone missing.'

'I'd like to know who you heard that from,' I said with a forced smile.

'Oh, well, I'll tell you – certainly not this director. What's his name?'

'That idiot Domori,' said Elettra, her eyes on the cards. 'Cassandra Sinistra' appeared to have joined the game.

'When I heard,' continued Alberto, 'I called him up, you know – just to enquire how the restoration process was going, and he didn't say a word about it. Everything was fine, apparently!'

I inspected my hand, glancing again at my 'partner' opposite. Giovanni Faidate wasn't giving anything away.

'You know,' said Alberto, 'I actually organised club membership for him, seeing as he was new to the city. We've played with him and his wife at this very table.'

'The Comandante was saying you're Toni Fausto's . . .'

'Brother. Elettra, here, is his . . .'

'Niece,' she said.

'As I understand it,' I said, 'the film had not been completed when your brother was . . .'

'That's right,' said Alberto. 'Most of the movie had been shot, but it had yet to be edited, pulled together, so to speak.'

'So what happened?'

'We did it,' said Alberto. 'Well, not Elettra here, obviously – she would have been a mere seed in her mother's womb – but the rest of the family. I took the lead. Worked with the director of photography, editor, actors . . .'

'Including Ron Manchester, George Malouf?'

'That's right. To complete the movie. We thought,' he shrugged, 'we did well enough.'

'It won the Special Jury Prize at Venice.'

Alberto smiled laconically. 'In the circumstances . . .'

'You didn't think it was good enough?'

'It's not for me to say. I am a mere businessman, an engineer. But following the shock of Toni's murder, well . . .'

'Indigo loves it,' said Elettra. 'I mean, otherwise he wouldn't be remaking it.'

'You speak as if you know him personally,' I said. 'Although I suppose Hollywood is a small town.'

'Ha!' She held out her left hand, waved her ring finger. 'Indigo Adler is my husband.'

***

We took a break. Elettra went to the bathroom while Alberto rose to chat with another industrialist-looking fellow by the bar. The Comandante and I faced each other across the wreckage of hands that had conspicuously failed to 'meld' – our apparent lack of teamwork thrown into sharp contrast by the intuitive gameplay of the opposing side. It was fortunate the Faustos were not actual clients, otherwise they might have been wondering if they had selected the right company.

'So,' I said. 'Director Domori's attempt at hushing this up has plainly failed.'

'Hardly surprising,' said the Comandante.

'I'm still not clear what they actually want from us.'

'To know what we know. And for us to know that they know.'

'That was one twist I hadn't expected – Indigo Adler being married to Elettra Fausto.'

'She has a role in the remake, herself,' said the Comandante. 'A minor part, I believe.' Fausto *nonno* and *nipote* were closing in from opposite directions. 'We were wondering,' the Comandante smiled as they took their seats, 'if there was any specific reason someone might have selected this particular film. There was nothing about the circumstances in which it was produced – no commercial disputes, nothing like that?'

Alberto shook his head with the same grave manner he had introduced 'Italian rules'. 'No,' he said. 'Nothing at all springs to mind.' He looked at his granddaughter. 'What does Indigo say? He's the expert, after all.'

'So, Mr Adler also knows . . .' Even as I muttered this, I realised it was a stupid thing to say – of course he did.

'Indigo hasn't mentioned anything,' said Elettra, 'except

he's furious. He says he should have been permitted to buy it.'
She scowled at me as if I was a stand-in for Director Domori.
'That it would have been safe.'

Now Alberto looked at me. 'And tell us – how *is* the investigation progressing?'

Burraco.

'Well enough,' I said uncomfortably. They may have known about the missing film, but they weren't actually our clients. 'We appear to be getting closer to finding out what happened and, hopefully, recovering the negatives.'

'So what was it?' said Elettra. 'Do you know who has them?'

While these might be Italian rules, I decided I wasn't Italian just yet: 'Comandante?'

The Comandante, looking like he would prefer the cover of cigarette smoke, cleared his throat. 'We can't go into too many details, dear, but I can confirm we believe we have ascertained how they were stolen.'

Alberto chuckled, Elettra scowled: 'It was my uncle's film. We have a right to know what's going on.'

'He who pays the piper calls the tune,' I said.

'If there's one thing I can assure you, young man,' said Alberto as he began to shuffle the pack, 'sooner or later, we will be writing a cheque.'

Chapter 5

'I'm sorry, so sorry.' Director Domori burst out of his office looking flustered. 'Valeria, my secretary, is absent.'

Signora Varese and I, having been sitting in awkward silence, followed him inside. The director took my arm. 'It's embarrassing really,' he confided to me in English. 'In the UK and Germany, I didn't even have a secretary – just used the admin pool when I needed something – but back here, in the stone ages, you know, it's remarkable how quickly we adapt, or perhaps that should be – regress.'

Like many Italians I encountered who had lived for long stretches abroad, the *direttore* clearly felt he had more in common with me than his compatriots, something hardly likely to endear him to the likes of the chief archivist here, who may indeed have been well-travelled, but you could be sure bore an epigram by the 'divine' Dante Alighieri etched upon her soul. Neither was she very appreciative of my suggestion that her archive might be being used as a cash and carry. Yes – I had drawn the short straw on that one.

'But every. Single. Reel,' she spoke in punctuation marks, her fists squeezed tightly, 'is scanned in. And. Out. *Punto.*'

'It's not about that, signora.' I lifted my laptop onto the desk and showed them the CCTV footage.

'How long do you think this has been going on for, Daniel?' asked the director.

'I've no idea, it depends upon how long the door was out for. It could be as much, even more, than a year.' The director nodded, poker-faced.

While Signora Varese looked wholly bereft, I was impressed by *dottore* Domori's calm demeanour – after all, from a 'reputational' point-of-view, this could be an utter disaster for CineBo – but I could almost see the cogs whirring through that smooth skull of his, reframing the narrative into one where 'fresh leader uncovers widespread incompetence and corruption in complacent and moribund organisation he turns around', before leaving to achieve greater things, preferably in northern Europe or America.

And the first head on the chopping block, I thought, would almost certainly belong to Signora Donatella Varese here.

The director's phone rang.

'Excuse me.' He picked up the phone. Signora Varese looked down at her now open hands. Perhaps she had arrived at a similar conclusion.

'I . . . oh . . .' The colour drained from the director's face. 'But she was only here yesterday. I called her earlier and there was no answer, I'd asked . . . uh-huh. Uh-huh.' He cleared his throat. 'But what?' He winced. 'But – that's just terrible. I can't believe . . . She's . . . I just . . . all right. Okay – I will speak to our human resources people. Yes, of course.' He rocked back in his chair, the phone's receiver in his lap. He raised both hands to his face.

'*Direttore*,' said the chief archivist. 'Is everything all right?'

He rocked forward. 'It's Valeria,' he said. 'She's dead. The police say – murder.'

Ispettore Umberto Alessandro was the only person I knew who could make vaping appear elegant. The sixty-something head of the Comandante's former Carabinieri command stood outside the entrance to Valeria Vignetti's *palazzo* in plain clothes looking, as ever, like an advertisement for an upmarket gentleman's outfitters.

The context may have helped, although Via Lame was not supposedly the most glamorous of locations – just around the corner from CineBo itself, it was a hotchpotch of modern and medieval buildings fronted on both sides by porticoes, with 'Porta Lame', the old city gate, standing at the far end – but it exuded enough intrinsic style to comfortably feature in any advertising campaign that might reproduce a 'typical' Italian setting. Seeing the *Ispettore* lit like that between the long shadows, fixed in the target of the tunnel-like portico as surely as Ursula striding down Via Saragozza, I could almost imagine myself in a Toni Fausto film.

The street itself was full of dark-blue Carabinieri squad cars and vans. Otherwise the portico remained open. Behind the *Ispettore*, a reporter and photographer were hanging around the front door chatting to a uniformed officer. I recognised the hack – Miranda, from the *Carlino*. She gave me a hopeful look – I shook my head. Not now, it said, although as ever with the press, it implied – maybe later. You never knew when you might need them.

'Come,' Alessandro ushered me into the lobby. It was

reasonably smart – fifties-era emerald green marble with potted plants and the distinct whiff of polish. Highish service charge, references required. Up the stairwell, I could hear the sound of activity – men's voices, mostly. They could be builders or decorators, although I suspected their overalls would serve a different purpose.

The *Ispettore* took another vape, his sculpted mouth absent its usual half-smile. He was plainly not in a teasing mood – this was plainly not teasing business. 'So what can you tell me about the young lady, Daniel.'

I knew if I wanted access there could be no messing around: 'I was with her boss, the director of CineBo, when he heard the news. We've been asked to look into the disappearance of a valuable set of negatives.'

He frowned. 'Negatives?'

'They're the constituent parts of a film – photography and sound reels. You mix them together to make the print that's seen in the cinema.'

'And what about them?'

'Well,' I said. 'They've disappeared. They were negatives of Toni Fausto's *Amore su una lama di rasoio* which is being remade by Hollywood, partly here in Bologna. There's been a fair amount about it in the press.'

'I'm not sure this has got anything to do with a missing film, Daniel.'

'I actually saw the signora – she was involved in looking for it.' I was stretching things a bit, but any connection would do.

'Is it worth anything, this film?'

'Hundreds of thousands, most probably,' I said, having no real idea. *'Comunque, un sacco di soldi.'* In any case a lot of cash. The *Ispettore* gave me a sceptical look. He knew what I wanted.

'If we weren't old pals,' he said, 'I would leave you outside with the hoi polloi.' He called the lift.

'Good job we're old pals, then.'

Valeria's apartment was on the fourth floor, the corridor a bustle of uniformed cops and white-suited forensics. Another old pal greeted us as I snapped on a pair of shoe coverings and latex gloves.

Massima, almost filling the corridor in her puffy white boiler suit, saluted the *Ispettore*. 'You can tell the coroner's men we're done, they can take the signora away. Oh, hi, Dan, what brings you here?'

Alessandro gave me a sideways glance. 'She was involved in a case I'm working on,' I said. 'I thought it might be helpful to take a look.'

Massima shook her head sadly. 'Stalking, was it? Domestic abuse? The bastard did a job on her.' She looked like she would like to do one on him.

I shook my head.

'Well, prepare yourself – it's not a pretty sight.'

I followed the *Ispettore* along the corridor towards the front door. 'The cleaner found her this morning,' he said. 'At around ten a.m., after she would have usually left for work.'

There was an air of deference as we approached the apartment, not altogether common at crime scenes. Popular portrayals of cynical cops bantering around the blood-splattered corpses of crooks are not so wide of the mark, but

they tend to be more respectful when it comes to 'civilians' –
folk who could be their wives or husbands, daughters or sons.

The door opened onto a corridor – facing us, a *soggiorno*
with a view of the *palazzo* opposite, and above it, the cloudless
blue sky. A pleasant aspect, I thought, for a pleasant, albeit
small apartment – quality wood floor, marked with age. A
coat stand by the door, a shelf with a box containing keys,
beside it a pile of flyers and post.

I followed the *Ispettore* along the short corridor, past a
bathroom – relatively new fittings – to a room at the end,
where a forensics officer pressed himself against the wall to
allow the *Ispettore* and I to pass. Clearly the sole bedroom.
'Rented,' I said out loud. To myself: a single-bed apartment
for a single young woman – late twenties? – affluent enough
to afford a cleaner. A way station, a stopping-off point. Only
– I stood in the doorway as Alessandro stepped around the
bed – it had all stopped here.

'So there you have it,' he said. 'She the one you saw?'

She was the one I'd seen, although I felt ashamed I had
barely noticed her at the time. She had 'just' been a secretary – an attractive young woman with long curly dark hair,
although in truth as I grew older, simple possession of youth
itself was attractive.

But in this context, her young age only served to amplify
the *ugliness*. This probably accounted for the *Ispettore* apparently finding my interest unsavoury, Massima's impulse for
violent revenge – because although not every crime scene feels
like a violation, this one did.

She wasn't undressed, and neither was there blood and gore,
at least that I could see as I followed the *Ispettore* around the

bed. In a sense, it was the very absence of drama – Valeria laid in her pink pyjamas with their Rupert Bear pattern as if she was still a child, her long dark neck – part from the holidays, part her natural pigmentation – crooked and darkened with bruises.

Her mouth was open and frosted around the corners from her saliva and possibly bile. Thankfully, her big eyes were closed – I suspected Massima's team had done this at the earliest opportunity. It would have felt even more indecent to have had her witness her own murder scene.

But were it not for those bruises, the *deadness* that casts all corpses at a little after five o'clock in the morning, she might have been an ordinary young woman, asleep in her ordinary bedroom with its hopeful, unmade double bed, generically attractive framed prints upon the walls, lotions and tissues and digital clock crowding the bedside cabinet.

Only someone had shattered that illusion, the one we all shared, from me and the *Ispettore* here to the forensics crew – that an ordinary, peaceful life would be permitted to us, providing we abided by the rules.

If she had abided by the rules, I thought, and felt almost ashamed for doing so.

'She's barefoot,' I observed. Alessandro didn't reply. I remembered he had a daughter much the same age. I tucked in my tie and bent forward, hands behind my back. Noted: two of her nails had been broken. I glanced up at Alessandro, but he was now looking out of the window. In any case, the forensic stuff would all be covered.

There was really not much more to be seen here, and it felt wrong to linger. Without saying anything more to the *Ispettore*, I left the room.

I paused in the bathroom, had a look around. Peeped outside to check no one was watching, and opened the cabinet. Nothing jumped out – the usual mix of first aid and medicines. I took a quick photo just in case.

I went four steps further down the hall and turned into the *soggiorno*. A cosy set-up with an over-stuffed *Maisons du Monde*-style sofa facing the TV. A small balcony onto Lame, framed black and white and colour movie stills and, possibly, an original poster of *The Bicycle Thieves*. Valeria was proud of her job, the place she worked.

I went over to the kitchenette. The grey-flecked marble-effect counter that separated it from the living space was tidy but 'mid-week': I could imagine those bottles of olive oil and balsamic vinegar remaining in place if she had friends over at the weekend, but not the rolls of yellow – for plastic – and blue – for paper – recycling sacks. At the end of the galley were three bins – black, yellow and green. The black was already open and for cans. The green, obviously, organic. I lifted up the yellow lid – more flyers and circulars and torn-up bills in a blue sack. I checked over my shoulder, the room was still empty. I reached in and grabbed a bunch, flicking through them. Nothing jumped out.

I was about to place them back inside when I spotted a batch of CineBo programmes.

I lifted it out and spread them across the counter.

Sounds outside, people coming through the front door. Likely the coroner's. I thought about ducking down, but it was too late. I stood at the counter waiting for them to pass.

Gone. I looked down at the programmes spread across the work surface.

There: the month I was looking for.

The programme opened up into a single sheet. The bottom corner had been torn off – straight through *The Seven Samurai*.

I spread it fully out on the counter and began taking photos.

The sound of further activity, people coming back along the corridor.

I folded the programme up, shuffled it back together with the rest, and pitched the lot back into the bin.

Massima came in as I was moving around the counter.

'You saw her, then,' she said.

'It's very sad.'

'Bastard. Anyway,' she comforted herself. 'They're bound to catch him.'

'What makes you so sure?'

'I've done enough of these to know – it's like I was saying, a jealous ex or boyfriend, most likely. Possibly married lover, but either way, always a fucking man.' She looked me square in the eye, she wasn't about to apologise. 'It might take a while, but they'll get the bastard.'

I walked over to the doorway, ducked my head out of the *soggiorno*. Alessandro was standing outside Valeria's bedroom deep in conversation with one of his uniformed subalterns. It didn't feel like a great time to confess I'd been tampering with evidence.

'I've got to go,' I said. 'But do me a favour, will you? Don't throw out the trash.'

Chapter 6

'You're really too kind. *Really.*' Indigo Adler had the slightly perturbed look of any non-Italian celebrity confronted by the sheer exuberance of the local welcome – be it the dozen or so members of the media who had buzzed around him ever since he had descended the steps of his private jet on the tarmac of Bologna's Marconi airport, or now at the press conference at Palazzo d'Accursio against the backdrop of a fresco depicting the coronation of the Holy Roman Emperor, Charles V.

'I would just like to say it is an honour, and a pleasure . . .' Elettra Fausto, in a white lace dress and smiley Californian mode, a hand clasped over her husband's, translated for him. She nodded permission for him to continue. 'To be here, and to get to know the streets, the people, the . . . well, it would have to be the *atmosphere* of the city, that's what it's all about, right? The location of so many of the *gialli* of Toni Fausto, his master, um, work, *Amore su una lama di rasoio.*' He made a pretty good fist of the pronunciation, albeit with a strong American accent. I wondered what had come first – Indigo's love for the filmography of Toni Fausto or his niece, Elettra? I suspected it was the former – his puppyish enthusiasm shone through.

A muscular, middle-aged man in a Marvel T-shirt with a mop of sandy hair, his wide-open, farm boy face might have pointed to Germanic Mid-West origins if a google hadn't informed me he was actually a Jewish Brooklynite.

Adler was flanked on one side by his raven-haired wife, on the other, blonde Anna Bloom, who was to play Ursula and, notwithstanding a recent career hiatus, had shot to fame as Aphrodite in a Spielberg movie. Every straight man in Sala Farnese – and watching on TV, as I was, in a bar on Piazza Verdi – was probably thinking: some guys get all the luck.

'Anna,' someone shouted from the pack. 'What do you think of Bologna?'

Aphrodite flashed a heavenly smile. 'Well, I must say,' she said. '*Bologna* is absolutely *belliiisssima*.' The hacks burst into obsequious applause.

'Hey, Marco,' said one of the guys who stood taking a coffee at the counter. 'I hear they're going to build studios here in Bologna like in Cinecitta in Rome. Maybe Anna will become a regular here.'

'Oh yeah,' said the *cameriere*, busy at the espresso machine. 'I already have her number. She keeps calling to ask if there's a table free, but I have to tell it's full up with you bastards.'

The bar erupted into laughter.

I had headed back to CineBo after Valeria's apartment. Despite having found evidence apparently linking the director's secretary to the theft of the negatives, I wasn't feeling especially pleased with myself. Whatever she might have been involved in, she hadn't deserved that.

The director's door was open, Rocco Domori sitting at the desk, looking at his screen. I knocked softly.

'Oh, Daniel. Please.' He gestured for me to come in. 'I was just seeing if there was anything in the news. Poor Valeria – how was it?'

How do you think it was, I thought, picturing her lying there. Then I heard Massima's words: *possibly a married lover.* The boss and his secretary? He would definitely be a suspect, especially here in Italy. But he had only been in the job a few months – he would have had to have worked fast.

'I would rather not go into details,' I said.

'No, no, I'm sorry, I shouldn't have asked. Of course not.' Now he was probably imagining a scene out of Jack the Ripper.

'However,' I said, 'there was a small thing that may be relevant to our enquiries.' I told him about the programme.

'So this means that Valeria was involved in the theft? My God, you don't think this is what got her murdered!'

'The programme,' I said, 'is of interest, but it does not necessarily mean she was involved. It could just be a coincidence.'

'A fairly big coincidence!'

'A lawyer would argue it was circumstantial – anyone may have found it, torn it off, etcetera. And ultimately, there's nothing to explicitly link it to the missing film.'

'But we are not lawyers,' he said.

'And although I will draw this to the attention of the authorities,' I said, 'even if she was involved with the theft, that certainly wouldn't mean her murder was connected to it.'

'Ah! Correlation is not causation you mean.' He swung back in his chair looking pleased with himself. Then his face clouded. 'But how?' he asked.

'How what?'

'What on earth would she have been doing in the archive? She didn't have access.'

'Remind me who has access, *direttore*. The archivists . . .'

'And me, that's it.'

'And where did you keep your passcode?'

'On my compu—' It dawned on him.

'"No man is a hero to his valet," I said. Domori looked at me questioningly. 'An English expression – basically, a boss has no secrets from his secretary. Do you know who Valeria was friendly with?' He shook his head.

'She seemed to get on with everyone.'

'Who were the people she went to lunch with?' He looked blank. I realised that, much like me, Rocco Domori had barely noticed Valeria Vignetti, even though in his case she had been sitting in the office next to his for three months. 'The other secretaries?' he said. 'Maybe?'

I walked to the end of the hallway where I knew the rest of the 'secretaries' – who actually *were* CineBo's administrative staff – sat. An announcement had been made while I was away, so the atmosphere throughout the building was one of shock, which didn't particularly help me – her colleagues and friends were hardly likely to appreciate my throwing accusations about at a time like this. On the other hand, presuming she *had* been involved in the disappearance of *Love on a Razorblade*, judging by the mysterious figure filmed at the rear door, I doubted she had been acting alone, and while I may have discouraged Rocco Domori from linking the theft to her murder, I couldn't help doing so myself. Let the police investigate the obvious leads, I thought. In the meantime, I would do some legwork on their behalf.

'*Signore.*' I stepped humbly into their room. There were three middle-aged women and one young one, who was dabbing her reddened eyes. 'You've heard, I see.'

'We still can't believe it,' said one of the older ones. 'Murdered!'

'And in her own home, right around the corner!'

'I've asked my husband to pick me up tonight. I'm sorry, it's my nerves.'

'Do you know anything more?' asked the first. 'You're that private detective, right?' I was only momentarily surprised she knew who I was – of course she did.

'I'm afraid I don't,' I said. 'I'm as shocked as everyone else. I've actually been asked to help build a picture of her life, for background purposes. Were you very friendly with her?' I directed this at the weepy young one, who seemed most likely. She blew her nose.

'Not really.' She shook her head. 'Valeria was . . . *Mio Dio.*' She crossed herself. 'I can't believe I am talking about her in the past tense.' She stifled a sob.

'Calm yourself,' said one of her colleagues.

The young one continued: 'Valeria was,' and now she used a very Italian word: '*particulare.*' Literally 'particular', its meaning is in the way you say it, and the way the secretary said it, I understood – standoffish.

'So she wasn't very friendly with you ladies, then?'

'It wasn't that.' She rushed not to speak ill of the dead. 'She was always very professional, helpful, pleasant, and so on. Only she kept herself to herself. Socially, I mean.'

'She thought she was better than the rest of us, that's the truth,' said a colleague who clearly had no such qualms. 'She was always going on about her fucking PhD.'

'*Anastasia*, really.'

'She had a doctorate?'

'I asked around – it turned out she'd started one but never finished, although hearing her speak you would never know.'

'It was in?'

'Oh, something to do with film, or watching films, or something. It's all to do with film here, obviously.'

'Then I might be better off speaking to people in archives, or restoration?'

She shrugged. 'You can try, although I'm not sure they had much to do with her either – I think they were afraid she was after their jobs! No, the only people I ever saw her hanging around with were those down the road.'

'I'm sorry, what do you mean, "down the road"?'

'The Department of Communication.' She nodded towards the window. 'Her old "Alma Mater".'

Chapter 7

The university department in question was quite literally down the road from CineBo. Housed in the very same street in a new, purpose-built building, it was the brainchild of semiotician and novelist, Umberto Eco, who had devised its courses and directed the school until his death. The *Dipartimento di Filosofia e Comunicazione* might have been considered the new kid on the block in the oldest university in the world, but it had pedigree.

The lobby was full of student bustle, yet despite my age and attire, I somehow felt immediately at home – after all, when I hadn't been 'watching films all day', much of my degree had actually been inspired by the likes of Eco, whose dry semiotic texts, breaking language down into units of meaning and wrestling them into mathematics-like equations, had formed a substantial part of my studies, albeit a part I had almost entirely forgotten. These were my people, I decided, although I'm not sure they saw me quite the same way.

'Vignetti?' The group of students gathered by the notice-board shook their heads warily, as they might to the police.

'Do you know where I might ask?'

'Try the office,' said one of the guys.

'What office?'

'I don't know.' He waved his hand in a general direction. 'The office.'

I headed deeper into the building, where I came to an office not unlike the 'secretaries' at CineBo, except there were two instead of three women, and they exuded a hostility inevitably born of dealing with students all day. There could be no pussyfooting about, I would have to evoke the nuclear option – family.

'I'm sorry to bother you, *signore*. I'm trying to trace anyone who might know a PhD student of this faculty who has a family emergency – Valeria Vignetti?'

'Oh? And you are?'

'Her uncle.'

'Vignetti . . .' She turned to her colleague. 'Do you know a Vignetti?' She shrugged, and consulted her terminal. 'A family emergency you say?'

I nodded gravely. 'I'm afraid so.' I wasn't going to share any further details, but my suit presumably lent me further authority.

'She's associated with the film studies laboratory,' called her colleague. I gave them a questioning look.

'First floor, at the end of the corridor.' I gave them a solemn bow.

'Grazie, *signore*.'

'*Prego*.' They emoted motherly sympathy.

I decided to employ a different tactic at the film studies office where the occupants were both younger and clearly more academic – the man and woman looked like they could

be working at CineBo themselves. I leaned in the doorway
and smiled:

'Are you guys friends with Valeria? Valeria Vignetti?'

'Valeria?' The woman, a twenty-something brunette in a
black short-sleeved turtleneck, nodded. 'Sure. What about her?'

'She said to speak to you about some films.'

'Films?' She laughed. 'You'll have to be a bit more specific
than that!'

'Seeing some old films, something like that?'

'He's talking about The Secret Cinema,' said the man, not
looking away from his screen.

'Oh, Secret Cinema, is that it?'

'Sure,' I said.

'Well, I . . .' She hesitated. 'I'm sorry, who did you say you
are?' In this case, the suit had probably worked against me.
The age gap probably hadn't helped either.

'I'm interested in a specific one – *Amore su una lama di
rasoio*. Is that part of the programme of The Secret Cinema?'

'I . . . I'm sorry, but you didn't say who you are.' Now the
guy had turned to look at me with curiosity.

'I've been asked to see if I can find anything out about this
film, that's all. Don't worry, I'm not looking to get anyone
into trouble. I studied film myself, you know.'

'Who's asking?' she said. 'What I mean is, I don't know
anything about this film you're talking about, and you *still*
haven't told me who you are.'

To hell with it: 'I'm an investigator,' I said. 'A private investigator, and I've been asked to track down this missing film.'

'Wow.' The guy sat back. 'A real private eye. Where are you
from? You're not Italian.'

'England.'

'*Accidenti!* Like Sherlock Holmes!'

I laughed. 'If I had a penny for every time . . .'

'Who's employing you?' asked the woman, who was clearly less amused.

'Ah, that I can't tell you, signora. But, given that they're negatives for *Amore su una lama di rasoio*, you might be able to guess.'

'I don't know what you're talking about,' she stonewalled.

'*Patrizia*,' said the guy.

'Shut up.'

'*Patrizia*,' I said softly, 'it's like this: I don't give a damn about this secret club of yours. Hell, if I was a student myself, I would probably be a member. But I've been tasked to find these missing negatives and it would certainly be in your interests to help me clear this up before the police get involved.'

She looked neither shocked nor surprised, rather as if she was seriously considering my offer. Italians grow up with an understanding that, in contrast to supposedly 'free-born' Britons, they are born into a web of laws, so in a country where you might unknowingly be guilty of perhaps half-a-dozen crimes before breakfast, even the most innocent among them can be as perspicacious as a hardened criminal.

'You'll have to speak to Valeria,' she said finally.

'I've tried Valeria,' I said. 'But I can't find her. That was why I came here.'

'It's a Valeria thing,' she said airily, crossing her arms. 'I really don't know anything about it.'

'Are you *sure* about that?'

'*Sure* I'm sure.' She smiled sardonically. 'And I'd say the same to the police, *Meester* Sherlock.'

'Very well,' I said. 'Thank you, *Patrizia*. And you?' The guy held up his hands.

'Oh no,' he said. 'Nothing to do with me!'

'Well, if anything occurs to you . . .' I left my card on the table.

I was hanging about in the lobby deciding on my next move, when I noticed Patrizia come down the stairs. She was half-way across, apparently on her way to the noticeboard, when she spotted me and veered towards the exit, heading outside. A few minutes later, acting as if she hadn't seen me, she walked back in, crossed the lobby, and took the steps back up to the office, but by that time I had checked the board and seen the flyer for THE SECRET CINEMA.

Black and white, with a photo of Alfred Hitchcock with a finger to his lips, it simply instructed people to follow an Instagram account @thesecretcinemabo.

I called Dolores to come over. While I was waiting, I scrolled through the account. There were stills from about a dozen films, mainly Italian movies from the seventies and eighties, among them no less than three Toni Faustos. Whoever ran The Secret Cinema was clearly a Fausto fan.

Dolores pulled up on her bike. I went outside to meet her, showed her a photo of the flyer and asked her to hang around the foyer and keep an eye out for Patrizia, who would presumably emerge again to remove it.

'And if she goes anywhere, speaks to anyone . . .'

'On it, chief.'

Chapter 8

I had just sat down with the Comandante to debrief him on the morning's events, when I got the call.

'I'm in Via Cartoleria,' Dolores said breathlessly.

'What are you doing there?'

'This Patrizia took down the flyer, then a guy turned up on a scooter.'

'And?'

'They had this intense conversation and she showed him the flyer. He took off, so I followed him.'

'Good job. But what are you doing on Cartoleria?'

'It's the Department of Literature. But before that, he went along the Viale to the Department of Engineering.'

'And he's taking the flyers down?'

'That's it.' I looked at a map.

'Okay, it seems as if he's doing the peripheral university departments, then working his way to the centre, Zamboni-Belle Arti. Keep tabs on him and I'll meet you there.'

'Progress?' said the Comandante. I went onto Instagram and refreshed @thesecretcinemabo. The account had been deleted.

'Of a kind,' I said.

I caught up with Dolores outside a bar at the top of Via Zamboni, the sweeping street of sixteenth-century *palazzi* now home to many of the university departments.

'That's him there.' She nodded to a skinny youth standing at the counter nursing a coffee. He was dressed head to toe in black with a mop of bleached blond hair and a pair of headphones around his neck. 'He's done the bottom half of Zamboni, which leaves maths, psychology, minerology, and the Accademia.'

'Okay,' I said. 'Let's get him on his own and see if he's a little more amenable to discussion.'

We followed him as he moved between university departments busy with students, but it wasn't until we arrived at the art school – the Accademia – and I discovered an empty studio, that I gave Dolores the nod. While she approached him, I stepped inside.

The studio looked like it was used for sculpture – it was filthy with clay and cement. An exposed tap was dripping into a drain, the high, dusty windows were spidery with cracks. If they hadn't been making art here, they could have been waterboarding.

I moved to the side of the door and waited.

The door finally opened. 'Ah,' I heard Dolores saying as she came in, 'this should do fine.'

'But I'm not sure what you want?' he was saying as he followed her in. She closed the door behind her.

'I saw you with the flyer. I wanted to ask you how to join your Secret Cinema.'

'Oh no,' he said. 'Actually, I was just taking . . .' That was when he saw me. He bolted for the door, but I stepped in front of it, my palm held out flat like a traffic cop. 'Be cool,' I smiled. 'She just wants to ask you some questions.'

'Who are you?' Panic flushed his face, his eyes instantly brimmed with tears. He was just a kid, I realised, late teens, no more than twenty.

'What's your name?' I asked. He looked at Dolores. She nodded.

'Romano,' he said.

'Romano,' I pulled out my official-looking company ID, 'we're investigators. Did Patrizia tell you what this was all about?'

'She just said to take down the flyers quick. The police were onto us.'

I shook my head. 'First of all, don't worry – the police are not onto you. And you, Romano, are not in any trouble – we're *private* investigators, we're not the police. We're on your side. Anything you say to us will remain *private* – nothing to do with the law, I promise.' He looked again at Dolores.

'It's true,' she said. 'I mean – do I look like a cop?'

'We don't give a damn about any illegality,' I said. 'That's not our problem. I can understand Patrizia's probably panicking – she wants you to get the job done. But what *we* want to do is locate some negatives that have gone missing from CineBo – *Amore su una lama di rasoio*. Ring any bells?'

He shook his head.

'This club,' I said. 'From what I can tell, you were basically borrowing films from CineBo to show, am I right?'

'I think so. I mean, I had nothing to do with that. I just

did the publicity. I didn't even realise it was illegal – I mean, as far as I know they always put them back.'

'It was nothing,' I agreed. 'A bit of harmless fun. The only problem is that one of these films has disappeared, and we've been asked to find it.' I shook my head as if, frankly, I could do without the inconvenience. 'That's all we're interested in. We know it was Patrizia, you, Valeria Vignetti.' He nodded. 'Was there anyone else involved?'

'Just Valeria's boyfriend, Gianni. We used to screen them at his place.'

'And tell me, Romano, where is that?'

The bar TV had cut to the studio where the presenters were having a light-hearted chat about what Bolognese sights Anna Bloom should visit, and inviting their viewers to send in selfies with her: 'And let us know if she is nice or *un po' "snob"*.'

'Ricardo, you can't tell people to do that, we don't want Anna to think we Bolognese are *maleducati!*'

I finished my lunch then downed a swift coffee before stepping back outside.

We'd already tried the address the kid had given us but there had been no answer, and no one responding to the other bells either, so I had let Dolores go and gone for some lunch in the nearby piazza. I wasn't about to try picking the lock of the front door on a busy portico, no matter how slick my skills might be getting.

Piazza Verdi was at the very centre of Bologna's student life, blazing with banners and political murals, and dominated by the opera house – the *Teatro Comunale* – where, when its portico wasn't busy with the great and good, drunks and drug dealers pitched up between the columns. If Bologna had been a kind of medieval Manhattan, then this remained its Times Square.

The piazza encapsulated the contradictions of the city, and was often my first port of call when tasked with hunting down an AWOL student or runaway, buying a prof coffee in return for their forensic expertise, or, far less commonly, attending an actual performance at the *Teatro*, but today I continued on to cobbled Via Petroni, which had its own reputation: Petroni was the party street, and more protest banners – this time by residents – hung wanly from second- or third-floor apartment buildings complaining about the 'degradation' of the area.

Number 19 was an ordinary, lightly graffitied brown door between an Asian-run grocery and kebab takeaway. The buzzers were a mess of indecipherable names and peeling stickers – this was a place of sub-lets of sub-lets – and there was certainly nothing indicating 'Gianni' or 'Colline', which the kid had assured us was his surname. But I kept the faith – Romano was too scared to lie, especially since we had taken care to photograph his ID card before letting him loose.

The door opened and a guy appeared with a dog who looked much like he did – a mongrel.

'I'm looking for Gianni Colline,' I said. He walked past me without a word – in my suit and tie, I clearly had nothing to sell he wanted to buy.

The closing door met my foot, and I stepped into the hallway.

The letterboxes were more revealing. There: '*G. Colline.*'

No apartment number, however.

I was standing in a gloomy space beside a stone stairwell.

It was fairly typical for a building 'inside the walls'. Probably thrown up around the seventeenth century, its gloominess was more or less deliberate: thick stone walls had been the only means of keeping cool during the summer and warm during the winter. Despite being smack in the city centre, these places were dirt cheap to rent because they were grim to live in any time of the year.

I tramped up the stone stairs. There weren't any names on the doors of the first floor, so I buzzed. One door didn't answer, the other took an age to get there. Finally, a half-starved-looking student girl peered through the crack, bleary-eyed. 'Gianni Colline?' I said. She shook her head, closing the door. 'Do you know him? Where he lives?'

She shrugged. 'Try above.'

I tried above. A middle-aged man answered the first door and shut it just as promptly, shaking his head before I had even finished explaining, while the security gate was closed outside the neighbouring apartment and there was, predictably, no answer. I ascended to the third, and final floor.

The voice of an elderly lady – clearly viewing me through the spy hole – 'Gianni? *Un bravo ragazzo* – a nice boy – he's next door.'

I thanked her and buzzed. Tried again.

No answer. Tried one last time.

Shook my head and made my way back down the stairwell. Reached the bottom, gave it a minute, then crept back up the stairs. Even if the old dear had continued to view me through the peephole, she had presumably lost interest by now.

I dug into my pocket for my pick wrap. Here I felt a little more confident about testing my skills – I had some privacy and it was an ordinary lock so shouldn't present too much of a challenge.

I worked the rods until I heard a click. I gave them a firm twist. The door opened. I let myself in and closed it softly behind me.

'Gianni?' I said. No answer.

I was standing at the end of a long, cabbage-smelling corridor weakly illuminated by a skylight, grey with grime and bird droppings. I felt around for a light switch. A dusty, bulbous paper shade mid-way along added a weak pall.

'Gianni,' I called. 'Are you here?'

The corridor was lined by crinkled, full-size film posters. All the classics – *La Dolce Vita*, *Casablanca*, *Bicycle Thieves*, *Taxi Driver*, *Kill Bill 1* and *Kill Bill 2* – attached by Blu Tack. Lying flat in front of me on the red, ceramic tiled floor: a collapsed clothes horse, its dark T-shirts, underwear, jeans splayed on the ground.

There were three doors off the corridor. The first opened onto a startlingly large, ripe-smelling, windowless room.

In the near corner was an island of domestic life: a mattress with a twisted chocolate brown duvet and pillows and, partitioning it off from the rest of the room, a listing clothes rail, largely unused, with a pile of dark clothing heaped at its feet.

Around the 'bed' were a couple of art school paintings flanked by a pair of Toni Fausto posters – *Kiss of a Gunman* and *Smash and Grab* – but beyond this squalid little corner, the remaining grubby cream walls were bare. Unsurprisingly: the sheer size of the room, equivalent to an entire apartment or trendy loft space, mitigated against it – they would have been swallowed up.

The room, in fact probably the entire flat, would have once been a granary – the Bolognese had traditionally stored their food at the tops of their buildings to keep it away from vermin. Now these huge, unwieldy spaces, scrupulously protected from alteration by the authorities due to their historic status, offered the very cheapest accommodation in the very cheapest buildings.

But I could see why a place like this might appeal to Gianni – the rest of the room was indeed a 'secret cinema'. An old reclaimed projector had been raised upon a scaffold and positioned upon a platform with cables trailing downwards, while spread out on the floor were cushions and mats for an audience which would sit facing a white PVC screen tethered to poles propped against a wall around fifteen metres away.

But before you could reach the 'auditorium', you had to navigate something of a scrapyard of old film gear – reel-to-reel machines, more projectors in various states of assembly, an editing table with a cutting block, and there at the end, throwing shadows against the wall like an alien emerging from the wreckage of its spacecraft, a Moviola machine like the one at CineBo.

I walked over to the cheap white Ikea-type desk next to it, where some kind of digital movie camera sat on a stand. Spread across the desk – brown paper packaging lined by bubble wrap. I picked it up – beneath the packaging was another sheet of stiff white paper, creased and torn where it had clearly been sealed around whatever had been inside. On its reverse: a movie poster consisting of washed-out pinks and reds – *Letter to Brezhnev* – featuring a woman in the arms of a

Soviet sailor, kicking up her heels. The paper, brittle between my fingertips, felt as dated as the film.

On the floor beside the desk was a large Apple Mac box, opened but not yet unpacked, which appeared to contain a state-of-the-art computer.

I heard something.

'Gianni?' A silence as dead and cold as those stone walls. I put the poster down and went back into the corridor.

The next door along – a bathroom. I flicked the switch – the fluorescent light stuttered then fizzed into life. In contrast to the gloomy pall of the corridor, it exposed the grime like a plaster ripped off a weeping wound.

It was more like another corridor than a bathroom, narrow enough for me to touch both sides with my hands, but almost as long as its neighbour, with the toilet, wash basin and bath positioned at the very far end.

'Gianni?' Nothing.

The grey-tinged black and white tile floor glistened with water, and as I neared the filthy, standalone bath, my footsteps began to splash.

'Gianni?'

Feeling a little sick, I peered into the bath.

It was half-filled, but otherwise empty. I suppressed a shudder. One corpse had been enough for today. I tested the filmy water with my finger, it was ice cold – the kid was clearly just a slob and had made a mess as he got out. It was no coincidence the place stank of mould.

I was splashing irritably back up the bathroom, when I heard it again. This time more distinct – the crash of crockery.

'Gianni?' Still nothing. I sighed. Well, there was only one room remaining – the kitchen. It was probably a cat, if it wasn't a fucking rat.

The kitchen was at the end of the corridor. In contrast to the other rooms, it appeared shallow and boxy, but at least it contained a window, which faced me as I approached the open doorway.

Beneath the window, a sink and draining board, piled with washed-up cups and plates, and sure enough, shattered upon the tile floor – a cup. I stepped inside, looking edgily around for the furry culprit.

I was jolted backwards.

Chapter 9

The arm was around my throat and tightening fast.

I grabbed at it, but as I did, felt myself being hoisted back onto my toes.

A man's coffee-scented breath against my ear, his gravelly voice strangely soothing: 'Don't struggle, pal, don't struggle and it'll be easy, don't struggle . . .'

I struggled. Tried in vain to wrench back the arm compressing my windpipe, my hands digging into the sinuous material of his jacket. Beneath – iron-hard muscle squeezing ever tighter. Relentless, like a hinged machine.

'Don't struggle, pal. Let it happen, it'll soon be over, I promise, just let go.'

I would not let go, but dusk was falling, and terrifyingly fast. A gathering, greying dimness seemed about to overwhelm me.

I began to panic – flailing in the desperate flight of life.

'There's a good boy. Let go, just let go . . .'

When I saw it – a wink of metal, perhaps the only truly clean thing in that kitchen.

I let go – of the arm – and went for it.

Through the haze something toppled.

The knives emptied across the draining board or fell onto the floor.

I was wrenched back.

That one – wobbling upon the precipice.

I lunged again.

Seized the hardwood handle and swung it backwards. Felt the resistance as it pierced nylon and cotton and flesh, his muscle-hard body, but then something gave and I buried it, buried it with every last ounce I had.

Air – rushing down my throat.

Air – hitting the floor hands first, oblivious to the edges of knives and broken crockery.

Gulping like a horse at a trough, not even thinking about what was behind me until through the rushing blood I heard a scraping, a mumbled swearing.

I scrambled forwards, smacking my head against a cupboard door before swivelling around, to look up.

A startled, middle-aged man, a man older than me – in his fifties, maybe, but fit with it. Neat grey beard with a matching quiff. Functionally dressed – jeans, bomber jacket and dark T-shirt, sculpting a muscular build.

The carving knife dug half way into his side, blood blossoming black against the green of his jacket.

He closed a hand around the blade, visible through his thick fingers, more in an effort to stem the bleeding, I think, than to remove it.

Our eyes locked. He looked at me as if to say – *now why did you do that?*

A squeak – talk. He was wearing an earpiece. He looked back at the knife, then at me.

'*Cazzo.*'

He swung himself towards the door and marched stiffly back along the corridor, the knife sticking out of his side like the key to a clockwork toy.

Chapter 10

I was still sitting nursing my bruised throat when the Carabinieri rocked up. My assailant had not bothered to close the door, so I watched them come along the corridor, the first with his baton at the ready, his partner at his shoulder with a yellow taser.

'Here!' I tried to shout, but nothing came out. I tried again, this time more softly. Something managed to escape, but my throat felt like needles. Instead, I banged on the kitchen floor, waved.

As they approached, I began to pull myself up. I fell back down again.

'Raise your hands!' said the one with the taser. I did as I was told, gesturing at my throat as I did so.

'Can't speak,' I whispered.

'Get to your feet!'

I tried again, this time with more success.

'Hands!'

The one with the baton swept my hands behind my back and cuffed me. 'What the fuck happened here?'

'I was attacked,' I whispered.

'What did he say?'

'Something about being attacked.' He switched on his torch and aimed it down the corridor. 'Have you seen that?'

I saw it now – a drizzle of blood. The Carabinieri turned me around to face them. 'Where's that from?'

'I was attacked. Strangled me.'

'And the blood?' I shrugged. I wasn't about to confess to a stabbing, even if it had been in self-defence.

'Nice suit. He doesn't look like a burglar.'

'Private investigator,' I whispered.

'You're a snoop?'

I nodded.

'I'm not liking this, Dario,' said the first. 'Snoops, break-ins, blood. Let's close it off and get him back to the *caserma*.'

'I concur.'

'Are you all right. . .' He reached into my pocket and pulled out my ID. 'Daniel Lie-chester?'

'It's him, *the bloody English detective.* Comandante's son-in-law.'

'You need a doctor?' I swallowed, shook my head. 'Be that as it may, this is still what it is.'

'It is what it is.'

'We'll take him in, let the higher-ups decide.'

'Affirmative,' said 'Dario'. 'Leave it to the higher-ups.'

My phone rang as I was sitting in the back of the *gazzella*. The cop reached around and plucked it out, showed it to his colleague at the wheel.

'Have you seen this?'

'Higher-ups.'

'They must have some sixth sense or something.' He showed it to me. It said ISPETTORE ALESSANDRO CALLING. 'Want me to get this?' I nodded. He put it on speakerphone.

'Pronto, *Ispettore.*'

'Who's this?'

'*Carabiniere Geldi. Comando stazione, Galliera.*'

'What are you doing with Daniel Leicester's phone?'

'We've arrested him, sir, on suspicion of breaking and entering.'

A long sigh, followed by silence.

'Sir?'

'And this address, it wouldn't happen to be the dwelling of a young man by the name of Gianni Colline, by any chance?'

The Carabinieri looked at each other – I realised they had no idea. They looked at me. I nodded.

'It appears so, *Ispettore.*'

'All right, then. Where are you?'

'In the car, sir, almost at the station.'

'No, bring him here.'

'And where's "here", sir?'

The River Reno had once loomed as large in the character of Bologna as its towers, positioning the city at the crossroads of Italian trade and feeding a network of canals that criss-crossed the city. But like those canals now buried beneath the city streets, today it was largely out of sight, out of mind, winding through the flat Emilian countryside on the outskirts, its banks punctuated by clumps of trees amid an otherwise unremarkable landscape of reddy-brown fields.

Our destination was clear even through the dust thrown up around us as we headed along the dirt track – the caravan of dark-blue Carabinieri vehicles gathered around one such copse. '*Gazzelle*' – Alfa Romeo 159s – Jeep Cherokees, and a forensics van.

We got out.

An airliner screamed in low, landing flaps up and wheels down. The airport was little more than a kilometre away.

The *Ispettore* was standing by one of the Cherokees dressed as immaculately as before, only wearing Wellington boots. He looked down at my shoes sunk in the ploughed earth.

'You would be surprised how often it ends in a muddy field,' he said. 'Go on, then.' He nodded to the uniforms either side of me. They turned me around and uncuffed me, then turned back to face him. 'Are you all right? You're looking rather . . . peaky.'

I pointed at my throat. 'I was attacked,' I whispered, although it was beginning to sound a little stronger. 'Someone tried to choke me from behind.'

'In Gianni Colline's apartment, you mean?' I nodded. 'And what were you doing there?' I was about to answer when he shook his head. 'Perhaps better to save your voice. Was it something to do with this business about the rubbish you mentioned to Massima?' I nodded. 'And thanks to that, you ended up at this fellow's apartment.' I nodded. 'On the hunt for those negatives?' I nodded. 'Did you find them?' I shook my head. 'Well, I may be able to help you with that.'

I followed him down a path leading into the copse. A short way in – just enough to be shielded from the road – a Fiat 500 had been parked and set on fire. It seemed that traces of smoke were still swirling around it, until coming closer I realised they were clouds of mosquitoes.

But the car was not quite inert – it was creaking as it cooled, and giving off a pungent, pork-sweet, yet rubbery, odour.

The heat had seared the paint off the car to leave only its grey shell. A fire-blackened interior was visible through glass-less windows, but as we moved around the vehicle, I realised it wasn't just combusted upholstery – melted into the mass was a person, slumped forward so their head rested upon the wheel, although they might just as easily have been transported there from Pompeii, such was their charcoaled anonymity: no hair, nose, lips, eyes, but recognisably human – side on, the entire jaw was burnt back, exposing its teeth in a skeletal grimace.

'You see, there, on the seat beside him,' the *Ispettore* observed dispassionately. 'The petrol can.'

'And here.' He moved to the backseats and indicated a large melted blob. 'I suspect we have what remains of that film of yours.'

The contents were utterly ruined, but it was true – you could tell by the curves and spindles, the sharp, chemical tang that cut through the sickly rubbery smell even in this state and recalled the CineBo archive; the shrivelled scraps and loops of celluloid that had fallen out or floated upwards, the black and brown lump the size and density of what might once have been a large CONAD shopping bag containing the negatives of *Amore su una lama di rasoio*.

'Case closed?' enquired the *Ispettore* dryly.

I took a step back. Tried not to dwell on the grinning corpse.

'And how,' my voice was coming back, 'do we know this is Gianni Colline?'

He gestured me to accompany him deeper into the copse.

We arrived at the river bank. The Reno rushed below in a torrent of silty grey. Resting on the bank above, a log. In front of it, an empty bottle of rum, a framed photo of Valeria Vignetti, and an ID – Gianni Colline.

'Convenient.' I coughed. It still hurt.

'Which lends it credence,' said the *Ispettore*. 'Suicides can be very obliging – after all, the act itself is unequivocal. People who take their life don't tend to be keen on ambiguity.'

'No note, though, I'm guessing.'

'Is one really necessary? The act – or should that be acts – says it all. He killed the woman and then himself. This is her car. Given your presence here, I presume you will be able to enlighten us further.'

'He was her boyfriend,' I said. 'They were running a kind of cinema club together with two others – a woman at the university and a student. They appeared to be borrowing films from CineBo to show there.' I watched the river water rumble by. 'All right, let's say he killed the woman. It *was* a personal thing. Why would he incinerate the film?'

The *Ispettore* shook his head. 'I'll say this for you, Daniel – you are single-minded. Who knows? Maybe it was the source of the friction, maybe they argued about it and it triggered all of this. Or maybe it was just sitting in the back of the car and its presence is coincidental.'

'And the attack on me in the apartment? That seems less than coincidental.'

'Although it could be – it is Petroni, after all.'

'This guy, he didn't strike me as your typical opportunist druggie. Too old, fit. Expert – he might have killed me.'

'Not expert enough, apparently.'

'I got lucky.'

'How?'

I hesitated – but this was the *Ispettore*, not a pair of uniforms. We had history. 'Stabbed him.'

That provoked the *Ispettore's* interest. 'Oh?'

'Not fatally, I think. In the side. He made off before your guys arrived. And – *he was wearing an ear piece.*'

'That's . . . curious.'

'Professional.'

'All right,' said the *Ispettore*. 'You have my attention. But I'm still treating this as murder-suicide.' He looked back down at the framed photo – a selfie, Valeria Vignetti standing on the edge of a volcano smiling, especially bronzed, in a pale-blue T-shirt and shorts, her long curly hair hanging loose around her shoulders.

'Poor girl,' he said.

Chapter 11

La Residenza Faidate, or Faidate Residence, was aptly named. Although the size of a modest *palazzo*, it was definitely not one of Bologna's palaces, trumpeting its status, complete with state and ball rooms (although almost all of the city's *palazzi* had now converted these into impractical residential or office spaces). Neither was it exactly a *casa*, or house, at least as commonly understood. You might pass *La Residenza* without the foggiest idea what lay behind the four-metre-tall ochre wall that ran along a section of narrow, otherwise porticoed Via Mirasole, although its bricked-together battlements might suggest there was something inside worth protecting, as indeed there once had been: *La Famiglia Faidate* had historically been merchants specialising in luxury items for Bologna's aristocratic families, from books and scientific instruments to spices, ointments and, mostly, medicinal herbs.

Entering through the now automated, iron-strapped oak gates, you would step onto a gravel path that crossed a grassed area complete with an ancient silver elm beyond which, where there had once stood a well, were spaces for a couple of cars.

Overlooking you on three sides were frescoed 'Romeo and Juliet' balconies rising three storeys, albeit that over time – and there had been as many bad as good times for the Faidate across the preceding five centuries – those Biblical scenes had been touched up by cruder hands, if not lost altogether: upon our landing we had armless saints and bugle-less cherubs exhorting across concrete-patched clouds, while just to the right of our door, a little flock of sheep floated upon a pale-green pasture riven permanently asunder from their half-faced shepherd.

The ground floor of the Residence had traditionally been used for stores and workshops, although I was waging a campaign to persuade Jacopo, who had most recently been hiring them out as studio space to his pals, to let me convert one into a garage so we could have more room for the garden.

Nearest the gate was, actually, a small 'house' – in fact another former workshop, where Alba lived with Claudio – and along the stretch of path running outside it, the dinner table had been set.

'All in all,' I said, coiling the *tagliatelle al ragù* around the side of my plate, 'terrible. A terrible, terrible day.' I shuddered to think of Valeria lying there like a broken doll, Gianni's charcoaled corpse.

'How's the throat?' asked Alba. 'You seem to be eating okay.'

'Your cooking is evidently medicinal.' She nodded as if it evidently was. 'But seriously,' I said, 'it seems better, just a bit bruised.'

'Well, eat up.'

We liked to dine outside this time of year, before the

summer heat forced us inside. In fact, in the years before the family had invested in air-conditioning, we had soldiered on through July until we escaped to the seaside, but now, once the evenings passed thirty degrees we scuttled inside and luxuriated in the cool – less romantic, perhaps, but also a sight less sticky.

'The pair of you, however,' said the Comandante, a fork of 'Roast Beef' topped by rucola and Parmesan paused halfway to his mouth. 'Yourself and Dolores, you did good work tracking down the lead to the film.'

'And a lot of good it did us.' Rufus, our Lagotto Romagnolo – a springy-haired truffle-hunting dog – appeared in the space between my daughter and me, looking mournfully up at us. Rose scooped up a forkful of *ragù* and lowered it to muzzle level. He polished it off in an instant. She responded to my scowl by reaching for the fork in the bowl of *tagliatelle*.

'I'll use this,' she mouthed.

'So it seems,' the Comandante admitted. 'However, this incident at the apartment, well, that is . . . intriguing.'

'I'm glad you see it like that,' I said. 'Your successor didn't seem to be unduly concerned.'

'The *Ispettore* was right to react the way he did,' said the Comandante. 'His reasoning appears sound. The deaths of two young people clearly take precedence over some missing film, and as someone with more experience of these kinds of tragic incidents than yourself, he is right to prioritise the more banal explanation – certainly I found that in the course of everyday life *passion* tends to trump *plot*.

'On the other hand, *we do* have the luxury to ruminate on your encounter. The most likely explanation is of course that it was an opportunistic burglary. It is just around the corner from Piazza Verdi . . . In his fever, the boy might even have left the door open, and from what you are saying, there was plenty of valuable material – this computer, for example. Isn't that precisely the kind of thing drug addicts favour?'

'Except, this guy didn't seem like a typical druggie. He was neat, strong, seemed like a pro. *And he had an earpiece.*'

'Most curious. Although – are you sure it was an earpiece for communicating, and not simply the kind that people use to listen to music?'

'It was one of those squiggly ones behind the ear bouncers use. It was definitely for communicating. I'm presuming someone outside tipped him off about the cops, which is why he got out.'

'Still,' said the Commandante. 'Although we can't discount that this was somehow connected to the film, the fact is there was so much other material there. He could have been interested in any of these other items.' He caught my sceptical look. 'I am simply playing devil's advocate, Daniel.'

'But the film's gone now,' said Rose, who rarely took any interest in 'work talk' as she put it. 'So, "case closed", no?'

'Have you been speaking to the *Ispettore*?' I said. 'But I suppose you've got a point. Although there may be some wrapping up to do – to work out the extent this "secret cinema club" has been pilfering the films, and if there are any further ones outstanding.'

'I expect CineBo will want to keep it under wraps, though, no?' replied Rose. 'Can you imagine the publicity if it got out?'

The adults around the table – at least, the Comandante, Alba, Jacopo and I, Claudio was too busy with his meal – surveyed my daughter with surprise.

'A most astute comment,' said the Comandante. 'And what has prompted this sudden interest?'

She shrugged. 'I just like CineBo, they put on some good films.' Indeed they do, I thought. I had a sudden vision of her among the student bustle in the Department of Communications a couple of years hence, although I realised her preference would almost certainly be art school.

'Dan.' Alba was looking meaningfully at me across the table. *'You were going to mention.'*

What? Then I remembered. 'Yes, well, actually, it was the Comandante's idea.' I nodded at Giovanni. For once, let him carry the can.

The Comandante cleared his throat. 'Very well. We thought,' he glanced at Alba, sitting back, idly rubbing her belly, 'when your cousin takes her leave, it could be a good time for you, perhaps, to take the reins at the firm . . .'

'Me?' Rose straightened as if accused of a heinous crime.

Alba chuckled.

'Don't worry, *amore*, he's not actually asking you to *run the company*,' which was, in fact, her role behind the reception desk. 'Just answer the phone and, you know, do what you do best – look pretty.'

'But . . .' Rose began.

'It would only be for a few weeks,' I interjected – it seemed unfair to have her think she was about to be pressed into child labour. 'Before we close for summer. And, let's face it,' I added mischievously, 'you could do with the money.'

'But . . .' She looked between us, furiously calculating. 'Let me think about it.'

'Sure,' I said, 'but don't take too long. When are you due off, Alba?'

'Ten days,' she said. 'She'll have to come in for a few days beforehand, learn the ropes.'

'So let us know soon,' I said. 'Otherwise we'll have to think of an alternative, and your Uncle Jac here is not too keen to be staffing reception.' Jacopo spluttered on his wine.

My phone buzzed. A WhatsApp. 'It's from Director Domori,' I said. 'Wants an update. He's also asking for a meeting tomorrow.'

'Why the frown, Daniel?'

'The venue,' I said. 'It's not CineBo, it's at the headquarters of Fausto SpA.'

Chapter 12

It was one of those spring mornings when the crystalline bright dazzled as if the sun was reflecting off a rippling sea, even though Bologna was an hour's fast drive from the Adriatic.

So it seemed natural for all three of us to be in sunglasses as I drove the Alfa along Via Stalingrado – me in my Aviator-style Polaroids, the Comandante in the passenger seat sporting a pair of surprisingly trendy blue-lensed tortoiseshell Wayfarers I suspected Rose had picked out for him, and Dolores stretched out in the back with 'vintage' eighties glasses that, along with the padded shoulders of her red jacket and that henna bob, could have won her a walk-on part in an old MTV video.

'This is the one,' said the Comandante.

There was a certain predictable irony that the radical-left filmmaker's family fortune would be embodied by such a blatant Fascist-era monument. Mid-way along one of the main roads out of the city, the building housing Fausto SpA would have seemed even more at home when Via Stalingrado had had its more innocuous, although still somehow implicitly Fascist, moniker, Via Nuova.

Set back from the road proper, the four-storey white stone edifice with its ranks of geometrically aligned square windows either side of four columns, stood alone among a wilderness of abandoned industrial land stretching all the way up to the *autostrada*, more like a war memorial than a company HQ.

'They might have moved outside the city, with all the others,' said the Comandante, 'but they couldn't vacate the premises unless they could get someone else to move in, and it would have been too expensive . . .'

'Couldn't they just have pulled it down?'

'Oh no,' said the Comandante. 'By that time, it was listed.'

In any case, the impression of decline was misleading. It was true *Famiglia Fausto* hadn't been able to abandon their old building, but they had a series of state-of-the-art packaging plants along the *autostrada* towards Imola and even the wasteland they currently occupied was in the process of redevelopment – their HQ would soon be surrounded by custom-built, futuristic plants hosting the mega computers of Data Valley. In fact, at first I had presumed the trucks and trailers in the car park, along with the cranes rising around an abandoned factory to the side of the building, were connected with this, until I saw the RAI livery and realised that it was associated with the remake of *Amore su una lama di rasoio*. I had read somewhere that the film was a co-production with the Italian broadcaster, and it would make perfect sense to utilise the facilities available at the family firm – of course, Indigo Adler was family too – precisely as Toni Fausto had: scenes from the original would have been shot at the very same factory before it had fallen to ruin.

We walked up the steps between the columns and pushed

through revolving doors into a huge reception illuminated by the largest Murano chandelier I had ever seen. But at least its frondescence took the edge off what would have otherwise been an oppressively stark granite and black marble interior dominated by a long reception desk flanked by a pair of slate-grey staircases. They may have been building a film set outside, but I felt as if we had just stepped into one – probably a noir from the 1940s, and certainly in black and white.

The receptionist directed us to a lift and we ascended to the fourth floor where we were met by a young woman in a dark suit and heels who led us along a panelled corridor lined by photographs celebrating company milestones: foundation layings, factory openings; mechanisation, computerisation.

We were shown into the company boardroom.

They were already in some kind of discussion but stood as we entered: Alberto and Elettra Fausto, Rocco Domori, and, coming towards me, hand held out ready to pump my own, Indigo Adler.

'You're the English detective, right? Daniel Leicester?'

'That's right. And you're Mr Adler.'

'Indigo,' he said solemnly. 'It's been intense, Rocco tells me.'

'It has,' I said.

'And they found the guys who did it.'

'Allegedly.'

He nodded to himself. 'You know, it's only now I truly think I'm beginning to get it – that Toni Fausto menace. Of course, he had the backdrop of the *Years of Lead* to help rack up the tension along the *blood red* porticoes – a Kodak 25 filter I'd say, but I'd need to check the shooting notes. Anyhow, what I'm saying is – for all their prettiness, the devil's walking these porticoes, too, right?' He gave me an intense look.

'I don't know about the devil,' I said, 'but it's true, I sometimes have the sense the city's alive, and has claws.'

'That's it,' he said. '"Claws",' he repeated as if making a mental note. 'Then how to convey it? Toni could use the politics because that was the context for the audience, too, see? But it's a *subtext* that no longer exists, so it becomes *literally* meaningless to the modern audience. I need to capture that same sense of life-on-the-edge – of a *razorblade*, right? – that around every corner . . .'

'Roeg managed it,' I said. 'With *Don't Look Now.*'

Indigo nodded appreciatively. 'You've got it.' He turned to Elettra. 'Wasn't I saying that?' She smiled affectionately.

'You were saying a lot, Indi, as usual.'

'She thinks I talk too much. She's right. I think that's why she's making me learn Italian – she's hoping it will slow me down, but they speak so quickly, *mamma mia* . . . Anyway – anything new?'

'Well . . .' I looked at the others who had presumably viewed our exchange with varying degrees of comprehension – only Rocco and Elettra could speak really good English, with Dolores bringing up the rear. 'Shall we sit down? Maybe your wife could translate?'

'Oh, yeah, sure, sure.' We took our places at the end of a glass-topped conference table so long that each place included a microphone and speaker set.

I quickly summarised what they apparently already knew about Valeria and Gianni, hoping to skip over prurient speculation.

'But they were screwing, right?' said Indigo.

'Well, they were apparently going out,' I said. 'Gianni Colline was on the same course as Valeria when they were at university, which was presumably where the connection came from.'

'Valeria was appointed by my predecessor,' interjected the director. 'I barely knew the woman.'

'There was a mini theatre at Gianni's home,' I continued. 'We have spoken again to the other woman involved in their so-called "secret cinema" – another doctoral student, Patrizia Bussoni – who claims Valeria and Gianni were the driving force behind the project.'

'As well she might,' said Alberto.

'She said Valeria got the idea after she began working at CineBo and described how she and Gianni got the films out in the early hours of the morning, which is consistent with what we had already discovered. She also provided us with a full list of the movies they had borrowed.' I pushed it over to the director. 'Which she said, as far as she was aware, had been replaced.'

'She was very cooperative, this woman,' observed Elettra.

'I gave her the impression that she could either talk to us, or the police.'

Director Domori looked alarmed. 'But we're not going to go to the police? About the negatives, I mean.'

'We don't have to, if you don't want us to.'

'We don't want them to, do we?' Alberto and Elettra shook their heads.

'Although I can't guarantee the police won't come to you,' I said.

'But that would be about the bodies,' said Domori. 'Not the negatives.'

'Yes,' I said. 'I think they will be more interested in the deaths.' He nodded, apparently oblivious to my irony.

'I should add,' he said, 'the *Ispettore* in charge of the crime scene passed on a sample of the small amount of material that had not been entirely consumed by the blaze, and from the stills in question, we can confirm they were the negatives from *Amore su una lama di rasoio*.'

Silence around the table.

'Then all in all,' said the Comandante, 'I believe we can bring this matter to a close. I am very sorry we were not able to achieve a more satisfying outcome.'

'But that's what I don't get,' said Indigo.

Elettra sighed. 'This again, *amore*?'

Her husband ignored her. 'You say "film", Signor Faidate, but they were negatives. Go on, sweetie-pie, please.' With a roll of her eyes, Elettra translated.

'I'm sorry, Signor Adler,' said the Comandante, glancing at me. 'I'm not sure I understand your point.'

'These kids were screening *prints* of the films, right? On a projector?' I nodded. 'Well, you couldn't screen these because they were *negatives*, right? You use them to *make* the prints, but you can't actually project them.'

'I think I get your point,' I said. 'I actually saw a Moviola machine in the room, too. My guess is they were using that to view them.'

'But why?'

'I suspect, like you, Indigo, Gianni was a Toni Fausto fan – he had his movie posters on the walls – and, having access to a Moviola, the temptation . . .'

Indigo slapped the table. '*Now I get it.* Yup, I can see that. Hell, if I'd been one of those kids, I'd have probably done the same. But then, that's the real tragedy.' He corrected himself. 'For art, I mean, obviously – those negs going up in smoke.'

'You mean because of the out-takes?' I said. 'Bloopers? Otherwise, as I understand it, the rest of the negatives are, ultimately, replaceable, no?'

'*Oh no, man,*' said Indigo. 'That's not it at all. It's the ending.'

'What do you mean, "the ending"?'

Indigo looked at Alberto and Elettra. 'Didn't anyone tell you? I came across it in his papers before I left the States – the version of *Amore su una lama di rasoio* deposited in the CineBo archives had a whole different ending.'

I looked between father and daughter. 'But I thought . . .'

'You're right, Giovanni.' Alberto Fausto rose, followed by Elettra. 'Our business here is concluded.'

Alberto Fausto had begun to lead the Comandante, arm-in-arm, along the corridor towards the lift when Elettra took me aside. '*Sensitive subject. Nonno* didn't like my uncle's ending so he changed it. Nobody complained at the time and he was quite happy to let his brother take all the credit. He had no idea the footage "on the cutting room floor" had even survived. He didn't really understand much about how films are made, despite having to complete one himself. As you can imagine, it's brought up a lot of unhappy memories.'

'I never would have noticed,' said Indigo Adler. 'The papers were at the bottom of a box file. I was actually looking for his photography notes for the Bologna shoot, when I came across the receipts and out of curiosity checked what had gone into the store and then to the CineBo archive.

'It was then I realised the editors must have kept Toni's cut for posterity and given Alberto new masters to work from, only the poor sap never realised.' He shook his head in wonderment.

'Look,' he continued. 'I was wondering if you'd be free to meet up outside office hours? I promised Anna lunch tomorrow but Elettra's out of town, so we're sort of missing our local Bologna expert-stroke-translator.

'It'd be cool to hear what it's like to be an English detective in Italy and,' he winked, 'maybe I'll even be permitted to tell you about Toni Fausto's original ending.'

Elettra rolled her eyes. 'I'm sure he's got better things to do than play the tour guide, Indi.'

But I was intrigued, and not only by Toni Fausto's finale. 'That's Anna . . . *Bloom*?' I asked.

'Anna, yup.'

'Sure,' I said as casually as I dared, adding – even as I was saying it, wondering if I was entirely sane – 'would you mind if my daughter joined us?'

Chapter 13

Rose, however, had not given me quite the reaction I had expected.

'Not Elettra Fausto?' she said in the English we habitually spoke to each other. I looked into her disappointed brown eyes – her mother's eyes – and understood that while to an oldie like me, Elettra Fausto was a nobody compared to, well, *Aphrodite*, in the universe of a sixteen-year-old *Bewitching* fan, Cassandra Sinistra, a supporting witch on a Netflix series, was by far the larger planet in the solar system.

'Well, you don't have to come,' I said. 'If you've got something better to do.'

'Oh no,' said Rose, looking down at her phone. 'I'll come. You're right – I've got nothing better to do.'

'Fine.' I silently posed the question universally asked by all parents of teenagers – *why do I bother?*

Happily, Rose's disinterest was short-lived – perhaps she had simply needed to consult her fifth metal and glass limb before being able to properly commit herself – because as I returned from walking Rufus the following morning, she was full of fun facts about Anna Bloom.

'Did you know she was first choice for Lady Luck?'

'I didn't, but I don't know who Lady Luck is.'

Rose rolled her eyes. 'It's from the Stargaze franchise.' CUE: amazement at my unbelievable ignorance. '*Scarlett Johansson* is Lady Luck.'

'Okay.'

'She dated Jamie Taverner.'

'Oh, yeah, I knew that.'

'*Do you even know who Jamie Taverner is?*'

'An actor?'

'*Dad*. Jamie Taverner is from Young Blood. You know – the group.'

'You mean that dreadful boyband of dancing vampires?'

'She was the older woman.'

'I suppose she must have been,' I said, feeling vaguely disappointed. 'But wasn't she married to Clive Cornwall – you know, the Shakespearean actor and Oscar winner?'

'It was after they divorced. Apparently, she's now going out with her personal trainer.'

'I suppose there comes a time in every celebrity's life when they date their personal trainer,' I said. Rose looked at me with great seriousness.

'I should find something to wear,' she said.

'Yes, you'd better get a move on, we've only got . . . five hours.'

As this was a Saturday, I indulged in my weekend habit of listening to BBC Radio 4 which, considering how immersed I otherwise was in Italian culture, could sometimes feel like the World Service, so detached from my reality were the concerns and passions of that Island People. Although I suppose Italy is also, effectively, an island – her knee-length boot stretches into the Mediterranean and is topped by a formidable mountain range. Certainly, she has that inward-looking island mentality, and is parochial to a granular detail that can make the British – be they English or any of the Celtic nations – seem like a homogenous blob. The difference is, of course, the 'island' of Italy has not gone unmolested for a thousand years, so instead of investing in a shared national identity, solidarity finds expression through: *family, locality, profession*. Italian society is essentially one great 'closed shop'. Over the generations, these identities evolved their own peculiarities, and while there are of course a range of personalities in every profession, characteristics tend to be shared between members as they might within a family, something as true for *camerieri* and *criminali* as for *professori* and *avvocati*.

And *that* was what had been troubling me: despite what I had said to the *Ispettore*, there had been something a little 'off' about the supposed 'professional' criminal who attacked me. I had come across a few in my time – from London gangsters to Bologna's local hoods, the Nonnies. But when they weren't keeping it in the family, the Nonnies tended to contract out to guys up from the south – probably lying low after some especially heinous mob business – spindly, skinny types with sharp haircuts in their teens and twenties.

But this one had been local, well built, older, with a definite Emilian accent. I simply hadn't come across any local mobsters of that generation who would still be willing to get their hands dirty. That was a young man's game.

'Don't struggle.' I could still smell his coffee breath. He had got me well and good – until I got lucky.

He was a professional, then, *but what profession?*

'No!'

It had come from Rose's room. I went to knock at her closed door.

'Is everything all right?'

'You can come in,' she replied miserably. She was standing in front of the mirror in her best dress – the white, jewel-necked Gucci the Comandante had bought for her mother Lucia for our wedding reception. Rose had last worn it a little over a year before for a friend's birthday party, and even then I'd thought, although it fit her slender teenage frame well having been adjusted a few months previously, it ended a good inch above where it was supposed to. One year and a late growth spurt on, it was verging on a mini.

Despite trumpeting her Englishness at every opportunity, and that auburn hair licking her long pale neck, Rose presented me with an ineffably Italian expression of horror – hands on hips, jaw jutted out, the unmistakable pose of outraged Latin womanhood. Actually, to my eyes the dress didn't look so bad – she had plenty of contemporary ones the same length she ventured out in during the evening – but I appreciated what might be appropriate for teenage boys, my daughter did not consider right for meeting a movie star and famous director. Perhaps that was also the Italian in her – these young girls had the heads of old women.

'You've got other dresses that fit you perfectly,' I said. 'There's the yellow one . . .'

'It makes me look like a child.'

'Then the red one.'

'Too showy.' She opened her wardrobe, bursting with dresses. 'Nothing!'

She gave me a look I knew too well.

'Rose,' I said. 'We've got four hours before we meet them.'

'That's plenty of time.'

'To buy you a dress, perhaps, but a *designer* one? You don't think I know that's what you're thinking?' I shook my head. 'I'm not going to spend that kind of money in a hurry. That's a birthday and a Christmas present together.'

'It could be,' she said as if she was making me an offer. 'Even birthday, Christmas, birthday.'

'Which is why it shouldn't be rushed. And a Gucci would certainly be out of the question.'

'It doesn't have to be Gucci, Dad, I'm not mad! Just something . . . nice. Can't we at least go and check? I think there are sales on.'

'You "think"?' I gave her a sceptical look.

'Oh, come on, Dad. Don't you want me to be,' and she said it as if she really meant it, '*elegant* for you?'

A mere twenty minutes later we were in Galleria Cavour, fortunately, or unfortunately, depending on your point-of-view, just a few hundred metres down the hill from *La Residenza*, across from where Via Garibaldi met placid Piazza Cavour with its fountains and flower beds.

The Galleria occupied a section of Palazzo Vasse, although as ever in Bologna, both the ancient origins of the *galleria* and the full grandeur of the adjacent *palazzo* were largely obscured by portico. As you entered Bologna's most expensive stretch of retail space you could be forgiven for imagining with all the glistening marble and glass this was in fact a modern development instead of inhabiting a structure five hundred years old. At least, these were the kind of thoughts that occurred to me as I used it as a shortcut to Piazza Maggiore or *Il Quadrilatero*, or simply dawdled in its air-conditioned cool to escape the heat of summer. Rose undoubtedly took more notice of her contemporary surroundings.

She made a beeline for Miu Miu.

As my daughter glided between the rooms like a seal through water, shadowed by an attractive young male assistant providing a cheerful commentary on the garments as if he were Rose's new bestie, I flipped the label on one of the dresses she had momentarily considered, before letting it drift back onto the rail.

Seized by a sudden panic, I thought: We need to get out of here.

But Rose had disappeared. I retraced my steps through the store, reassuring myself that however dazzled she might become by the luxury on offer, I was still that indispensable accessory – the wallet.

'Signore?' It was the assistant.

'What have you done with my daughter?'

He smiled. 'She has excellent taste, signore, very refined. Very beautiful. Come,' he took my elbow, 'she is upstairs.'

'There's more?'

'Oh yes. Come, come . . .'

I'd missed the stairs. I followed him up to the first floor, which would have been part of the *piano nobile* of the old palace. The restored staterooms, with their frescoed ceilings and eighteenth-century damask wall coverings, felt like entering an antechamber to the Palace of Versailles, a feeling hammered home when I spotted my daughter modelling a slight cream dress in front of Marie Antoinette.

'It's okay,' said the Queen, looking up from the velvet cushioned *chaise longue*, her bare arms stretched back, head cocked thoughtfully to one side, 'but with your cold water complexion and that lovely natural hair, I think you could do better with something that draws attention to the contrast. Ah, there you are.' She meant the assistant. 'Have you got anything in . . . emerald green, ideally – she's like a lovely colleen, you're not Irish, are you?'

'English,' said Rose.

'Oh, I'm an eighth English, but mainly Scandinavian stock. Or navy,' she said to the assistant. '*Bold* blue.' She turned back to Rose. 'With looks like yours you shouldn't hide yourself away, especially in this country where simply everyone is beautiful, but all *the same kind* of beautiful, you know? You stand apart. And I see you've located the sugar daddy!'

'The *daddy*,' I said. 'Anna Bloom, I presume.'

'Guilty.' She rose, holding out a long, slender hand. We were eye to eye. If she had been wearing heels I would have had to look up to her. 'Your daughter tells me we're actually due to meet for lunch today.' She spoke in the West Coast American of Oscar acceptance speeches – as indeed she had early on in her career, for Best Actress in a Soderbergh film. 'You must be Bologna's very own Sam Spade.'

'It makes a change from Sherlock Holmes.'

'Ha. I can't exactly imagine you in a Deerstalker. Ah, yes,

now we're talking!' The assistant had arrived with a dress over each arm.

'Our new collection,' he said. As he passed by, I tried and failed to glimpse a price tag. He handed them to Rose, who took them into the changing room. I had the sickening sensation of being overtaken by events.

'So Indigo is hiring you as a consultant,' said Ms Bloom.

'That's news to me.'

'Oh, he didn't tell you? Well, that's what he told me, but don't take my word for it – he's a law unto himself, like all directors. She's sweet, your daughter – has she thought of modelling?'

'Please,' I said. 'Don't plant that idea in her head.'

Anna Bloom threw her head back and let out a loud laugh. Again, I couldn't help picturing Marie Antoinette in the Luc Besson movie, this time the scene at the theatre before things turned pear-shaped, although in truth there was little to otherwise identify her with the role – her tied-back blond hair was hidden beneath a black baseball cap and she was wearing a plain white T-shirt and jeans. 'You know,' she said, 'I started off as a model, but I get your point – after I got into acting I never looked back. Rose doesn't want to act?'

'She wants to be an artist. She's actually very good. She's already had a joint exhibition with Stella Amore.'

'*Really?*' she said. 'And who's Stella Amore?'

Rose drew back the curtain. The assistant gasped. Rose brushed back a lock of hair that had fallen across the night-blue shoulder of the dress. Anna had been right – it was a stunning combination with her almost translucent skin and flame hair.

'Well,' my daughter said sheepishly, 'what do you think?'

Anna clapped her hands together and gave me a broad smile. 'Well, what do you think, *Daddy*?'

'Elegant,' I said. 'I think you look very elegant, darling.'

We arrived at Leonida around two hours later and twenty minutes early, not that I was nervous, exactly, but I did want to make sure we had secured the private room at the back I had taken care to book – naturally, news of the film was all over Bologna, and I didn't want the famous director and actor to be interrupted throughout the meal. I'd chosen Leonida because it was a reliable, traditional restaurant down a side street off Piazza Santo Stefano, a little on the expensive side, but nothing over-the-top. We came here at weekends ourselves. But while the clientele of one of the pricier joints might be more likely to restrain their enthusiasm for selfies with the famous duo, I couldn't be quite so sure about Leonida. On the other hand, I was also confident the proprietor, the venerable Signor Dante, wouldn't give a damn about who they were – his was not the kind of establishment that placed pictures of its famous customers on its walls.

While Rose waited inside, I stepped out to make a call. Frankly, I also needed to get away from her. I was still fuming that, having spent *six hundred euros* on that dress – and this with a fifty per cent discount requested by Anna Bloom, who had an 'arrangement' with the designer – she had declined to actually wear it to the lunch.

'She's already seen it!' Rose shouted back at me. 'It will look like I was just getting dressed up for her!'

'She'll appreciate it – she loved it!'

'But you don't want her to think I've only got one dress!'

'I honestly don't care what she thinks!'

'Well, I do!'

It picked up: 'Alessandro.'

'*Ispettore*, I had a thought about the guy who attacked me.'

'Daniel, it's the weekend. Even Carabinieri take the weekend off occasionally – in fact, we are on the way to Forlì, there's an exhibition.'

'You're right,' I said. 'I'm sorry to disturb you.'

'Now you have – tell me.'

'I was thinking – that blade went in pretty deep. I probably did some serious damage. And if I had, he might be in hospital.'

'He might. Or they might just have left him to fester somewhere. Or put him out of his misery.'

'That's just it – this guy. The earpiece. This didn't feel like an ordinary break-in to me. The guy was older . . . he didn't strike me as the type likely to be, or to be treated as, quite so "expendable". He probably had a family to support. I think his pals would have wanted to look after him.'

There was silence at the other end, then the sound of a navigator telling the *Ispettore* to make a left turn. 'All right,' he said. 'We'll look into it.'

The navigator now told the *Ispettore* to take the second exit at the roundabout. 'Incidentally,' he said, 'we found something interesting when we searched the apartment of the young man.'

'Oh?' Coming along the lane, I spotted Indigo Adler and Anna Bloom – still dressed in her T-shirt and jeans, I noted. Perhaps, I hated to admit, the Miu Miu might have been a bit much.

'Twenty thousand euros.'

'Oh?'

'Stuffed into his mattress.'

'Which might explain the guy . . .'

'It might.'

'But where . . .'

'Did the cash come from?' said the *Ispettore*. 'Precisely. It's quite the mystery.' Indigo and Anna began to near. I gave them a wave.

'It wasn't just the guy. There was something wrong about that place – the bathroom was flooded.'

'And what do you think that signified?'

'I . . . don't know. Only that it appeared to have come out of the bath. What do you think?'

The *Ispettore* laughed. 'Well, Daniel, I have absolutely no idea. Only that, like you, I have been distracted from enjoying this lovely weekend. Mysteries are for Mondays. I suggest you get on with your day, and I'll get on with mine.'

I ended the call. Anna and Indigo were standing before me.

'You're looking worried,' said Anna. 'Is it to do with Indigo's case?'

I shook my head. She arched her eyebrows. 'Another one,' I said. 'It was a police contact.'

'Man,' Indigo patted me on the shoulder. 'You're the real thing. This is what I was talking about: an inside track on the underbelly of Bologna – *A Room with a View* meets *Mean Streets*.'

I laughed. 'I'm not sure about that,' I said, leading them inside. 'Either of them.'

***

The pair were, as I had expected, charmed by Leonida. Sensitive to the proclivities of Hollywood folk, I had warned Indigo in advance to expect meat-heavy cuisine, but he hadn't batted an eyelid. He had a *cotoletta alla bolognese*, which Signor Dante reluctantly agreed to serve without prosciutto in recognition of Indigo's Judaism, although he made a great deal of emphasising it wasn't a 'proper' *cotoletta*, while Anna went for *faraona*, or guineafowl. I had my usual *tagliatelle al cinghiale*, while Rose chose the same with mushrooms. The meal was accompanied by a bottle of the local Otello Lambrusco, which the Americans found a tremendous novelty.

'*Cold fizzy red wine,*' said Anna. 'They never served that at Venice!'

'She means the festival,' said Indigo.

'Hardly,' I said. 'It's local to Emilia Romagna. Venetians would likely be a bit snobbish – it's a country wine, a peasant wine. But it's low alcohol and very moreish.'

'I'll say,' said Anna, refilling her own glass. Rose offered hers up. I shook my head.

'Moreish for adults,' I said.

'*My God, you're right,*' said Anna, steering the bottle away. 'I'm already getting seduced by your permissive European ways. If this was the States I'd have been arrested for child abuse! Speaking of which.' She exchanged a glance with Indigo.

'*Speaking of which?*'

She let out that big laugh of hers again. 'Well, *child exploitation* would probably be the phrase.' Now she looked at Rose. 'How would you like to come to work for me?' Rose's eyes widened. 'I was saying to Indi how much fun we had in the store, and although RAI have been very helpful, you know, the assistants they've provided, well . . .' She lowered her voice. '*None of them can really speak English.* Oh, they can do the "goffer" thing – "go for this, go for that" – but they're not exactly *conversational,* fun to be around. I really need a mother tongue, someone with a bit of personality, just to hang out with, and I thought . . .' Now she looked at me.

What could I do? I smiled at Rose, who was twirling the *tagliatelle* around her fork. She looked between us.

'I'd love to,' she said, 'but the thing is, I've already got a job.'

'Oh.' Anna looked surprised. 'Well, obviously, it was just . . .'

'Of course you can,' I said.

'But don't you need me?'

'We can find someone else. It'll be a great opportunity for you to see how films get made.'

'Are you sure?'

I nodded. The excitement my daughter had heroically dammed swept her face. Anna reached across the table and squeezed her hand.

'We'll have such fun!'

'In fact, I also meant to ask *you,*' said Indigo Adler, 'if you would be available as a consultant.'

'Are you looking for a family discount?' He laughed.

'Well, that's how things get done here, isn't it – *the Italian way?*'

'What do you want me to "consult" upon?'

'Oh, you know.' He gave a vague wave. 'A bit like Rose, I'd like you to hang around, check we're getting the detail right . . .'

I wasn't sure I fancied 'hanging around' a film set like a spare part, but with the CineBo contract closed, I didn't feel I could turn it down, especially if I wanted to keep my girl in Miu Miu.

'You were going to tell me,' I said. 'About this ending. I mean, the version Toni Fausto produced that went up in smoke. What happened?'

Indigo's eyes lit up. 'You see, that's the thing, man – the ending everyone knows wasn't *Toni Fausto's* ending. According to his old script, in the ending *he* filmed there was no editing studio climax, not even a gun. That's what I was looking forward to seeing, and the version I'm planning to shoot in *Razorblade*.'

'So what's so different about the Toni Fausto ending?'

'Only – everything! Instead of heading to the editing studio, Ursula gets the cab to the airport with the brother, Franco, and it's *then*, as they're boarding the plane, the husband confronts them. There's quite a scene, but finally, as there's the final call, she goes with Franco. Cut to credits. Of course,' he smiled, 'the flight is Itavia 870.'

'I'm sorry, you've lost me.' He smiled again.

'Ustica,' he said. I sat back with surprise. 'Yeah,' continued Indigo. 'I guess that's the sort of reaction Toni was hoping for. To be honest, when I first read it, I didn't get the significance myself, and why should I? Another place, another time. *Ustica* – sounds like brand of pasta. Then I read about the plane crash, the controversy – jeesh, the *continuing* controversy. Do you know they're still trying to get to the bottom of it over forty years later?'

'The *muro di gomma*,' I said. 'That's what the families

called it when they tried to work out what had really happened. They were greeted with a "rubber wall" – everything just bounced off. A huge cover-up. So the actual crash isn't depicted or mentioned in the film?'

'Nope. I guess back then the local, or Italian audience, would have gotten it, but for a foreign audience . . .'

'Maybe that's why they changed it.'

'Maybe, although it killed the movie artistically, as surely as Vanessa stopped Ron's bullet. Toni more or less invented the "flip emergency exit".'

'I'm sorry, the what?'

'The great Douglas Sirk called it the "emergency exit" – the unlikely but satisfying ending that flies in the face of everything that's come before. Toni Fausto flipped it to slam the door shut on that exit. He clearly intended for the audience to think they were watching a kind of high-stakes melodrama with a predictably happy ending, but what they were actually witnessing was just one of the stories behind the eighty-odd victims on board the ill-fated flight.'

'That's . . . intriguing.'

'Isn't it? Toni's original script was a footnote in movie history, it's always circulated among us Toni Fausto nuts – but the negs surviving, now that was a surprise. We're actually filming out at the memorial to the victims at the moment. Gonna set some scenes there.'

Signor Dante appeared with the bill. I took it.

'No, no,' said Indigo.

'I insist.'

'This is a business lunch, right? We'll charge it to RAI.'

Chapter 14

In contrast to the usual pace of things in Italy, it only took RAI two days to courier over the contract setting my fee at €1000 a day for a minimum of thirty days from the date of delivery, with an automatic rollover. This sweetened the pill – I hadn't set any terms, but as I had read by then that the production had a $40 million budget, I figured they could afford it.

Although Rose had begun 'hanging out' with Anna Bloom more or less from that first day – mainly accompanying her on chauffeured sightseeing trips around Emilia Romagna, and a shopping jaunt to Milan – her own contract came through at the same time. Three hundred daily, basically under the same terms. She was over the moon. I told her not to go crazy, to save the money and decide what she wanted to spend it on when the circus left town – as indeed it would at some unspecified time later in the year to shoot the US scenes (there was quite a diversion from the original plot). How much of that she took in I had no idea.

It was another day before I got the call, which meant I had already earned two thousand euros 'for nothing', although I had passed the time either working from home or in the office. Admittedly, as I justified it to myself, it had constrained me from committing to any new cases which, after meeting the clients, I had handed over to Dolores: a missing husband who had probably just had enough, a suspicious employee who may or may not have been siphoning funds, and a batch from an insurance company asking us to check out health claims. In short, bread and butter work.

Rose actually had the day off as Anna was studying her lines, although my girl had secured a copy of the script to run through with her and was reading it with her legs draped over the armchair in the *soggiorno* as I left.

'Good luck,' she called. 'And don't be overwhelmed by all the activity, it seems crazy at first but everybody knows what they're doing.'

'I'll try,' I said. 'Have you packed me a lunch?'

'What? Oh, ha ha.' But Rose's words came back to me as I walked across scrappy Parco della Zucca in Bolognina.

Half the park had been swallowed up by vans and trailers, and I wandered along a taped-off cordon until I came to a woman with a clipboard.

'And you are?' She was flanked by a pair of security guys, one of whom I recognised – he used to work for us.

'He's *Meester* Daniel Leicester.' He clamped his huge hand around mine, and we kissed in the Italian fashion.

'Dino.' The big guy had been part of our security operation before we had sold it off – a former Carabinieri parachutist who had spent more time patrolling the streets of Kabul than Bologna.

'You're early.' She looked at me accusingly.

'I'm English,' I said apologetically.

'It's okay,' said Dino. 'I'll look after him.' The woman shrugged.

'Just don't disturb the director before it's time.'

'She's the really scary one,' he whispered as he led me away.

We emerged between trailers into a world of activity. What looked like an oversize kids' railway was being set down beside the footpath, while standing lights were being positioned along it and a camera set at the far end. Thick black cables ran everywhere. Across them stepped production assistants, actors, caterers – who knew? There must have been a couple of dozen people wandering about. At the far end of the path was the memorial – an old brick railway shed spruced up with a glass reception area and metal shutters.

We stopped at a refreshments trailer and Dino ordered us coffees, from, I noted, a proper machine. There was no stinting on catering here.

He downed his *espresso* in one go, the pair of little Ace of Spades tattoos – for terrorist, or mafia kills – showing just beneath his sleeve line.

'So what are you seeing the boss about?'

'Apparently I'm supposed to be a "consultant",' I said. 'You know – make sure everything's authentic.'

He laughed. 'Authentic? What do you know about authentic? You're a Brit!'

'I've applied for Italian citizenship.' This was greeted with predictable amusement.

'But then,' he said solemnly, as if it had just occurred to him, 'I suppose with *La Brexit* they'll deport you otherwise.'

'Not exactly,' I said. 'But it will certainly make things

easier. Hey,' I pointed my fingers at him in the shape of a gun, 'I'll be legally entitled to carry a firearm. Maybe you can teach me how to shoot straight.'

'From what I've heard, boss.' He laid a heavy hand on my shoulder. 'You've done all right by yourself so far.'

'How do *you* know about that?' The deep ridges of Dino's brow crinkled upwards.

'Are you really sure you should be advising them on "authenticity", *capo*?'

At the appointed time, I was led to Indigo Adler at work beneath a spacious canopy rather as one might imagine a general during battle. Inside, there was almost as much bustle as outside, with artists bent over draughtsmen's tables, technicians gathered around computers powered by yet more trailing cables, and the director himself standing by a white-board populated with Polaroids, stick men, and arrows.

'You mean that narrow little lane with all the greengrocers'? Nah.' He plucked off the photo of *Il Quadrilatero* and tossed it onto a seat. 'Too touristy, I want something a little more . . . it sounds crazy, but modern. Modern, *but also* . . . Italian.'

'I . . . don't get it, Indi,' said a grey-haired Italian man. 'Modern Italians still shop in the market like that. It *is* modern. You're saying you wanna supermarket?'

'Too bland.'

'Then what you want?' Indigo Adler looked over their heads.

'Daniel? Any ideas?'

I hadn't realised he'd noticed me. 'You're thinking about a shopping scene?' He nodded. 'How about Barberino?' I was remembering the dress Rose had finally selected for her lunch at Leonida. 'It's an outlet for designer clothes – it's not in Bologna, it's near Florence, but it's modern, yet they've tried to reproduce an Italian – Tuscan actually, but it may not matter – town, and there's piped music.'

'Piped music! Bullseye! *That's* what I'm talking about.'

The others looked at each other, plainly mystified, then around at me.

'Daniel's going to be advising us,' said Indigo. 'How about you guys scope out this Barbery place and get back to me with some video. Dan – let's go and have a proper talk.' He gestured outside.

We walked along that path toward the memorial.

'Great idea that,' he said. 'Thanks. This Italian crew – well, these Italians, the photographers especially, they're simply the best in the business. Always have been – Stanley always used them. Something about Italians – they have that eye for beauty, everything's "*bello*", right? It's a visual culture . . . you know, like us Jews – not for the looks but the stories, we're a storytelling culture. *Ciao*, Antonio!' He waved at a lighting guy.

'And don't get me wrong – Sorrentino, Diritti, Adriatico, there are some great directors, but this RAI team,' he continued confidentially, 'their storytelling . . . *meh*. There's a kind of schmaltzy quality, even the stuff for local consumption, I realised: *Italians buy into the myth of Italy themselves*. That suggestion about the market. Great example! I'm not making some fucking travel commercial.' He shook his head. 'But they don't get it. It's not deliberate, it's just . . . what they're used to.'

He opened one of the smoked-glass doors of the building and I followed him inside. 'You know this place, of course,' he said.

'Of it,' I said. 'I've never actually visited.' We pushed through a second set of doors onto a gantry and I was momentarily dazed by the scale of the place: it had been built to construct railway engines, only now there sat an airliner, once exploded into thousands of pieces, now painstakingly reconstructed to sit on the workfloor as if on a runway, with lamps, mirrors, and speakers gathered around it like landing crew.

A red stripe ran the length of its fuselage, beneath it the words *ITAVIA*.

'So that's our idea,' he said. 'This is Ursula and Franco's meeting place in a kind of homage to Toni's version.' I followed him down a ramp onto the floor.

As we reached the ground, the imagined thoughts of the deceased began to drift out of the speakers.

A disembodied, child's voice: 'When we arrive, I'll go straight to the beach.'

A man: 'I still haven't received that invoice.'

I followed Indigo around the plane.

'I wonder if I left the iron on,' said a woman. 'No, you remember, surely, you checked before you left . . .'

'At first they put it down to a terrorist bomb,' said Indigo. 'Meantimes, just about every witness died – the air force pilots flying nearby, both air traffic controllers; a dozen deaths in all, mostly violent – hanging, car accident, or straightforward murder.' He scoffed. 'The investigators called it "suspicious", no kidding.

'In the end they tried some air force generals, but they were let off because the proceedings took too long.'

'What was it, then?'

'Most likely a NATO plot to assassinate Gaddafi,' he said. 'But the missile hit the wrong target. At least, that's the theory . . .' He began to climb the stairs into the fuselage.

A gantry continued down the corridor of the plane, which had otherwise been reconstructed as it would have been with what they had recovered from the sea – seats, luggage, other stray belongings – a child's shoe, a water-bleached seventies paperback.

'We actually want to do a scene in here,' said Indigo. 'Although we're still waiting on permissions.' He turned to face me. 'It'll be respectful. I mean – they'll fuck in a hotel.' He glanced out through one of the many holes torn in the fuselage. 'So,' he said. 'What do you *really* make of all this business, English Detective?'

'You mean the deaths of the young people?' I said. 'Standing here, well, I wouldn't want to get too paranoid.'

He nodded thoughtfully. 'Rocco told me you got attacked when you went to that kid Gianni's house. You left that out of your debrief, I noticed.'

'I didn't want to . . . complicate matters,' I admitted. 'I informed the police, who believe it might have been a coincidence . . . We had uncovered this secret cinema, the theft of the films. And of course, the negatives had been destroyed.'

'Yeah, about that.' His eyes drilled into me. 'You got that hiring you as a consultant was bullshit, right? For appearances sake? Although don't get me wrong – I appreciated your suggestion. I meant it. We'll check out that mall.'

I tried to act as cool as he was. 'Then what is it precisely that you want me for, Mr Adler?'

He let out a hollow laugh. 'You can still call me Indigo.' A smile creased his mouth, but now there was nothing puppyish about it. 'Just treat me like a mister.' He shook his head. 'Shit's never been the same since it all kicked off. First there's this tragedy with the kids. Then the negs, man! Toni's ending! What the fuck? And Elettra, well . . .'

'Well?'

He drew a deep breath. He looked like a child peering over the edge of a very high diving board. I said nothing, let him take that first step into mid-air.

'She's playing "Deborah",' he said.

'The boss's secretary, right?'

'She's been skipping rehearsals, not sleeping . . . I wake up and find her on her phone, sending messages.'

'Does she say to who?'

'Her grandfather, about this business. Friends . . .'

'She's been discussing it with her friends?'

'No. Not as far as I can see – I mean, we're not in Bologna often, it's normal for her to want to be back in touch with her old pals. Only . . .'

'Excuse me, Indigo – you said "not as far as I can see". Have you been checking her messages?'

He shifted uncomfortably. 'All right, I took a look at her phone when she was in the bathroom. I guess that makes me a suspicious prick.'

'You're worried about her,' I said. 'You wanted to check everything was okay. What did you find out?'

'It was pretty much like she said: friends, stuff about

meeting up, appointments with Alberto, that kind of thing
. . .' The diving board look again.

'There's something else,' I said.

'A guy,' he replied flatly. 'Deleted messages. All the rest –
well, they're still there. But she's been messaging this guy and
deleting everything. Well, almost.'

'Do you know him?'

'Paolo Mestre. I didn't know the name, but googled – I
think we've been introduced at a couple of events, weddings,
that kind of thing. Family friend – I think they grew up
together, they're about the same age.'

'You said she had deleted *almost* everything.'

'Look, I know what you're thinking, but she'd never texted
this guy, at least as far as I could see, until she got over here
about a month ago, and the first message is from him shortly
after they discovered the negs were gone: "They agreed," it
says. Then there's a thumbs up from her, and she writes: "We
should meet, I'll call." Just that. And then a couple of days
later from him – a bunch of photos, maybe seven or eight, of
them as kids, teenagers, whatever, at school, family parties,
and she's all smiley emojis, and some trivial stuff in Italian,
like look at my hair, whatever, and then – the deletions,
maybe a dozen of them. The last was yesterday.'

'*They agreed. We should meet?*'

'Yeah, fucking spooky, isn't it, what with all this other shit.'

'Have you mentioned anything about this to her?'

'How the hell could I? What am I gonna say?'

There was a creak. It was just the aircraft, shored up by
steel, held together by wire, but we both felt them – the
phantoms.

'As I was saying,' I said flatly. 'Standing here, it's easy to feel paranoid.'

'And the folks on this plane would have been right to feel that way,' said Indigo. 'Instead, they thought they were going on holiday. Two dead kids? You getting jumped like that? My wife with those mysterious fucking messages? Call me a Yankee fool, Dan, but you know what? I'll choose paranoid.'

Chapter 15

I googled Paolo Mestre myself in an attempt to answer whether Indigo had after all stumbled upon his wife having an affair which, regardless of their mysterious exchange of messages, seemed at least as likely as something more sinister.

'What do you think?' I asked Dolores.

'Looks like Harry Potter ate all the pasta.' It was a photo from Paolo Mestre's graduation, perhaps a decade earlier. He was standing tall among a group of family and friends – Elettra was not among them, I noted – in a dark suit and tie wearing a wonky laurel wreath atop his shoulder-length brown hair. He was overweight with a rather broad, cheery face, his owlish features emphasised by those large round spectacles. He looked like a guy who played a lot of Dungeons and Dragons.

He was barely recognisable in a more recent Facebook profile. His hair had been cut to a crop and he'd lost the puppy fat around his jowls, and with it the jolly demeanour. Metal-rimmed rectangular glasses reinforced the more severe impression.

There was just one other image, this time without the

glasses – showing off a bulging bicep decorated with rune-like tattoos. The guy was clearly into body building.

'Quite a transformation,' I said. 'Especially for someone who apparently runs a bookshop. Would you say he's attractive?'

Dolores snorted. 'Would you?'

'I suppose it's an improvement on the previous Harry Potter look,' I said. 'But I wouldn't say you'd fall for him across a crowded room, more likely give him a wide berth in a dark alley.'

'Some women like that.'

I gave Dolores a sideways glance. 'What do I know,' I muttered.

We certainly had a tried and tested system in place when it came to philandering couples – infidelity was a popular national pastime, and for a particular type of bourgeois woman, an appointment with the private detective was almost as routine as the aesthetician. But regardless of my suspicions, I was mindful of my 'terms of reference' – to establish whether Paolo Mestre could somehow be associated with the business surrounding the negatives. If we happened to come across anything else in the course of our investigation, then so be it, but I doubted Indigo would thank me if I interpreted his instructions purely as an excuse to discover whether Elettra was straying. He had said he would keep an eye on her WhatsApp, otherwise he didn't want her 'spied on'. Which was fine by me – I honestly didn't give a damn if Elettra Fausto was playing away. I was more interested in what Gianni Colline was doing with twenty thousand euros stuffed in his mattress, and who that bugger was who had jumped me.

***

Mestre wasn't hard to locate – in fact, we knew precisely where he would be between nine and one and three and seven, five days a week (Libreria Mestre was closed on Sunday and Monday). The store was at the two towers end of Strada Maggiore, a pretty prestigious spot, if not on the central Rizzoli-Paviglione axis.

There was certainly no shortage of independent bookshops in Bologna, stuffed full of obscure and often second-hand volumes, the survival of which, along with many of the other dim-lit stores occupying the porticoes, was something of a mystery in itself, at least from an Anglo-Saxon perspective. From an Italian, less so: work was so intertwined with identity many of their ageing proprietors continued to open simply as a signal of their continued existence, while for others, in such a static job market, they had no other option; for most, actual income was derived from the property they had acquired, or inherited, in the building above.

The profession of bookseller also maintained an elevated status in this education-obsessed culture in this education-obsessed city – Feltrinelli and Coop chains might occupy the prime positions in the centre, but tweed-jacketed university professors could most frequently be found among the towering stacks of volumes beneath the arches, enquiring about out-of-print tomes (sometimes their own) to patient men (and it was almost always men) with a proper appreciation of their philological passions.

The 'Harry Potter ate all the pasta' Paolo Mestre was easier to picture in this environment than the 'body builder', at least until I was standing outside the store. I must have passed it on numerous occasions – it occupied three arches along Maggiore, so wasn't easy to miss – but I had never bothered examining the books in the window. Now I realised it could fall into that other category of store – one that might actually be thriving. It had customers, for a start – men with their noses in books or gathered around a desk where Paolo Mestre was checking a computer screen, tattooed biceps bulging from his black T-shirt.

The window display did not feature the usual literary or antiquarian finds but volumes like *Panzer Tank Warfare* or *The Italian Russian Campaign 1941-3*, biographies on Second World War General Messe, Benito Mussolini, ranks of books on military uniforms across the ages, and a display of old photo magazines dating from the 1930s.

There was noticeboard by the front door and I risked stepping in – Mestre appeared absorbed by his computer. As I examined it, I listened to the conversation.

'The seller seems legit,' Mestre was saying. 'They've got 4.5 on Trustpilot.'

'But what I want to know is – how can I be sure it's an original?'

'You can only really know for sure if you examine it under a black light.'

'A . . . ?'

'Ultraviolet – modern paint will glow and you can also check for repairs. But what you really need is this, it's in English but it's the pictures that count. *Uncovering Forgeries: Third Reich Militaria, A Collectors' Guide*. It's the bible. I wouldn't be without one.'

'And what does it cost?'

'It's not cheap: seventy euros.'

'You're right, it's not cheap.'

'It's your choice, obviously it's for someone serious about militaria.'

'They've got 4.5 on Trustpilot, you say.'

'Sure, although I couldn't say how many of those reviewers would know the difference between an SS *Ehrendolch* dagger and a SA *Feldherrnhalle* . . .'

Judging by the noticeboard, there would be no shortage of local expertise – a patchwork of typed and written flyers advertising 'Top Quality Reproduction Webbing (Bersaglieri, US Rangers, Wehrmacht)', 'Tour of the Gothic Line', 'Lecture: Italian Social Republic', 'Frontline Military Uniforms – 1922 to 1945'.

At the centre of the noticeboard was a colour A4 printed poster featuring a battleship grey German Second World War tank emerging through rusty smoke, across it written: 29th MILITARY MEMORABILIA FAIR. It would be taking place at a site on the outskirts in a week's time, and listed among the attendees: Libreria Mestre.

Someone brushed behind me and exited the shop. Paolo Mestre called:

'Can I help you?' I raised a hand without turning around.

'I'm fine, thanks.'

I waited until I heard another guy approach the till, and left.

I was heading back to the office, when I got a call.

'Is this Signor Lie-chester?'

'It is.'

'This is Patrizia Bussoni, from the university. Can we speak?'

'Sure, go ahead.'

'What I mean is – can we meet?'

I waited for Patrizia in Piazza Maggiore – took a seat outside La Linea, the cheap bar the locals used on the unfashionable side of the piazza, technically not actually on it, in fact, but facing the road. Still, the coffee cost a third as much, and the company was usually a little more interesting.

Patrizia arrived a few minutes later, dragging a suitcase behind her and with a rucksack over her back. She swung the bag onto the ground and sat down. As soon as she had, she looked as if she wanted to get up again.

'Are you all right?'

She looked nervously around.

'Can I get you something?'

She shook her head. She didn't look so cool now. She looked, actually, terrified.

'What happened?' I asked.

'You told me . . . It's just . . . *the police came.*'

'Ah,' I said. 'Well, yes, I'm sorry about that, but with the death of your two friends, that was inevitable.' She looked around again, then back at me.

'The first, an *Ispettore*, he asked me questions. About Gianni and Valeria. The club. What we did. Anyone else involved, anyone who knew them, and so on.'

'Uhuh.'

'He went away. He said he didn't think they would prosecute.'

'Okay.'

'But then, this other one. In a uniform. He wasn't so nice. He came to my home. He was asking questions like you were – I mean about these missing negatives. He wanted to know what I knew.'

'And what did you tell him?'

'Nothing! I knew nothing about them! It was Valeria and Gianni who got the films, I had nothing to do with that. I knew nothing about any negatives, which we couldn't have shown anyway.'

'Because you can only actually project prints.'

'*Giusto*. That was nothing to do with me, or Romano.'

'The kid, you mean.'

She nodded, looking into my eyes. I could see hers were gleaming.

'I can see he really scared you, this cop,' I said.

'There was something . . . It wasn't that he shouted, raised his voice even. He was very calm, but there was something about him that made me think that if I gave the wrong answer . . .' She shuddered. 'He wasn't like a normal cop. In truth, despite the uniform, he wasn't like a cop at all.' She swallowed, spilt tears. I handed her a napkin but she used the back of her hand, smearing her mascara.

She leaned forward: 'Please, tell me: *what have I gotten in to?*'

Chapter 16

'Christ, this place smells even worse than before,' I said. 'Are you sure there's no one actually mouldering away in here?'

'Of that,' said *Ispettore* Alessandro, 'we can at least be certain, unless someone's been walled in. Wouldn't be the first time.' He winked. 'Now, explain to me why you've dragged me here. The Comandante told me your company had a renewed interest.'

'We have a fresh contract – apparently there have been some . . . unexplained messages between Elettra Fausto and a childhood friend that our client believes might be linked to the stolen negatives.'

'This "childhood friend" is a man?' I nodded.

'And the client, I presume, is her husband. The messages?'

'A couple of ambiguous ones, the rest deleted.'

'Are you sure you're in the right place, Daniel?'

'We're on the guy, but I was interested in taking a closer look. As you know, the last time I was here, I was . . . disturbed. I don't suppose you've made any progress on the hospitals?'

The *Ispettore* shook his head. 'Perhaps you didn't stab him as deeply as you thought.'

'Well, I did my best.'

We were in Gianni Colline's 'bedroom'. The main differences: spotlights, which reminded me of the ones I had seen on the film set, and the mattress, which was displaying its foam and springs as if it had been savaged by some sharp-fanged beast.

'Where you found the money,' I said. 'Any news on that? Small or large bills?'

'Large, which suggests he didn't expect whoever gave them to him to go to the police.'

'Didn't put them in the bank, though.'

'This is Italy,' said Alessandro. 'People tend to keep income outside the purview of the authorities when they can't explain its origin.'

'Which means you believe he wouldn't have been able to explain its origin?'

'You heard me correctly the first time.'

'I see that everything's still in place.' I walked over to the desk with its movie camera, the green metal bulk of the Moviola machine beside it.

'On this, we have made some progress,' said the *Ispettore*. 'Signor Colline was planning to make a film.'

'Hence the new computer,' I said. 'Which he presumably paid for . . .'

'With the money from the mattress – yes, we have actually traced it to the Apple Store on Via Rizzoli.'

'Making a movie is not a one-person job,' I said, picturing the scene at the museum. 'Others must have been involved. Patrizia Bussani told you about the cinema club?'

'Yes, she gave us the details of a group of likely associates, also mainly from university. They were all, in their own ways, trying to break into film or TV. He had spoken to them about a project he "had in the pipeline" as he put it. They were sceptical, as he was always coming up with ideas, but when he started purchasing equipment they began to believe it was the real thing.'

'Did he explain how he could suddenly afford to do this?'

'He claimed a grandparent had died, left him a legacy.'

'Presumably . . .'

'No.'

'And did they have anything to say about Gianni and Valeria?'

'Only that they had been *fidanzati* since university. However, they weren't able to enlighten us any further about why he might have killed her, and then himself. But that means nothing – all relationships are unknowable to outsiders.'

'The second man you sent to see Patrizia,' I said. 'He really put the frighteners on her.' Alessandro frowned. 'She asked to see me. There were tears. She's fled Bologna to her parents in Trento.'

'And what frightened her?'

'She said it was his manner, she found him threatening. He was asking what she knew about the missing negatives.'

'One of mine?'

'A Carabinieri, uniformed.'

'Did she get his name?' I shook my head. 'ID?'

'I guess a uniform is enough.'

'Would she be able to furnish a description?'

'You could call her in Trento. But surely you know who you sent.'

'I never sent another officer, Daniel.'

'Maybe he was part of the wider investigation.'

The *Ispettore* tutted. 'I have full overview and know precisely who is asking what to whom.'

'Because this guy was apparently very intimidating,' I said. 'He clearly scared her – enough for her to flee the city.'

'I will give her a call,' he said solemnly.

I tilted back one of the shoulder-like canisters on the side of the Moviola's viewfinder. There turned out to be a spool of film inside.

'And this?'

'I . . .' The *Ispettore* looked surprised. 'I must confess, we may . . . have overlooked that.'

I tilted back the canister on the other side of the viewfinder, and sure enough there was a smaller reel, presumably the soundtrack.

I nosed around the machine, wishing I had paid a little more attention to the chief archivist's lecture at CineBo. There was always Dolores, I thought, who was a bit of swot when it came to this kind of thing, but the thought of her smugly reaching for a switch spurred me on.

Well, nothing gained . . . I flicked a switch myself, and the thing came to life, light beaming out of the viewfinder.

'Actually,' said Alessandro, 'my father had a Super 8 projector, which presumably shares the same principle.' He pressed a button and a spool began to rewind in a hiss of hot dust. Another, and I heard the second canister follow suit.

'They used the Moviola for editing negatives,' I explained. 'Don't ask me the details, but negatives can't be projected, otherwise they'd be reversed like photo negatives.'

'Of course, it's all digital now,' the *Ispettore* said ruefully.

'But not then, hence they needed this machine to see the films as they would be on screen.' I lifted up the second canister. 'The sound track would run in sequence with the film track, so they would be in sync.'

The spools flapped for an instant before clunking to a halt.

'Now if we toggle this switch forward?' said Alessandro.

'I'm guessing that we should be able to see what's on the negatives.'

'Here's hoping.' The *Ispettore* flicked the switch.

And there they were: in the hand-sized square of the viewfinder. Those blood-warm hues again – had Indigo said something about a Kodak filter? – immediately recognisable as the claustrophobic, almost womb-like atmosphere of *Amore su una lama di rasoio*.

Vanessa Tramonte – Ursula – sat in the vast *soggiorno*, a current affairs magazine upon her lap. Although it was apparently day outside, the room was dark and dated, even by eighties standards. It was illuminated by a pair of chandeliers that shivered as a tram passed outside. The shot cut to the blue sparking lines outside the tall windows of the *piano nobile*.

I knew these kind of apartments – I'd interviewed clients in a few – vast, airless spaces where you had to keep the windows closed at all times because of the external noise. Perhaps the kind of place Toni Fausto grew up in, certainly the kind that would appeal to Ron Manchester's character: more like a hotel lobby than a home, and the lobby of a staid hotel at that – the kind where you were expected to dress for dinner.

Indeed, despite being at home, Vanessa Tramonte's Ursula

was outfitted in a bottle green silk dress and heels, sat upright on the kind of eighteenth-century baroque sofa you can only imagine being sitting upright at, when CUT to an old-style black Bakelite phone, its tinny ring crackling through the Moviola's speaker. CUT to Ursula answering.

'Pronto?'

CLOSE UP of her made-up powder-pale face, those bright red lips, the expressions that washed over it as she listened to the indecipherable voice at the other end: shock, horror, then a leak of relief before she forced the corners of her lips downwards as if she was aware that we, the audience, had her under observation. CUT to the phone being replaced.

WIDE SHOT of Ursula standing in the *soggiorno*. She picked the receiver up again, held it to her ear, her long finger dialling one number, another, then stopping. She replaced the receiver. Smoothed her dress. Walked out of shot, a fist raised to her mouth (a theme of the film – her husband likes to introduce her as his 'tarnished trophy wife' because she is always chewing her knuckles. She tries to make light of it by saying as a child she used to bite her nails, which obviously now is out of the question).

CUT to a dimly illuminated portico, in fact a portico lining a courtyard. Ursula sitting alone on a bench. A nurse approached. *Now I recognised it* – instead of using the more modern high-rise Ospedale Maggiore, Toni Fausto chose the old maternity hospital on Via d'Azeglio, which was still in use back then. Those haunting pools of shadow, that sense of enclosure . . . we might as well have been in a Dario Argento movie. It was no coincidence the pair were firm friends: Argento shot his horrors like *gialli*, while Fausto his *gialli* like horrors.

CLOSE UP on Ron Manchester's bruised face. CUT to Ursula sitting on a wooden chair by his bed, as upright as she had been at home. She held his hand while – CLOSE UP – Ron Manchester, or Vittorio, dubbed in Italian, explained that as he faced death it was not his former wife he thought of, but her. How he had been afraid to show her his true, tender self but he swore that, from now on, everything would be different. CLOSE UP on their fingers threading. Ursula leaned over to kiss Vittorio tenderly upon the forehead. Ron Manchester closed his eyes in peace.

DAY, EXTERIOR. The private detective sitting at an outside bar table, an empty cup of coffee in front of him, smoking. A ray of sun, almost certainly reproduced by artificial light, bleached his skin. He put on a pair of black-lensed sunglasses. CUT to the door of the *palazzo* on Strada Maggiore opening. Ursula emerged in a low-cut blue dress and heels. WHITE. The white of pure light, the flap of the unspooling film.

'That's it,' said Alessandro. We sat in silence, in the light of the blank viewfinder.

'Well, that's odd,' I said. 'It's the scene in the film before the ending, only – what's it doing here at all, when it should have been in the car?'

'Colline forgot to take it out?' said the *Ispettore*.

'We might be able to overlook your people missing the Moviola canisters, *Ispettore*,' I said. 'But a film maker?'

'He was in a state of . . . distress.'

'But clearly he intended to keep the films together, for one reason or another.'

'You think these are some of the missing negatives, then.'

'It would appear so.'

'I will send these over to CineBo.'

I went back to the desk where, beside the movie camera, there remained the packaging that included the poster of *Letter to Breznhev*. I crouched down – beneath the desk, among the detritus of discarded electronics, university papers, a shoebox full of badges and loose change – a small pile of flat grey and white boxes. I put them on the desk, switched on the lamp.

There were half a dozen of them, all empty – the larger, grey ones for film reels, the smaller white for sound. Each had written on top *Amore su una lama di rasoio,* along with numbers ranging from 3/8 to 6/8.

I set them together, then closed the packaging around them – the folds fitted a consignment like this, albeit perhaps twice or three times the size.

I removed the boxes and lifted up the outer, brown paper packaging.

Gianni Colline's name and address was written in thick black felt-tip. There was a patchwork of cheap stamps and a blurred postmark. I held it up to the light but couldn't work it out.

'What do you make of this?' I asked.

The *Ispettore* produced a slim, egg-shaped container and flipped it open. He took out a metal-rimmed lens that unfolded to become a pair of reading glasses. He balanced them upon his nose.

'Well, I can't be sure,' he said. 'But I think it's from Venice.'

Chapter 17

I may have done stranger things in my life but driving across the Ponte della Libertà with Aphrodite by my side, I was hard-pressed to think of one.

Always a kind of revelation: Venice, *La Serenissima*, coming into view, her domes and spires balanced upon the sparkling Lagoon like the finial of a crown. Yes, glance right and there was the rather less picturesque multi-storey car park at Piazzale Roma, where we were in fact heading. Then there would be newly-installed turnstiles mobbed by indifferent hordes of tourists, but despite all this, Venice was the treasure of Italy and rose above the mob just as she appeared to rise above the water.

'Have you got any more gum, honey?' asked Anna Bloom. Rose leaned between the car seats and dealt her one. 'Oh,' Anna sighed. *'Che bello.'*

I drove the Alfa to the top of the multi-storey. As we got out, Anna popped on her baseball cap and sunglasses. She was dressed in a shapeless grey sweatshirt, skinny jeans and white sneakers. It more or less worked — there was clearly still a beautiful woman underneath it all, and if you knew who she was, you would instantly recognise her, but if you weren't expecting to see Anna Bloom, Marie Antoinette or, indeed, Aphrodite, you wouldn't.

'You're so lucky,' she said, 'to have Venice just down the road. Where I grew up, it took an hour and a half to get to the nearest town.'

'I can't believe America's that big,' I said.

'Okay, maybe I exaggerate – the nearest town with a *bar*. They don't call it the Bible Belt for nothing.'

'But it must have been so,' Rose slammed the rear car door, '*boring.*'

'Really, my dear,' she said in a pretty good Bette Davis impression, which would have been entirely lost on my daughter, 'how could you say such a thing? My, we had college football, cow-tipping, and church!'

'*God,*' said Rose.

'Yup, there was a helluva lot of that. "What do you need the internet for, missy, when you've got the *divine* internet – your pray-ers!" Mom was very devout, even though Dad had run off with another woman. She used to pray for them *both*, can you believe that? When *I* ran away . . .'

'You *ran away*?' I said.

'Well, wouldn't you? But maybe I'm exaggerating, just a little – I mean, I didn't sneak out during the night. When I graduated high school I'd got a place at the community college at that town with the bar, but a gang was driving to some kid's party in Dallas and I hitched along for the ride. I told Mom I'd be back in a week, but I didn't see her, in the flesh I mean, for two years, by which time I'd been picked up by Diamond, I mean the modelling agency, and spotted by a scout for Steven.'

'You mean, Steven Spielberg.'

'Hm. And thought – you know what, I'd better take some acting lessons!'

'Wow,' said Rose.

'You make it sound so simple.' I glanced at Rose. 'Perilously so.'

We had arrived at the dock. While I queued to buy the tickets, in the reflection of the *biglietteria* I glimpsed Anna take Rose's hands and lean into her, talking rapidly, but by the time I had returned with the tickets, the pair were standing casually, Anna's arm now linked in Rose's as if they were mother and daughter. Rose's eyes would have usually given me a clue, but these, too, were masked by dark lenses. Anna gave me a preppy smile.

'All set?'

'All set.'

We weren't going to Venice 'proper', but Lido. Anna hadn't had a film at the Festival that year so had stayed away, but now 'the dust has settled' was keen to meet up with an old friend connected to the Palazzo del Cinema, where the event was held. I'd asked if I could tag along. Rose hadn't exactly been thrilled – she took her position as Anna's minder seriously – but I had managed to ambush the pair of them when I'd visited the set, ostensibly in my role as consultant, actually to update Indigo on the progress of his case (inconclusive – the tail we'd put on Mestre hadn't led to anything, yet) and Anna had said she would be 'delighted' to have me along.

'Is it connected to those negatives Indi was so worked up about?' she asked.

'Well, to tell the truth, I thought it would be useful to meet this lady you're going to see.'

'Clara del Monte.'

'She sounds fascinating, and I was wondering if she had any recollection of Toni Fausto. Just background, really, nothing very important. If it would be an imposition . . .'

'You're kidding! I bet Rose could do with a break from my wittering. And Clara, boy can she talk! She'll love it!'

A man shouted: 'Cast! Positions!'

'That's me.'

We watched Anna step nimbly over the cables to her position on the set, where the uber-modern, steel-surfaced kitchen of a nonetheless stiflingly windowless apartment had been recreated and where Ursula (Anna, playing an American expatriate in Bologna) had just been scalded by a malfunctioning hot tap when Maurizio, her husband's assistant, arrives to pick up some important papers. The pair began to position themselves upon the lines chalked on the floor.

'You're lying,' hissed Rose.

'What do you mean?'

'You think I don't know when you're lying? What do you really want to speak to Clara about?'

'What I said.'

'And what else?'

'That's it.'

'Oh, so you're going to spend two days chauffeuring us to Venice just for some "background"?'

'Don't you want to pass some time with your old dad now you've got stardust in your eyes?'

'She's no fool, Anna,' said Rose. 'She'll know you're up to something.'

Because the *traghetto* would stop at St Mark's Square before going on to Lido, it was especially packed with visitors, many of whom, like us, had crammed onto the waterbus with their luggage, making it all the more crowded. By the time we had shuffled on board there were no free seats and we were obliged, at least until we reached San Marco, to stand near the middle by the disembarkation point and hang onto the plastic straps. Anna would later remark this was not the first time she had taken a *traghetto* – she had done so in her early modelling days when she and a Texan friend had interrailed 'after a gig in Paris' – but of late she had always been picked up by (water) taxi, which made me feel like a bit of a cheap-skate. Frankly, at those prices it hadn't even occurred to me.

Still, my fears of us being mobbed on the boat were unfounded. Anna's outfit seemed to be holding up. Chewing gum with Rose's North Face rucksack slung over her shoulder (Rose, meanwhile, had Anna's Louis Vuitton case) Anna appeared a rather typical tourist. But it was entirely an act: the 'real' Anna I had encountered that first time in Miu Miu was at least an inch taller and possessed a kind of grace that simply drew your eye, an indefinable 'star quality'. In the packed boat, she was simply playing a role – anonymity.

As expected, the majority of the passengers disembarked at San Marco and we were able to get a seat. The low-lying boat with its windows clouded by Lagoon salt was no sight-seeing vessel, so I only got my first good look at Lido as the *traghetto* docked and we were stepping off. I had mixed feelings – it had been a good while since I'd last visited, the year after my wife had died. Rose had been on a school trip (her days were one continuous whirl of activity back then in an effort to distract her) and the Comandante had insisted I take some time off myself. He had suggested I return to the UK, but that would have been the very worst thing: to suffer the sympathy of family and old friends. Instead, I took myself to Lido in a semi-conscious echo of Dirk Bogarde's von Aschenbach in Visconti's *Death in Venice*. I even brought the book by Thomas Mann, which remained in my luggage.

While not ailing physically like von Aschenbach, I was heart-sick, although I didn't for a moment expect the island to still resemble the haunted territory of the film. I was wrong: with its fin de siècle villas and hotels, placid, close-of-season Lido had very much that same sense of gentle mourning, and I spent five days alone at café tables, deserted restaurants; walking leafy lanes, sitting on the quiet beach, visiting old fortifications. It served its purpose – it gave me the time and space and, most importantly, privacy, to properly bid Lucia farewell, at least in this world. And, unlike von Aschenbach, I never once left the island, until I took the *traghetto* back to Piazzale Roma and drove home.

But Rose knew none of this. 'Wow, it's like a whole other Venice,' she said as we walked along the Gran Viale. 'Why have we never been here?'

'We've got the house in Cesenatico, remember?'

'It's not *quite* the same,' said Rose.

'There's always somewhere better, Rose,' said Anna. 'But you can be sure there are a helluva lot of places worse. You ever been to an Oscar ceremony?'

Rose gasped. 'Of course not!'

'Christ, I hate 'em – all the dressing up, photos and fake smiles, and the shit you know you're going to get the next day in the press for wearing the wrong damn dress, and gawd, the *sitting* for hours on end, ass aching, making small talk, it's so dull. But it looks glamorous on the "telly", that's what you Brits call it, don't you?'

'Winning probably makes up for it,' I said.

'You would think so, but then doesn't Brad have half a dozen, and Angelina another clutch? Like I was saying, there's always somewhere, or someone better. "We seldom think of what we have, but always what we lack."'

'Very true,' I said. 'Is that from a play or film?'

'That's Schopenhauer, honey.' She flashed me a very white smile. 'You think I'm just a pretty face? I picked up a Masters in Philosophy while I was hanging around set. I'm not your average *Yokey from Okey*. Ooh, there it is! Don't you love it?'

The Grand Hotel Ausonia could have easily accommodated von Aschenbach, had he not chosen to stay at the now abandoned des Bains. He would have certainly passed five-storey Ausonia as he promenaded along the Viale with his powdered face and blackened moustache, where its mosaic-covered façade embodied the opulence of Belle Epoque travel for the wealthy – yesterday and today.

'I always stay here instead of the Excelsior,' said Anna as we walked up the red carpet, 'which is like a hostel during the Festival. This place is so much more chilled, you know?' She whipped off her disguise and the reception staff stiffened, smiles frosting their faces. A deep-tanned, elderly man in a cream suit with a crimson cravat emerged from the velvet curtain behind them. He rushed around the desk.

'Ms Bloom! So *wonderful* to have you back with us.' He took her hand in both of his, bowed and kissed it. 'We missed you last year, signora.'

'Well, I can't have an entry *every year*, Maurizio. A girl's got to get some rest!'

'Not you, signora, never! I see you are making a film with Mr Adler. There's not a scene set here?'

'This is strictly pleasure, Maurizio. I couldn't come to Italy without catching up with Clara. She would be furious.' Anna frowned. 'She's well, I hope?'

'Ah, yes, Signora del Monte is very well, *meno male*.'

'And you?'

'Very well, signora. You know I was conceived in the Ausonia, and it's said, providing I do not step outside its grounds, I will never die.'

'Your wife must miss you, then.'

He chuckled. 'She barely knows I exist these days, with the grandchildren.'

'How many is it?'

'Seven. And how are your Brian and, of course, *Sonia*.'

Anna looked at us. 'I named my daughter after this place, although I couldn't guarantee she was actually *conceived* here. Oh.' She turned back to Maurizio. 'You know, *padrone*, they barely know *me* these days, what with the nanny, and their telephones!'

'*Questi maledetti telefoni!* You have my sympathies, signora!'

'These are my companions. Rose will be sharing the suite with me, and you've got a room for Daniel?'

'Signora Rose.' He shook her hand formally. 'Signor Daniel.'

We followed Maurizio along the corridor, trailed by four of the hotel staff, although our luggage could have easily been handled by one. We reached the end and Maurizio opened the door. 'Your usual suite, signora.' He stepped aside.

While British interiors tend to reflect their exteriors, their owners making great efforts to retain – or install – 'original features', the Italian sensibility to fashion and design more often means that ancient façades will conceal modern interiors, albeit below surviving beams or frescoes. As such, Anna's suite looked like something out of *Vogue Design*, as well it might have been. A grey leather modular sofa faced a flat screen TV, with a coffee table shaped out of a huge piece of driftwood between them. The walls were decorated with abstract art, while a glass-topped desk supported by thick black metal legs was set facing a window overlooking the Gran Viale.

'A home from home, I hope, signora,' said Maurizio.

My own room, opposite the suite on the unfashionable side of the corridor looking over the swimming pool, was a continuation of the grey theme, albeit without a living area. But it was certainly a step up on the last place.

I was unpacking when Rose came in.

'Not bad,' I said as she sat back against the desk. 'Five-star living. Don't get used to it.'

'We're meeting Clara in the bar in an hour.'

'There's no need to look so glum, you know I wouldn't say anything to embarrass you. I genuinely want some background from the lady and, all right, to grill her for some info about the film, but I promise, I'll be gentle.'

'It's not that.'

'What, then?'

'Nothing,' she said.

'Come on.'

She crossed her arms.

'Is it what Anna was saying to you while I was at the *bigli-etteria* in Piazzale Roma? Was she telling you off?'

'No!'

'Women's secrets?' Rose straightened and went over to the window, drew the curtain aside. She sighed.

'She was simply saying she always made it seem easy and fun because that's what everyone expected her to say but actually it was really "brutal", that was the word she used. But you know, Dad,' she turned to face me, haloed by the afternoon sun, 'you don't need to worry. I'm not interested in this world. I mean films, acting, modelling, all that. I want to be . . . *an artist*, create stuff, I don't want to be just *a body*.'

'I'm not sure that's entirely fair,' I said. 'Actors *act*.'

'In any case, I don't want my whole life, the whole meaning of my life to revolve around me.' She shook her head. 'What I mean, is: what I look like, who I might be *pretending* to be – I want the opposite. To be able to leave things behind, walk away, create something new. I don't want to have to tell people what they want to hear. I don't want to have to smile for the camera. I don't want any of that shit. I want to be . . . *precisely myself*.'

'Your mum would be proud to hear you say so.'

'*Mum* . . . You know, Dad,' her voice broke, 'you say that . . . you say that *a lot*, but I've got no idea what Mum would be proud of. I mean, I *can* remember her, but just as a kid. I never actually knew her as . . . *a person.* I'll *never* know her like you did, as a grown-up. I'll *never* truly know what she was like, what she would have wanted.'

I patted the bed beside me. Rose sat down. I took her in my arms. It was a long time since I had held her like this, and she felt both bony and womanly. I wished I could hold her forever, stave off the outside world.

I let go.

'Your mum would have been proud,' I said. 'Because if there was one thing she wanted you to be, it was *yourself.* That's all she would have wanted. Integrity was very important to her, she was the most honest person I'd ever met – sometimes too much! – and she'd have been proud of you for not being dazzled by all this, for remaining indomitably *you.*'

'Anna's not like Mum, then?'

'Not really, although that's not to say she's not a good person.'

'Stella?'

'Ah, Stella . . .' I thought of my ex who, as Rose's art tutor, had probably influenced my daughter's young adulthood more than anyone else. 'Stella's driven, that's for sure. I think your mum would respect that. But . . . I couldn't say they were especially similar. I mean, your mum was an activist, Stella's an artist.'

'Do you miss her?'

'Who? Your mum?'

'Stella.'

I shrugged. 'Sometimes.'

'I'm sorry.'

'For what?'

'It can't be easy, having a daughter in tow.' I took her in my arms again.

'Don't be silly,' I said. 'You're my joy, you're all that keeps me going.'

'Love you too, Dad.'

Speaking of Stella Amore, I may have been expecting Clara del Monte to be an eccentric old lady like Chiara, my ex's landlady, who had a penchant for saris and tutus, but the octogenarian who greeted us on the terrace bar at the Ausonia – 'Don't get up!' cried Anna – was cut from a very different cloth.

'Of course I'll get up.' Clara del Monte rose from the low, white leather seat with little visible effort, although admittedly she was carrying little visible weight. In a brown floral-design suit and white blouse with matching embroidered flowers, fashionably large-rimmed glasses, and blond feathered hair, she had the appearance of a woman who had once been a great beauty and earned, or came from, or married into, a great deal of wealth. She might have once been a model or an actor, but Anna had told me that she was, in fact, a screenwriter and had co-written ('It was all co-written in those days,' Clara told us. 'As the director usually insisted on a writing credit, but in fact they just put their name to it – the words were all mine!') some mainstream hits between the sixties and nineties. She was also the author of three novels ('They dismissed them as "women's fiction" because they're about – shock! – the lives of women, and were read largely by women. They're forgotten now – period pieces.')

but her bestseller was the autobiographical *Between Women – Me and Mastroianni* based on her long-standing affair with the famous actor ('It began between Faye' – *Dunaway*, Anna whispered – 'and Catherine' – *Deneuve* – 'and was on and off through the seventies, he came back to me when he tired of the actresses, no offence, dear' – she meant Anna – 'although he also soon tired of me breaking his balls and went back to them. "If I wanted a wife, I'd have stayed with the first one!" But the book's not just about the screwing, sorry, dear' – she meant Rose – 'it's about the life and times, that was what I was *truly* interested in' – she held up her bony, manicured fingers and pinched the air – 'that peculiar moment, those particular people. I wanted to capture it, for it to be almost . . . *anthropological*, you know?' She shrugged. 'But the only reason they're still printing it is the gossip.').

'And Toni Fausto? Did you have much to do with him?'

She gave me a writerly scowl. 'He's in the book! What about Toni?'

'He's a legend,' I said.

'*Beh*. What is a legend but a beloved lie? He was a legend to himself, perhaps.'

'So you're saying he wasn't such a great director? A political hero . . .'

'Young people,' she crooked a finger toward Anna, 'including your Signor Adler, they love to put these people upon a pedestal, so maybe they can clamber on top of it, too? It's been the same since Truffaut and Hitchcock. But Toni was no Hitch, and certainly no Truffaut – he was a hack director, he *begged* me to write for him, but I wasn't interested.'

'Such a sour face, Clara!' said Anna.

'Was it his politics?' I asked.

'*Poh*. Politics? Of course everyone was red, but Toni was exceptionally pompous. "Cinema for the masses"? He couldn't get the funding for anything other than *schlock*! Not even his family would stump up for it – they'd only back the films they thought they could get a return on. More fool them, actually, because some of that arthouse tosh is still earning decades after the big hits have been long forgotten. I should have got a credit on *Umberto D*, you know – I'd re-worked some of Cesare's scenes – but they wouldn't have that, a "script girl" being acknowledged beside the great Zavattini. Some fucking communists they were – sorry, dear.'

'But the politics didn't bother you,' I said.

'All a pose, just like today.'

'What then?' That scowl again.

'It's in my book. Although admittedly it's just a passing comment. I mean, they were all at it in those days, it was well known, expected, even, only that Toni was one of the most egregious examples. I suppose it came with the territory, he was hardly making masterpieces. His actresses were too desperate to say no and too powerless to be listened to even if they had.'

'So, he was a womaniser.'

Carla's face creased with distaste. 'My Marcello was a *womaniser*, and what woman wouldn't fall for *his* charms? No, that's far too soft a word for it, Toni was cheaper than that – even among the chorus line he had a reputation for forcing himself upon women, he once tried to force himself upon me.'

'And what, if you don't mind me asking, happened?'

'I was working at the time on *A Lizard in a Woman's Skin* for his pal Lucio, rewrites in the studio late at night, just me at the desk. Then I feel these hands around me, squeezing my breasts. I scream, and you know what the shithead says? "Go ahead, no one will hear you." He swivels me around, but fortunately I had a freshly sharpened pencil in my hand and I plunge it,' she made a stabbing action, 'straight in his fat face. He staggers back with the pencil embedded in his cheek, sobbing. He plucks it out and tries to stem the bleeding with a handkerchief. "You could have blinded me!" he wails. "I wish I had," I say, "I'd be saving *the masses* the agony of watching your garbage!" That's why, if you look carefully at his photos post '72 he's got this white patch on his cheek just beneath the right eye. I include the anecdote in the book, but say it happened with some anonymous b-movie actress.'

'Why?' I said. 'It's a great story.'

'You know, I think even now I find it so . . . degrading I just don't want to be associated with him. And maybe, I wanted to give one of the hundreds of wide-eyed girls he deflowered a moment of triumph, if only in their case it was fiction. They never fought back, or if they did, never got to tell the tale.' I followed her gaze to Anna, whose blue eyes gave nothing away.

Brutal, I thought.

'Well,' said Anna. 'We can't all be talented writers.'

Clara nodded slowly. 'It's a tough business. Always was, always will be.' An awkward silence.

'Dad,' said Rose. 'Didn't you want to ask Clara about the film?'

'Yes,' I said. '*Thanks*. Clara, Anna told me you're involved with the Festival. I've been trying to speak to someone at the archive for the past week but no one has got back to me.'

'Oh, Pietro Volpato and I go back a long way – we met in the eighties. He had just joined the Festival then, was keen to get hold of an early draft of a script I'd been working on – *Metello* if I recall correctly, very much of its time. Took itself *extremely* seriously. I remember it was entered at Cannes and I was put out not to receive an invitation. I was delighted when it barely won a thing! I'm sorry, what were we talking about?'

'The archivist, Pietro Volpetto?'

'*Volpato.* He hasn't got back to you, you say? It doesn't surprise me – because of the prep for the Festival they tend to take time off in the spring. In the past I would have said he'd have gone abroad somewhere, but he's mostly around Lido these days. His wife, Letitia, has crippling arthritis, poor darling, so he wheels her about. In fact, I often see them, either along the Viale or in their front garden – they live around the corner from me. What do you want from him?'

'It's about some negatives of *Amore su una lama di rasoio* we came across, the packaging had a Venice postmark and the Festival's archive is the sole film library in the city. In fact, it actually has an arrangement with CineBo to store its acetate films with the archive.'

'A bit thin, no?' said Carla. 'I've written enough mysteries to know that isn't much of a clue – it could have come from a private collector.'

'The film was wrapped in a poster from another film, which was shown at the Festival the same year.'

'Oh? What film was that?'

'A British movie – *Letter to Brezhnev*.'

She looked blank. 'Never heard of it. All right,' she said. 'If you'll walk me home, I'll show you where he lives.'

Unlike Bologna, where the warm evenings were already beginning to hint at the stickiness of a land-locked city, here the jasmine, lilac and laurel of Lido gardens met the sea air which, as we walked those quiet, dimmed lanes of darkened Belle Epoque villas, balanced flowery warmth with the light touch of a coming summer.

'Here it is,' said Clara. 'Hm, the lights are off – maybe I was wrong, perhaps they have gone away. But, look, the car's still there.' A gleaming navy-blue Citroën DS sat by the side of the house.

'But if they were flying,' said Anna, 'would they use the car?'

'Why would they fly? With Letitia it would be too much trouble. No,' she said with certainty. 'The most they would do is drive – Pietro has relatives in Rome, I believe, but even that far, at his age . . .'

It was a modest villa compared to some we had passed, but no less attractive. Behind the low green wire fence, the garden had strayed from what were clearly once strictly policed parameters to assert the wild origins of its seasonals and perennials; oleander had overgrown to narrow the stone path. It was a garden, in short, of a husband diverted to the care of an ailing wife, diverted from the care of her garden.

The two-storey villa with its faded salmon façade might have seemed as deserted for the season as others in the street were it not for that car, and the fact that the three ground-floor front windows were open.

'They might have gone to bed,' said Rose.

'At this hour?' said Clara. She checked her watch. 'It's barely nine. I've walked past here at twelve and used the lights from Pietro's to help see my way. They were always late to bed, and now with Letitia sleeping downstairs he stays with her.' For a moment I wondered at the old lady, venturing out alone so late at night along these dark lanes. 'Ring the bell,' she said.

I wasn't sure if disturbing Pietro Volpato's sleep would be the best way to get him to tell me about the film.

'Maybe we should leave it until morning,' I said.

'Nonsense,' said Clara. She was reaching a bony finger across to the copper buzzer set in a speaker phone, when Rose whispered:

'Hold it.' She pointed to the second storey. 'I thought I saw something.'

'What?'

'There, see? A flash.'

Now we all saw it, the unmistakable track of torchlight.

'Do you think the power's out?' said Anna.

'Possibly,' I said. 'That would explain a lot.' I stepped onto the low wall in front of the fence and, taking hold of the metal post, pulled myself up.

'What are you doing?' said Anna.

'I'd better check.'

The fence was not designed to deter intruders, and I easily made it over, even if it did mean grazing a pear cactus on my way down which managed to penetrate my trousers and propel me back against the fence.

'Are you okay, Dad?'

'Yeah, yeah.' I irritably rubbed my leg.

Respectfully bordering the cactus, I limped over to the metal column set back along the path and clicked the garden gate open. I put my finger to my mouth. 'Hang back,' I whispered. 'I'll go first.' The three generations of women, their faces silvered by the moon, looked as if it hadn't occurred to them any other way.

I tried the handle of the front door. It was unlocked.

I found myself standing in what appeared to be an open-plan *soggiorno*. I fished out my phone and switched on the light. The silhouettes took form. To my right a large dining table and chairs bordered by mahogany cabinets displaying glass and silverware. A florid Murano chandelier hung above. Beyond these, a serving hatch that presumably led to a kitchen.

Ahead, a broad, dark wood staircase curving upwards to the second floor. To my left, an ample 1970s-style tan leather sofa and armchair, piled with bedding, was set against the far wall at an awkward right angle to a modern flat screen TV. Both had clearly been moved to make room for the hospital bed opposite the television. Beside it, another tan armchair and a ceramic-tile-topped coffee table which might, in another era, have displayed books on art and film, but was now busy with the paraphernalia of sickness – bottles of pills and disinfectant, boxes of plastic gloves and syringes, tissues and a kitchen roll.

'Signora Volpato?' I said softly. The shape beneath the white sheets was unmoving. Upstairs, I heard the creak of a floorboard. 'Signora?' I approached the bed, noting the medicinal smell, and, moving closer still, the acidic signature of urine.

The old woman was waxen in my light, lying flat, her

mouth hanging open, eyes closed. She might, conceivably, have been sleeping, had her chest not been still. A sparrow hand hung by the side of the bed. As I looked down, I noticed a pillow on the floor.

I lifted the wrist. Judging simply from the cold, let alone lack of a pulse, it was clear the old lady was dead. Smothered, I judged, by the pillow.

I rested the hand on the bed and swung my phone back to the entrance, where Anna and Clara were standing. Anna's phone light was on me.

'Get out,' I mouthed. 'Call the police.' They did as instructed but were quickly replaced by Rose.

'*Dad. You too.*'

'I'll be fine.' I waved her out.

'*Dad.*'

'*Go.*' A wave of anger swept her face, but she was already backing out, her phone glowing to life as she dialled 112 for the Carabinieri.

Creaking sounds were still coming from upstairs. They sounded unhurried as if whoever was up there had not been alerted to our presence. Well, that was something. I tested the first stair. It seemed solid enough. I switched off my phone's light, waited for a moment for my eyes to adjust fully to the dark – enough to make out the outline of the stairs – and took another step.

The creaking upstairs continued as I climbed step by painstaking step.

I finally made it, apparently undetected, to the landing. It was even darker up here, and there was definitely no sign of torchlight. I would risk it.

I turned the phone's light on again and found myself in a corridor – behind me, towards the back of the house, there were a couple of doorways on either side, open and closed. Ahead – two more: one to the right side of the corridor, another at the far end. This would have presumably been where the light, and the creaking, was coming from.

I stepped into the corridor, taking care to keep to the side, where I judged the floorboards were less likely to advertise my approach.

I managed to make it silently to the door. I pocketed the phone and closed my hand around the doorknob. I took a deep breath and slowly began to turn it.

I pushed.

The door opened enough for me to step inside, enough for me to see from the moonlight streaming through the unshuttered windows, that this was the matrimonial bedroom. Between the windows was a dressing table, and I could see my dim silhouette in the mirror, like a shadow of a shadow. To my left was a double bed, made, I noted, but then I remembered the bedding I had seen piled at the end of the armchair downstairs – it hadn't been slept in for a long time. Beyond it, the dark bulk of old wardrobes.

The creaking was coming from my right, however, where the view was blocked by the door.

I took a careful step into the room to avoid being whacked by whoever might conceivably be on the other side of the door and, bracing myself, pushed it all the way. I found myself staring at a chest of drawers topped by family photos. I realised: this room accounted for only two of the three windows visible on the second storey. The light must have been coming from the room next door.

I backed into the corridor but with my final step, the floor creaked loudly beneath me.

The sound next door stopped.

Chapter 18

The animal instinct might be to freeze, but if there's one thing I've learned over the years, a moment of disadvantage like this can be turned to your favour if you do precisely the opposite, namely: act first, act fast.

I snatched the doorknob and pushed the door open so hard it cracked back upon its hinges.

But this time I hadn't been fast enough – the torch was already shining in my face, dazzling me. That might have been it, had not the lights then come on.

Now it was not me dazzled but the youth who stood holding his torch aloft – a stocky kid, mid-twenties in a khaki T-shirt and denim shorts. I took a step forward and my shoes stuck to the floor.

I was standing in syrupy blood. I looked back up at the youth and he at me, brown eyes bulging beneath a mop of black hair.

I punched him in the throat.

The kid dropped the torch, his eyes popping as he sank to his knees in that soup, struggling to breathe. My instinct was to deliver a follow-up blow, but he was clearly done for, clutching at his throat, gasping like a landed fish.

I stepped around him, skidding a little on the blood, and forced him onto his front. I rested a knee on his spine and twisted an arm behind his back. He wriggled like a fish too, but I wrenched his arm further back.

'Don't even think about it,' I hissed.

As he heaved beneath my knee, I tried to take it all in. What was this place? Some kind of museum? The old film posters in front of us reminded me a little of Gianni Colline's, only these were framed, and clearly, judging by the creases and their relative obscurity, originals. Beneath them – framed programmes, invitations, black and white photos of movie stars, all signed. A soft cap stood on a pedestal. Beside it, a pair of women's patent leather shoes. Hanging from a hook, boxing gloves.

To the right, a pair of backlit glass-fronted cabinets stood on either side of the window. Inside: a golden lighter, a diver's watch (in the case beside it, stretched across a gold-plated Y frame, a pair of pale blue swimming trunks), a half-spent cigar resting in a crystal ashtray, a blackened figurine, a pair of tailor's scissors, what I now recognised as an editing block.

The kid was beginning to breathe more steadily and I felt him tense up for another go. I tightened my grip accordingly.

'Please,' he said, his face smeared with blood. 'Let me go. Please. I had nothing to do with this.'

'You mean the old lady?' I grabbed hold of his hair with my free hand and yanked him around.

Now I could properly see what was behind me.

Sitting in a gold filigreed throne, it might have been another prop – a dummy stand-in for a scene of *grand guignol*, or bog-standard gore – an old man incongruously dressed in a cowboy outfit, *sans* the leather Stetson in his lap, soaked in blood from the throat down.

His balding head with its horns of curly grey hair was cocked back, his grey eyes open but lifeless. As if to confirm this, a mosquito settled on an eyeball before taking off again.

'What the hell?'

'I swear,' said the kid. 'He was like this when I found him!'

I noticed there was still something attached to the man's neck – a blood-splashed square metal box with a handle. *'What did you do to him?'*

'I swear . . .'

A shriek from the doorway. It was Anna. 'Oh. My. God.' She stepped back into the corridor.

'Stop Rose from seeing this,' I said.

'She's downstairs with Clara. We found the power . . .'

'Make sure she stays there. Police?'

'On the way. Oh Christ.' She had her hand to her mouth. *'What the living fuck,* Daniel?'

'Is everything okay?' Rose called.

'It's fine,' I shouted. 'Wait down there, make sure the police don't shoot us.'

'Who's he?' Anna looked down at the youth. 'Did *he* do it?'

He turned his bloody face upwards, not a good look. He said in English: 'I don't do nothing, missus.'

'Oh Christ, though.' Anna pointed. 'And what is that *thing* attached to his neck? Is it some kind of saw?'

'Just go back down,' I said. 'Wait for the police. And stop Rose from seeing this.'

'Okay. Yeah. Okay.' She turned away. 'I'd better do that.' I heard her make her way back along the hallway.

'Boss,' the youth repeated in English. 'I don't do nothing.'

Blue lights pulsed outside. The slamming of car doors. 'Well,' I said in Italian. 'Good luck with that.'

The first police to arrive were actually the Polizia Locale – basically glorified, and armed, traffic wardens – who at least relieved me of the youth. They cuffed and steered him, along with the rest of us, into the front garden while we awaited the Carabinieri, who apparently had to make their way up from the far end of the island.

I asked if they could let the women go, but they refused. In their shock, I don't think they had yet recognised Anna, but they had definitely recognised the scene of a serious crime and were not moving until the big guns arrived.

Clara seemed more curious than concerned. 'A cowboy costume, you say? Ah yes, Pietro was particularly fond of that – it was Bud Spencer's from *Call Me Trinity*. He loved to wear it at parties or dinners, and I don't mean just fancy dress! He would sometimes even go out in it – I would see him wheeling Letitia . . .' Her face clouded for a moment. Then she brightened up. 'A "device" you said? A metal box with a sort of handle? Now that would be the "noose-o-matic".'

'The what?'

'Another thing he used to take out at parties. It was the murder instrument in Dario's first US horror, *Trauma*, back in the early nineties, I think. It's a sort of crude gun with a wire lasso the killer slips over the head of their victim and when he flicks the switch the wire tightens until it whips off their head.'

'But that was just a prop, surely.'

'Well, yes and no. In those days it was often cheaper to actually build a functioning device than create something that *behaved* like one, although naturally it didn't *actually* work like in the film – you could never actually lop off a head with one. In fact the wire they used in the film wouldn't even break the skin, although it might well garrotte you. Pietro had replaced it with cheese wire. Not to kill anyone, you understand, but to demonstrate – on marrows, cucumbers, that sort of thing – when he brought out all his toys at the end of the evening.'

A pair of blue-liveried cars pulled up beside the Polizia Locale and a group of uniformed officers got out. I was reasonably familiar with Carabinieri ranks by now and recognised the lead – a thick-set man with a bristly black beard – was a captain, probably the most senior officer on the island. He was pulling on his latex gloves.

The Polizia Locale saluted and handed over the intruder to two Carabinieri, who led him to the cars. The captain glanced over at us as the Polizia gave him their report. I wasn't about to pitch in – I knew the Italian police well enough to respectfully wait my turn.

Finally, the captain approached us and saluted. 'Signora Bloom,' he said, as if encountering film stars was an everyday part of his job. 'Please,' he continued in English. 'One of my officers will accompany you and your assistant,' he nodded at Rose, 'to your hotel. I apologise for the inconvenience, but we will be obliged to visit you tomorrow to take a statement.'

'And Clara?' she said.

'The signora is free to go, although we will also be asking her to make a statement.'

'Daniel?'

'I'm afraid I will have to ask the gentleman to accompany us to the *caserma* to take some samples and his statement. I apologise for the inconvenience, signora.'

Anna looked questioningly at me. 'I'll be fine,' I said.

'I'll speak to Uncle Umberto,' said Rose, meaning the *Ispettore*.

'Just message him,' I said. 'Tell him I'll be in touch if I need to.' I didn't want Alessandro on the blower to the local military until I had this straight in my head – as things stood, we had done everything, more or less, by the book, so the cops had no reason to believe I had anything to do with it, and I wasn't sure if I wanted to start discussing stolen films, mysterious stashes of cash, and dead film buffs with the Venice branch of the Carabinieri. Alessandro could let them know once I'd got off the island, otherwise I might be stuck here for days.

I sat in the passenger seat beside the captain as he drove to the *caserma*. A position of privilege, I presumed – *I hoped* – reserved for a witness.

It was a straight road along the seafront and we soon left the grand villas behind for more modest, modern dwellings, small stores, bars. As on the main island, Venetian life continued to cling around the fringes.

The captain turned off the coast road and into a patchwork of suburban-style streets before emerging onto a long, tree-lined avenue punctuated by empty fields and small workshops and warehouses. Away from the centre, it seemed Lido had plenty of land to spare.

As the captain turned the wheel, I noticed his wrist: three spades, almost like a bracelet.

'You've seen action,' I said. He gave me a sideways glance. 'The tattoos,' I added. He looked back at the road and navigated a roundabout. Looming out of the darkness ahead of us, the red brick of a Napoleon-era fort.

A modern blue metal gate opened automatically. The other car had already arrived and was parked in front of a grand white stone entrance facing the parade ground, the youth being marched up the steps.

Our car continued past and into a car park to the rear of the buildings, surrounded by garages that I guessed had once served as stables. The car park was almost deserted, and the captain drew up close to the single doorway giving off light. It opened, and another Carabinieri emerged, saluting as we approached.

'The corporal will take DNA samples,' said the captain before stalking off down the corridor.

'Not much of a conversationalist, your boss,' I said as the corporal examined my fingers like a manicurist. He took a Q-Tip and swabbed them before asking me to open my mouth and did the same. He then plucked out a couple of my hairs. The *omertà* apparently extended to the rest of the troops.

'Please,' he said when he had finished. 'Come.'

I followed the corporal along a series of corridors and up a set of stairs to a banner-lined anteroom, beyond which I could see the captain through art deco mahogany and glass doors, sitting behind a vast oak desk. He was looking at his computer. The corporal knocked on the door. Without looking away from his screen, the captain gestured for me to enter.

The corporal ushered me in and closed the door behind me. I hesitated for a moment, unsure if I should continue to stand as if I was one of his subalterns but decided that was ridiculous so sat down. The captain clicked on something and finally turned to look at me. 'Signor Leicester,' he said. 'Please tell me what happened.'

Perhaps the silent treatment had made me nervous, perhaps I just wasn't used to such a frosty reception – we were 'a Carabinieri family' after all – but my earlier resolve had weakened somewhat. I wasn't going to get away with stonewalling entirely. I would tell the captain what I had told Clara – enough to keep it plausible. I was interested in a film in Volpato's archive but he hadn't got back to me, so we paid him a visit.

'And this film . . .'

'*Love on a Razorblade.*'

'Why were you interested in it, signor?'

'Well, it was part of a case I was following up. This is confidential, isn't it?'

'Of course, signor, this is the Carabinieri.'

'A film had gone missing, and we had reason to believe there might have been some . . . connection with Signor Volpato. I wanted to discuss it with him.'

'I see.' He scratched his stubbly grey hair. 'Gone missing, you say . . . From where?'

'CineBo in Bologna, my client.'

'And this connection with Signor Volpato. What made you think this?'

I shrugged. 'We found a movie reel, some packaging . . . We thought perhaps there might have been some kind of mix-up.'

'But Signor Volpato did not return your messages so you decided to visit him at his home. That's rather extreme, isn't it?'

'It was a coincidence – I happened to mention it to Signora del Monte and she said she lived nearby and we should pay him a visit. There was nothing more to it than that.'

'Except you found the couple dead, the signore in the most gruesome fashion. And caught an intruder in the process.'

'If that's what he was . . .'

'What do you mean?'

'Only that it is for you to connect him to the crime and so on, I know nothing about that.'

'So you don't think he did it? He was covered in blood!'

'That may have been my fault, I mean, when I wrestled him to the ground.'

The captain gave me a long look. 'The corporal took the samples?'

'He did.' He frowned.

'Are you tired, signore?'

'Perhaps a little bit.'

'Then we will let you go, although we may have further questions for you tomorrow.' He stood up and held out his hand. As I shook it, he said, 'And when you get back to Bologna, do send my regards to Comandante Faidate, and of course, Colonnello Alessandro.' He used the *Ispettore's* official title.

'I will,' I said, trying not to sound too surprised. The captain nodded and the door opened.

'The corporal will return you to the hotel.'

Chapter 19

There was someone asleep on top of my bed when I got in.

'Rose?' She turned over, turned on the light. It was Anna.

'God, I must have dropped off.' She sat up. 'So you're okay? They didn't beat you up in custody? Try to pin it on you?'

'Nothing like that,' I said. 'It was like they said: to take a few samples, and ask a few questions.' She got up, went over to the desk beneath the TV where I noticed a bottle of Scotch whisky that hadn't been there before.

'I thought you might be able to use one,' said Anna. 'I definitely could.' She poured us both a generous finger. We clinked glasses. She sat on the end of the bed while I took the chair.

'I'm terribly sorry about what happened,' I said. 'How do you feel?'

'I've had better nights.' She winced at the taste of the Scotch. 'I'd . . . Well, I'd definitely not seen anything like that before. His throat was cut?' I nodded. 'I don't think I've ever seen so much blood. I mean, I guess I've seen my fair share of the *fake stuff* on set but, well, it's nothing like that.' She frowned. 'It's the *smell*, you know? The iron-y smell of all that blood. That's . . . oh my.' She took another sip.

'Are you all right?'

She straightened. 'Too real, altogether too much reality. Live a life like mine and you can avoid it, mostly. But sometimes . . .'

'Believe me, that wasn't "real". What I mean is, I've never seen anything like that before myself.'

'So how do *you* feel?'

'Like I could do with a drink.'

'But you do owe me an explanation,' she said. 'There's got to be more to this than some missing film, right?'

'It's beginning to look that way,' I said.

'Those two kids, then this guy and his wife. *What's going on, Daniel?*'

'I wish I knew. Maybe the intruder will be able to throw some light on it.'

'You don't look convinced.'

'I don't know what to think, honestly. I was hoping Signor Volpato would be able to explain how part of the film in his archive had apparently made it to Gianni Colline in Bologna . . . The guy I caught appeared more like an opportunist . . . saw the windows open, maybe knew there was some valuable stuff . . .' I took another sip of Scotch. Anna was right – it was precisely what I needed. 'This remake of *Amore su una lama di rasoio* . . .'

'Or *Love on a Razorblade*, as it'll be known.'

'Certainly seems to be . . . jinxed.'

'Toni Fausto was murdered, wasn't he, all those years ago?'

'He was.'

'And did they get anyone for it?'

'Apparently they convicted people for crimes associated

with the killing but were never able to pin the actual shooting on anyone.'

'Do you think all this could have anything to do with that? I mean it was decades ago, right?'

'Yeah, but here's the thing about Italy – the past tends to co-exist with the present, not least because people stick around for so long. Though it's a good point – we should ask around, see if anyone other than Alberto Fausto is still alive to give us their version of events.' I raised my glass. 'Cheers.'

'Maybe I wouldn't make a bad private eye myself?'

'There might be a little too much reality,' I said. 'And you could have trouble keeping a low profile.'

'Oh, I didn't do bad today, did I?'

'It's true – you managed to make yourself appear almost normal.'

'Hey, mister! That's going a bit far.' Anna reached across for the whisky and our hands brushed. She looked at me, and I at her. There was a long moment before she arched her eyebrows and sat back with the bottle. She splashed another finger into her glass and then into mine.

'But I guess at heart I'm just an ordinary gal from Okey,' she said. 'Down the hatch.'

'I did say "almost".' I put my glass down. Anna placed hers onto the floor. She sat back on the bed, smiling.

There was a knock at the door.

'Dad?'

Although Rose was surprised to find Anna, she didn't appear embarrassed for the interruption and took our explanation at face value – it was, after all, the truth, and she certainly seemed more like a teenage girl excited to discuss the night's events with her father than worried about barging in on something, if indeed there had been anything to barge in on.

And by the time she was ready to leave, the moment, if there had been a moment, had passed, and Anna left with her.

Chapter 20

Da Carlo was another one of the Comandante's 'old men' *trattorie*, although the menu of each was almost identical – meat-heavy *primi*, meat-heavy *secondi*, with *zuppa inglese* – Italian trifle – for dessert, plus meringue, and *tiramisù*, if you were lucky.

Like the menus, the décor for these places varied little – muted wallpaper, old paintings and sepia city scenes. Gold satin lampshades, white linen tablecloths.

Although menus in Italy might differ with the location and its signature cuisine, I had sat in the same kind of places from Naples to Turin. There appeared to be an implicit agreement among a certain breed of restaurateur that the summit of dining aesthetic had been achieved around 1936, the birth date of the typical proprietor.

What was unexpected was the Comandante's choice – a grilled breast of chicken accompanied solely by a crisp lettuce leaf. This from a man whose idea of light food was lasagne.

'Problem, Daniel?'

'Not a problem, Giovanni. Merely the deepening of a mystery – the other evening I noticed you had foregone pasta for the roast beef, and now . . .'

'It seems my training is paying off – you are most observant.'

'What training?'

'So subtle, my boy, you never even noticed. You might bear that in mind when hectoring your young lady.'

'Dolores, you mean? She might be young, but she's no lady.'

'You think so?' Giovanni gave me a pitying look. 'Then it seems you still have much to learn. In any case, since you've noticed, Enrico recommended I watch my weight. He prescribed me a diet.'

'Enrico? The coroner, you mean? How about a proper doctor instead of someone whose patients are exclusively dead?'

'He *is* a proper doctor, Daniel, and who better to advise than someone who is intimately acquainted with the causes of death? He formulated the diet himself, in fact, which he has been kind enough to share with me.'

'Well, what a pair of housewives you two have become.'

The Comandante tutted. 'That is very sexist, Daniel.'

'I can see *Lady* Dolores has got to you. Remember what you used to say about her?'

'That was before she smartened herself up. It's true, you have done a good job with her. I admit, I was sceptical at first, but your instincts were right. She is a credit to the firm. Now – *Venice.*'

I sighed. '*Venice.*'

'I understand this young thief is apparently sticking to his story that he spotted the windows open and chanced his arm.'

'As inconvenient as it might be, Comandante, I'm inclined to believe him – the congealed blood suggested that it took place a few hours beforehand, so unless he was some kind of ghoul who wanted to hang around . . .'

'The props were apparently quite valuable. Also Signor Volpato's manner of death . . .'

'As if someone knew what they were doing,' I said. 'Knew him, even, if Clara is to be believed about his demonstrations – possibly they bore a grudge. Or he may have been tortured in order to reveal a hiding place . . .'

'Except . . .'

'Apparently nothing was missing – and it silenced another voice that might have shed light on our case. I can't help having the sensation of a fist reaching out and pounding dead our leads. First these kids, then the Volpatos, even the assassination of Toni Fausto . . . It's all beginning to bear an unsettling resemblance to the events that followed the end of his version of *Amore su una lama di rasoio*.'

'Ustica, you mean?' the Comandante harrumphed. 'I was based out at Marzabotto at the time. I knew little more than anyone else.' He looked regretfully down at his chicken. I wondered how long it would be before it was replaced by the usual parmesan-smeared *cotoletta*. 'However, this name, Mestre . . . I went down into the *cantina* and dug out some old files.'

I straightened up. The Comandante's black filing cabinet in the corner of 'the strong room' as we called it – protected as it was by a security door in the basement – was a thing of family legend. Only Giovanni knew for sure what the cabinet contained, but as far as I had gathered it was mostly photo-copies of sensitive files he had amassed during his career in the more opaque branches of the Carabinieri. The fact he had smuggled out photocopies in the first place was highly irregular and almost certainly illegal. That he had felt obliged to do so said something about their potentially explosive nature and the requirement he felt to protect himself. In the event of his (natural) death, he had made me give him my word I would promptly destroy the files, 'and no peeking, eh?' I had agreed, although we both knew that while I could be relied on to undertake the former, I would struggle with the latter.

'As I suspected,' said the Comandante. 'Ettore Mestre was the retired general responsible for overseeing the Gladio caches in my area.' He closed his hands prayerfully beneath his chin as if this explained everything. Seeing I had no idea what he was talking about, he continued: 'It wasn't just in Italy, you know – Gladio was in place throughout Western Europe, including your United Kingdom. It was a "stay behind" operation – in the event of Allied countries being overrun by the Warsaw Pact, groups would undertake rearguard actions against the invaders – basically, Gladio put in place the framework and personnel for a resistance organisation in advance of invasion.' The old *padrone* came to remove our dishes and Giovanni sat back. When he had left, he leaned forward. 'That was the idea. The reality . . .'

'This is linked to the *Years of Lead*, isn't it?' I said. 'The terrorism of the seventies and eighties . . .'

'Gladio recruits tended to be associated with the right. With access to these arms caches . . .'

'So the Italian state could have been supplying weapons to right-wing terrorists?' My conclusions shunted into each other like cars out of the fog. 'Hence the "strategy of tension", right? I'd always thought it was left-wing propaganda, but this definitely gives it more credence: the state arming fascists to target the left, create a state of crisis, and keep the communists out of government.'

'*I'm* certainly not saying that, Daniel, but it has been said. One of my tasks in the countryside was to oversee the destruction of these caches after the existence of the arrangement was uncovered in the early nineties. My contact was General Ettore Mestre . . .'

'Is he still alive?'

'I very much doubt it – he was in his seventies, he would have to be well over a hundred now.'

'And this Ettore Mestre?'

'Yes, it appears he is the father of one Crispino Mestre, who opened the bookstore on Maggiore, but who has also now passed away.'

'They were childhood friends – Elettra and Paolo Mestre – apparently moved in the same circles, which means their parents must have. And their grandparents – Ettore and Alberto?'

'It is highly possible – the Fausto fortune was built by Elettra's great-grandfather during the 1930s, the Mestres had long-standing military ties . . .'

'You mean, going back to the Fascist era.'

'That's right.' The Comandante, whose own family history was not entirely clear of the taint of association, shifted a little uncomfortably. 'And as you know, Italian families have deep roots, long-standing relationships. Of course, it could simply be one of those coincidences . . .'

'Toni Fausto was assassinated by right-wing terrorists.'

'But there was no suggestion Ettore Mestre was involved

in the Fausto affair,' said the Comandante. 'His name didn't come up – that I would have known – and he was certainly not associated with anyone convicted for involvement in the murder.

'No,' he continued. 'In any case, I feel the links between the right and Gladio were exaggerated. *All* the caches were overseen by the military and leakage was not that widespread.'

'"Red" Bologna was a flashpoint in this undeclared civil war, though,' I said. I began to rub my temples. 'For the sake of argument, Comandante, let's just say Ettore Mestre and Alberto Fausto were friends, but Ettore *was* somehow connected to Fascists with access to these weapons, the question remains – could Ettore have been involved in the assassination of a friend's brother? Even when it comes to Italian politics, that seems pretty extreme.'

'And is there any reason Elettra would have contacted his grandson about it, years later?' asked the Comandante.

We looked at each other across our empty plates.

The *padrone* laid down our coffee. I noticed the Comandante produce a little bottle of sweetener. He offered it to me.

'I'll stick to the hard stuff,' I said, emptying a sachet of sugar.

'You need to stay trim in your situation.'

'What's *that* supposed to mean?'

'If you're going to step out with actresses.'

'Who told you? *Rose.* Nothing happened, seriously.'

'My granddaughter appears to be operating something of a dating agency – first her art tutor, now her employer . . .'

'*Basta*, Giovanni.' We got up to pay. 'There's really nothing to it.' I was opening the door to the street when it occurred to me. 'General Ettore Mestre,' I said. 'He was a general of what?'

'What do you mean?'

'When you first said it, I was thinking army . . .'

'Air force. Why?'

I linked my arm with his as we stepped into the bright sunshine.

'There it is again,' I whispered. 'Ustica.'

Chapter 21

Libreria Mestre turned out to have a rather sophisticated alarm system Claudio deemed too risky to try and bypass – 'It might be worth a punt if we were trying to rob Tiffany's' – so we decided to wire up the company van instead. This would not only enable us to track it, but also to see whatever Paolo – and possibly Elettra – were up to, thanks to a micro camera placed above the rear-view mirror.

But we faced a similar problem here – although it was an old van, Paolo parked it in a courtyard behind the store secured by electronic gates not unlike our own at home. Dolores was able to slip inside when a neighbour came to park their car, but discovered the bookshop garage secured with a further set of steel shutters.

We would wait for the militaria fair, then.

Early that morning, we tailed the van out to the event being held in the outer suburbs of Pilastro in the north of the city, where beyond the low-rise social housing, the city gave way to farmland.

The fair turned out to be better organised than I, at least, had expected – I had imagined we would simply follow Paolo into a car park, but his van was directed to an exhibitor enclosure while we were obliged to pull up behind a queue of cars that had already begun to form at a dedicated visitors' entrance.

There was no point queuing with the rest of the early birds if we weren't going to have direct access to the van. Instead, I had us pull out and continue along the road until we came to a bar where we stopped for breakfast and waited for the event to officially open.

I had expected the queue of a couple of dozen militaria fanatics to have disappeared by the time we returned, but there was quite the traffic jam. We finally made it along the secondary road to the public parking area. Beyond these fields, the tops of white canopies were visible, as if behind the hedges we would find a carousel, acrobats and a bouncy castle rather than the detritus of warfare.

There was certainly a festive atmosphere, families stretching their legs as they alighted Qashqais and people movers, some even producing fold-up chairs and tables from their open boots and having breakfast. This was everyday Bologna – part of the vast majority of folk who lived 'outside the walls' and made up the metropolitan city's population of over a million, who visited the malls at the weekend and were happy for the opportunity to distract the kids, and especially dad, for a morning at the relatively modest entry price of five euros a head for adults and three for accompanied children.

We were fielding almost the full team – once I had located Mestre, I would give Jacopo and Claudio the green light to sneak behind the exhibition tents and fit the device. Meanwhile Dolores, her henna hair hidden beneath a camouflage forage cap, would hang out in the exhibitors' car park to provide an early warning if he headed their way. That was the plan, anyway.

It didn't take me too long to locate the Libreria Mestre stand, which was in the main pavilion between a stall glimmering with polished shell casings, medals and military badges and another piled high with military surplus uniforms, boots and webbing, but instead of finding Paolo stationed behind the display of polythene-wrapped books and Third Reich paraphernalia, I found an elderly woman. I guessed she had to be Paolo's mother – she had the rotund build of her pre-buffed son, along with the same jolly wobble around her cheeks, as she chatted to the army surplus stall keeper, her fingers clacking at the knitting on her lap. Unusually for a woman from the north of Italy, she was dressed in the black of mourning.

I was about to move off to find Paolo when she looked at me: 'I'm just minding the stall, son, I've no idea how much any of this is worth.'

'Oh,' I said. 'Fine. So, he's coming back?'

'Don't doubt it.' She turned back to the stall holder. 'He wouldn't trust me with his treasures for long, be afraid I'd give them away!'

I nodded my thanks and wandered off to examine a table devoted to daggers, bayonets, and supposedly deactivated Second World War pistols and hand grenades much like, I hoped, any other militaria nut.

I was still frankly surprised by the sheer scale of the event and variety of merchandise – from stalls piled with rusting German, Italian and British helmets, spent munitions, trench shovels, ammunition cases, field telephones and tin cans, to proper antiquarian stands displaying Napoleonic era swords and banners, varnished muskets and bolt action rifles alongside ranks of German Iron Cross medals in glass cases. Between these, others sold camouflage clothing, old Wehrmacht army paybooks, Nazi-era postal stamps and crockery stamped with Swastikas; Fascist-era copies of the *Corriera della Sera* and occupation *Signal* magazine featuring handsome Aryan youth and heroic German soldiers on the cover. And that was just the main tent.

Outside, mingling among the mums and dads and the kids dashing from one stall to another, there strolled what looked like genuine soldiers, bearing their weapons as if they were patrolling the event, only they were dressed in US Army khaki from the Second World War, Fascist-era Italian army kit or, disturbingly even more prevalent, the uniform of the German Wehrmacht, including not a few with the SS flash.

I followed a couple of 'SS' into a smaller tent, at the end of which a book presentation was taking place. The elderly, ferret-faced author was being respectfully interviewed by a skinny, student-looking type with a black toothbrush goatee that might have been a Hitler moustache had it swapped his bottom lip for his top, on the subject of *The Abyssinian Campaign – A Timely Re-evaluation.*

Around half of the dozen plastic seats in front of the pair were filled.

This tent seemed a little more genteel than the main pavilion, with smaller folding tables, the men who were sitting glowering defensively behind them not dissimilar in their formal, if rather threadbare appearance, to the author of

A Timely Re-evaluation. Judging by the design quality of the book covers, they were mostly self-published authors, and it was hardly surprising no traditional publisher would invest in titles like *Il Duce's Black Brigades – Forgotten Heroes* or *How Communists Stole The Crown of Italy – A Monarchist's Lament.* Indeed, sharing, as many of the books on the stalls were, table space with busts of Mussolini and Hitler, paperweights bearing the twin 'Facia' or a Swastika, and calendars celebrating a century since Il Duce's March on Rome, much of this stuff was borderline illegal, but the laws were recent and oblique enough to make enforcement barely worth the while – unlike Germany (and there were also a good few German voices among the stallholders) Italy had never made a genuine effort to confront its past, not least because many of Fascism's fellow travellers had been left in place by the Allies as a bulwark against communism. Mussolini remains viewed by many as a hard man who made some wrong moves (indeed, his granddaughter Alessandra, an enthusiastic apologist for his legacy, is a popular TV celebrity) and Italy is rarely cast as a belligerent in the Second World War so much as one of its victims. It was hardly surprising, therefore, that in this corner of a Bolognese field, it was forever *Salò*: the Italian Social Republic.

I was stepping squeamishly out of the tent when I finally spotted Paolo Mestre: at an official Italian Army stand set beside the refreshment facilities.

There were two 'proper' soldiers at the stand, both apparently sergeants, their table displaying recruitment and publicity material. One was chatting to a father with two small boys, the other, his eyes obscured by wraparound sunglasses beneath a green beret, was standing beside a pull-up banner of troops spilling from a helicopter, talking to Paolo Mestre.

I pulled out my phone, ready to signal to the others when Mestre headed back to the pavilion, but instead, after chatting to the soldier, he went in the opposite direction – toward the visitors' car park.

I followed him through the exit and the ranks of vehicles, his height making him easy to keep an eye on. He pulled out his own phone, pressed it to his ear. Finally, he was waving, making his way to the far end of a line of vehicles where he stopped at the fence beside an empty, ploughed field. He began to look around. I ducked down, peering around the wheel of a car to see him shaking hands with a slight blond man in a Bologna FC tracksuit standing at the rear of a black SUV. They exchanged some more words before taking another look around, but I stayed put – they were clearly keeping an eye out for accidental witnesses heading in the direction of the fair rather than someone actively spying on them.

The man finally opened the boot and they peered in. Mestre reached inside and lifted something half-way out, but I couldn't get a clear view. He spent some time with his arms sunk in the boot, apparently supplying a running commentary while the man, who seemed too old and, frankly, weedy, to be in any way associated with Bologna Football Club, nodded away like a dog on a dashboard.

Mestre stood back, wiping his hands with a cloth, which he threw back into the boot before the man brought the lid down. Some more words were exchanged then Paolo began to head back my way while the man stood at the rear of the SUV watching him go. They did not shake hands.

I waited until the man had turned back to his car before getting up myself and following Mestre back into the fair. Waving my ticket, I was able to jump the queue in time to watch him detour by the army stand and give the sergeant a thumbs up before entering the pavilion. The sergeant responded with the slightest of nods before, although it might simply have been my imagination as his gaze was unreadable behind those wraparound sunglasses, looking directly at me.

Planting the bug appeared to have gone smoothly and we all met back at the car to see if the thing was working, although not before I had returned to where I had seen the SUV, but it had left. I kicked myself for not getting its number plate, although it would have meant taking my eyes off Mestre and his mother in the event she decided to nip back to the van for some biscuits, and that had been the priority.

We crowded around the open doors of the Alfa as Jacopo booted up his laptop. Google Maps came up and there was a bleep, with an orange flashing light.

'That's it,' he said.

'And vision?'

'Hang on,' he said. He clicked on a camera icon. The surprisingly clear colour image of the inside of the van came up.

'Sound?'

'Yeah,' said Jacopo. 'We'd need someone to actually be speaking to check that, Dan.'

'And what's the range?'

'Of the bug? It's on a phone card, so basically infinite so long as it's within the radius of a tower.'

'All we now have to do is wait, then.' I looked resignedly out of the window. Jacopo shook his head.

'It'll ping if the motion sensor picks up anything. The show's on all day, right? They won't pack up until six. May as well go home. Download the app and I'll give you the password, that way you'll get pinged yourself and can check on your phone.'

'What's going on in the van, you mean?'

'The look on his face,' said Claudio. 'It's the twenty-first century, Dan, it doesn't have to be difficult.'

'*Bene.*' I put the car in *Drive*.

'What's wrong?' asked Dolores. 'I thought you'd be pleased.'

'It's the convenience that bothers me,' I said. 'It's the death of field craft.'

'Field what?'

'See what I mean? For instance, when I started off as a reporter, you had to do a course, get a job on a newspaper or magazine, if you wanted to report the news. Now anyone can do it.'

'And that's a *bad thing*?' said Dolores. 'The news is out of the hands of the elites!'

'And how's that working out? It's the same with this "app". If it's this easy, anyone can do it, right?' This didn't seem to cut through. '*Anyone* can set themselves up as PIs. *Do our jobs.*'

'Not everyone can break into a van, Dan,' said Claudio.

'Or would want to,' added Jacopo.

'You know what I mean,' I said.

There was silence as we got onto the main road and began to head back to Bologna.

'Not really,' Dolores said finally.

Chapter 22

'Oh, you're home.' Rose twisted around from the stove as I came through the front door.

'There's no need to sound so pleased,' I said. 'Will there be enough for me?'

'I eat like a bird.' Anna Bloom came in from the balcony with the Comandante. 'I didn't realise you lived in such a romantic place – these balconies are something else.'

'It doesn't seem so romantic when Jacopo's playing Death Metal at two o'clock in the morning.'

'Jacopo?'

'My uncle,' said Rose. 'He lives across the landing. *He's* not coming, too?'

'He's gone off with Claudio to watch a basketball match. Apparently someone can sneak them in the back to watch Fortitudo-Virtus.'

'Claudio?'

'Auntie Alba's boyfriend,' said Rose.

'It's so Italian,' said Anna, 'all living together, one big happy family.' Rose turned back to stir the pot. The Comandante went to wash his hands. I removed my jacket to hang on the stand by the doorway. 'Well,' said Anna, drawing out a chair to sit at the kitchen table. 'One big family, anyway. I guess you're wondering what I'm doing here? Rose promised to treat me to some home cooking. In fact, she's asked her Auntie Alba to join us – apparently she's an expert at Bolognese cuisine.'

'She is.'

'And I was talking to Rose about that book, *Eat Pray Love*, and how she did this cooking course in Bologna and how I might do one in my down time and she said why not just ask Auntie Alba?'

'She's coming up,' called Rose without looking around.

'Three flights of stairs in her condition?' I asked.

'She offered, and she's not due for another three weeks.'

'She's pregnant?' said Anna. 'I'm sorry, I hadn't realised.'

'Don't worry,' I said. 'If Alba offered, I'm sure it won't be a problem.'

'Still, maybe we should go down.' She stood up.

'But . . .' Rose was holding the sauce-dripping spoon over the pot.

'You carry on,' I said. 'We'll not be long.'

'I feel awful,' said Anna as we went out. 'I hadn't . . .'

'Being sixteen has its limitations,' I said. 'Rose didn't think it through, and Alba probably over-promised.'

'*Over-promised*,' said Anna. 'Yeah, that's one of the down-sides of being, well, someone like me.'

'A star, you mean?'

'Yeah, a "star". I can't complain.'

'Oh, you can if you like, it'll make us mortals feel better.'

She laughed, taking my arm as we descended the

age-smoothed steps, although there was a perfectly functioning handrail on her other side.

'That's the rub – people don't treat us like "mortals". Most
of my pals, my fellow "stars in the firmament", lap it up, and
hey, I've been plenty guilty, in my time, but it can also be a
bit of a drag. The privacy. The, as you say, "over-promising"
– people don't like to say no, even when they can't deliver.
That's why some of us – never me, of course . . .'

'Never.'

'Get this diva reputation, like nothing's good enough.
It's often just exasperation – our time is so parcelled up, you
know, every minute earns someone some money, pays someone's wage *you're* responsible for, so when something doesn't
happen, well . . .'

'You throw your toys out of the pram.'

'Not me, obviously, honey. Well, not often, anyway,' she
winked. 'I'm just a *Yokey from Okey* . . .'

'So you say.'

'That's what I like about you.' I noted she was still holding
onto my arm as we crossed the courtyard. 'You don't seem to
give a shit.'

I frowned. 'I give plenty of shit.'

'I mean.' She drew me up before the house. I didn't look,
but I strongly suspected we were being monitored from the
balcony by that big happy family. 'About me.'

'I even give a shit about you,' I said. Anna nodded
thoughtfully.

'It's true what they say – you English are *so* charming.'

The crash of broken glass from Alba's house.

A shriek.

***

We were at the front door. As I knocked, it swung open.

'Is everything all right?' I called.

'No,' Alba gasped.

We passed through the snug *soggiorno* into the kitchen, which had once served as a metal workshop and where the refurbished benches now accommodated an impressive array of cooking equipment. Alba was upon her hands and knees on the brown ceramic tiles using a dishcloth to mop up a pool of clear liquid.

'What happened?' I said.

She looked up at me puce-faced. 'My waters broke!'

'But it's not due for three weeks,' I said.

'What did she say?' asked Anna. I explained. 'Don't be a bozo.' She crouched beside Alba and felt her cheeks. 'Honey,' she said, 'you're going to hospital.'

'What did she say?' Alba asked. I told her. 'I've called Claudio.' She picked up the phone. 'But he's not answering.'

'You should have called us,' I said.

'But I called him,' she said desperately.

'Honey.' Anna crouched beside her. 'How long have you been like this?'

'I cannot speak the English!' Alba wailed in English.

'Shush, shush now!' Anna tried to comfort her. 'Ask her how long she's been like this.'

'How long . . .'

Alba gasped as she was gripped by another contraction. She looked at Anna wide-eyed.

'I need to get to hospital!'

'Can you get up?' I asked.

'With your help!' Between us, Anna and I lifted Alba to her feet and began to walk her slowly toward the door. Before we reached it, Rose was coming through, followed by the Comandante.

'We heard shouting,' said Rose. 'Is she okay?'

'Get my keys,' I told her. She spun around and rushed out.

'Get a towel!' Alba shouted at the Comandante. He looked bemused but brushed past us to go to the bathroom.

By the time we had reached the Alfa, both Rose and Giovanni had caught up with us. Rose opened the front passenger seat. 'No, I'll go in the back,' said Alba. 'Put the towel down,' she instructed the Comandante. 'I don't want to ruin the leather.'

We looked at each other. 'Alba,' I said, 'don't be . . .'

'Just do it!'

Once the towel had been spread out, she set herself on the seats. She looked up at Anna. 'I am sorry, sorry!' she said, again in English, as I closed the door.

The Comandante came with us to the hospital while Alba continued trying to call Claudio – she finally got through as we drew up outside casualty, and was still shouting at him as the medics got her into a wheelchair.

'Don't leave me!' She dropped the phone onto her lap and grasped hold of my hand. Thus attached, I accompanied her through to triage, where she let go as she was helped onto the trolley, but grabbed hold again as the doctor began to examine her. He looked up between her legs.

'He's on the way,' he announced behind his mask.

'He's on the way!' Alba repeated. Her eyes bulged.

'Nurse!' the doctor called. 'Here! Quick!' Alba began to

puff frantically, her hand clamped to mine with an unnatural strength. I might have yelled out myself if I hadn't been infected by the same frantic terror that had seized the woman attached to my hand.

The nurse took one look and said: 'We need to get her into delivery.'

'No time – everyone, here, now!'

Alba and I became a still point as medics and equipment swirled around us as if changing the scenery upon stage, although in truth Alba was far from still, puffing and bucking and moaning and swearing and praying and puffing and weeping and yelping and puffing and . . .

'That's it!' said the doctor. '*Spingi, amore!* Push!' Alba, panting madly, sat forward as she bent toward her open legs.

'Push,' cried the nurse, peering over the doctor's shoulders.

'Push, Alba!' someone was shouting in English. 'Push!' I realised it was me.

The splash of liquid, the doctor dipping down – 'Quick!' – joined by the nurse.

They straightened awkwardly up, cradling against their hospital blues a blood-splattered, russet-skinned being with two arms, two legs and a head full of dark hair. It looked momentarily startled to find itself in the world, and then let out a furious wail.

'Congratulations,' the doctor said to me as he passed it, still attached to its sinuous cord, into the arms of its mother, 'you have a daughter.'

'I do indeed,' I said, rubbing my aching fingers, and finding myself, together with both Alba and half the medical staff, with tears running down my face.

There it was: the shock of life.

My hand freed from its responsibilities, I made my way toward the exit.

Sitting among the ranks of plastic chairs, the walking wounded and their friends and relatives – the Comandante. Seeing him there, I was reminded of another time I had come out to find him waiting anxiously like this, albeit in the pastel-coloured suite of the maternity unit rather than *Pronto Soccorso*. Now, sixteen years later, one of the sources of his anxiety was sat beside him, playing on her phone, while the other . . .

Claudio ran through the open casualty doors looking frantic.

'Where is she? What happened?'

'Congratulations,' I said. 'You have a daughter.'

'Where is she?' I indicated triage and he ran off.

'You're welcome,' I said. I went over and hugged Rose, then my father-in-law.

'Everything's all right?' he said. 'The baby was premature.'

'She certainly didn't look like it,' I said. 'She's a big girl, takes after the parents.' I looked around. 'Anna?'

'She wanted to come,' said Rose. 'But said she didn't want it to all be about her.'

'It's all about the little one now.' I spotted Jacopo coming in. 'Where the hell were you? Why didn't you pick up?'

He looked sheepish. 'There was a problem with the app.'

'What? You mean the app for the camera in the van?'

'Apparently it was . . . unstable. Anyway, Claudio had to download an update for his phone but it wasn't picking up a signal, so he said to wait until the game had finished and we went outside, and that was when he picked up the messages.'

'And this app.' I pulled out my own phone. I noticed the signal had also gone. 'What the hell, Jacopo?' He waved his hands.

'Really, there's no need to worry, you just have to get an update and the phone will work fine.'

'And the app?' Now he looked pensive and his hands, this time tilting from side-to-side, were less reassuring.

'Well, does it work or not?'

'To be honest, Dan, we won't know until it does . . . or it doesn't.'

Chapter 23

'Now do you see what I mean?' We were back in the Alfa which, despite Alba's efforts, had the faintly earthy whiff of a visit to the garden centre. Around us, the field which had accommodated visitors to the show, was beginning to empty as it came to a close. We would stay put, for now.

'Except,' Dolores said, lowering the window, 'that wasn't what you meant, was it – you didn't expect the app *not to work*, quite the opposite; you were moaning, like always, about the modern world.'

'I don't always moan about the modern world,' I said. From the back seat, Jacopo, fiddling with the laptop hooked up via a cable to his phone, guffawed. 'When it works,' I added testily.

'I thought you'd be happy we're having to do some "field craft",' said Dolores. 'Whatever the hell that means.'

'It means,' I said, 'cultivating qualities alien to your generation, like patience.'

'The game, you mean?' said Dolores. 'I have that on my phone. Never play it – boring. What do you think she'll call her, the little girl?'

'I don't know,' I said. 'Daniela? I could do with some credit.'

'*Che schifo!* What a horrible name!'

'And Dolores isn't? It isn't even Italian. "Dolore" means pain in Italian. Doesn't *Dolores* mean "pain in the ass"?'

'You're my witness, Jaco,' Dolores said without looking around. 'See how I'm being bullied by the boss?'

'You read too much *Guardian* – this is Italy, twenty-first century culture hasn't arrived yet, just the technology.' I noticed Jacopo's computer screen appeared to have frozen. 'And even that's patchy.'

'Anyway,' said Dolores. 'It's an old family name, handed down. It's Spanish. *María de los Dolores*,' she pronounced with a perfect Spanish accent. 'Our Mary of Sorrows. The Virgin Mary.'

'What were the Spanish doing in Italy?'

'The Kingdom of the Two Sicilies?' said Jacopo. 'Your part of the world used to be governed by Spain, right?'

'*Vero*,' said Dolores triumphantly. 'You should read some Italian history, Dan. Especially if you're going to become an Italian yourself – they might ask you in the exam.'

'There isn't a test on Italian history,' I said. 'Just the language.'

Now she turned to Jacopo. 'We still have some hope, then.'

'He doesn't stand a chance,' said Jacopo. 'It's advanced beginners.'

'*Advanced* beginners? *Mamma mia*. I'm so sorry, Dan, but we will come and visit you in England.'

'In the rain,' said Jacopo.

'In the rain and wind. We will send you pasta.'

'You're so funny,' I said. 'One thing I won't miss is Italian humour, oh I forget, there's no such thi—'

There was a ping that was echoed upon all of our phones. 'It's working!' said Jacopo.

I twisted around. 'So?'

'Look for yourself.' He turned the computer toward us. Paolo Mestre was sitting in the driver's seat, beside him, his mother. He helped her fix her seatbelt into the slot, then put the van into gear and pulled out.

'A good showing today,' she said. 'It was nice to see Riccardo, and did you hear? His boy Marco is in Bolzano now.' Mestre didn't reply. 'Working in a law office. They're expecting their third in the spring.'

'We ought to get moving,' said Jacopo. I put the car in *Drive*.

Although exhibitors and visitors had separate entrances, the exits merged as they opened onto the road, and both we and them became stuck in a queue. The Mestres sat in silence before things freed up in the exhibitors' line and they finally pulled out. As we edged forward ourselves, we watched the orange dot on the map move.

'Heading home,' observed Jacopo.

'We sold that silvery one, from Lapland,' said the mother. '*Lapplandschild.*'

'I thought he might also buy that lovely golden star with the black cross . . .'

'*Stern zum Großkreuz des Eisernen Kreuzes.*'

'But he wasn't prepared to cough up. If he had, it might have at least paid for hiring the stand.'

'Like I've said, mamma, that's not why I do it – it's for the visibility, the networking . . .'

'I don't think I've ever sold one of the Italian ones, or the British ones, for that matter.'

'German's where it's at.'

'A lot of would-be Nazis, I suppose.' Mestre made a slight smile.

'Collectors,' he said.

'I suppose it's simpler for Italians to be into German stuff. Less complicated. Do you think the Germans would be interested in the Italian stuff, then?'

Mestre let out a laugh like a bark. 'I don't think it would hold quite the same . . . *cachet*, mamma.'

Another period of silence, then: 'I'll warm up the lasagne tonight.'

'*Mamma*, I don't eat pasta in the evenings, you know that.'

'But you barely had anything for lunch!'

'*Mamma* . . .'

They continued in this vein until they returned home, and us with them. We pulled into the car park outside the church of Santissima Annunziata on the Viale close to the Faidate Residence as they trundled down Maggiore and Mestre pulled up outside his shop. We had expected Mestre to operate the automatic gates and enter the courtyard, but instead he helped his mother out of the van, then got back in. He turned on the radio – Radio Italia, *solo musica Italiana* – and headed off again.

'Okay,' I said. 'We'll hang on here until we know where he's going.' Sure enough, because of the one-way system he was obliged to exit the city centre on the opposite side from where we were parked, he took the Viale virtually all the way back around to where we were waiting, before turning up Via Saragozza.

As I started the car, I heard Mestre's voice from Jacopo's laptop. 'He's on the mobile,' said Jacopo.

'Right,' said Mestre. 'I'll be half an hour.'

Although he was at least five minutes ahead of us, the tracking technology now appeared to be working properly, and we were able to track Mestre's course along Saragozza, past the lengthy portico leading up to the rose-domed church of San Luca, and through the suburbs.

We finally arrived at farmland punctuated by *borghi* – hamlets – with a handful of houses and, if they were lucky, a roadside *osteria*.

'Why are you smiling?' asked Dolores.

'Just something the *Ispettore* said.'

'What?'

'How it often ends in a muddy field.'

'I'm not sure that's something to smile about,' said Dolores uneasily.

At Zola Predosa, Mestre took a minor road into the countryside proper, then another, the fields giving way to foothills that marked the beginnings of the Apennines – winding, potholed roads barely the width of a car, edged by trees and forest foliage, with increasingly steep drops glimpsed in the gaps.

Another turn, another tributary, this little more than a dirt track.

'How far is he ahead?'

'Hold on,' said Jacopo. I stopped the car. 'No more than two hundred metres. He's waving at someone. Pulling in. Getting out.'

I began to back the Alfa up to a lay-by set along the roadside to allow oncoming traffic to pass. With some difficulty, I swung the car around so it was facing the other direction.

'You stay here, Jac,' I said. 'Call us if he gets back in, anything else happens, and get ready to drive.' I looked at Dolores. 'Ready?' She opened the door. 'Well, at least you're dressed the part.' In her camouflage cap, tan T-shirt, cargos and DMs, she looked like she was set for Desert Storm. Me in my navy polo shirt and jeans, less so.

'If they spot us,' I said, 'we'll just say we're going for a walk.'

We opened the apps on our phones as we made our way down the lane. When we got within fifty metres, we moved to the side of the lane and began to take it more stealthily. Sure enough, we soon spotted the rear of Mestre's van butting into the road, beside it a navy Ford SUV and beside that, a black VW I immediately recognised as the one from the fair.

'First,' I whispered, as we crouched down behind them, 'we get the registrations.' I photographed the number plates.

The vehicles were parked in an elongated lay-by carved out of the surrounding woods. Keeping our heads down, we shifted around them – beyond was a kind of basin or plateau in the hillside. It was clearly some kind of picnic or activity area – there were a couple of tractor tyres set up as swings and a rudimentary zipline strung on a rope between trees. Logs sculpted into seats or benches and picnic tables, although it didn't look as if anyone had picnicked here for a long time.

Mestre was standing at the tree line diagonal to us with the other two men – the spindly chap in the Bologna FC tracksuit and the sergeant, *sans* beret and sunglasses but still in his military camo. He was one of those dark Italians, like a

Sicilian, an Arab or an Israeli, bald-shaved up top but, unlike Rocco Domori, he hadn't felt the need to balance it with facial hair below. If he hadn't been going bald he might have got rid of his hair anyway – he was one of the lucky ones it suited.

And while the sergeant was smaller than Mestre and less beefed up, there was definitely something more menacing about him. Maybe it was the camo, the way he held himself, the certain knowledge he was a trained killer. Or maybe it was because he was holding a machine gun.

'Let's video this,' I whispered to Dolores.

Mestre and Tracksuit stood on either side of the sergeant as he worked its mechanism, made some kind of technical explanation. He had the instinctive physicality of the military veteran, habituated to treating guns as tools of the trade. The rank of sergeant suited him: he looked like he could put a bullet through your skull with as little compunction as an artisan might drill through drywall. The pair jumped back as he promptly raised the gun and opened fire.

The sound ripped through the wood. Birds flew, leaves fell, smoke drifted, and with it the whiff of cordite in the subsequent, stunned silence. Gunfire is always shockingly loud and I understood why they were using this location to test a weapon – the dip, surrounded by trees, would serve to muffle the spread of the sound.

The machine gun wasn't modern – I had vague memories of playing toy soldiers, of plastic green and grey figurines, British versus Germans. It was one of those – a German machine gun with a stick magazine slotted vertically into the barrel. The kind of weapon that in the relentless diet of Second World War movies of my childhood had sprayed innocent civilians, British prisoners of war and heroic French Resistance.

The soldier said something to Tracksuit, who picked up a pair of bulging shopping bags and set off across the dip, their contents clinking. Mestre was meanwhile occupied with painstakingly reloading the empty magazine with bullets. The soldier laid the emptied gun upon a log and took out a pack of cigarettes, lighting up as he watched Mestre.

'Like this?' Tracksuit called. He had begun setting bottles out along a row of logs. The soldier nodded.

Mestre finished filling the magazine and slotted it into the machine gun, which he held reverently up to the sergeant. The sergeant offered him his half-smoked cigarette but Mestre shook his head. He flicked the fag away and took the gun.

By now Tracksuit had finished lining up the bottles and cans and was making his way back across the dip. The sergeant raised the gun and shouted with a fake German accent: '*Halt!*'

A skull-like grin crossed Tracksuit's chalky face and he playfully raised his hands, still coming.

The sergeant pulled the trigger. Gunfire screeched across the dip, flames spitting from the gun barrel.

Dolores let out an 'Oh!' but it would have been lost in the cacophony as Tracksuit dropped face-first to the ground and Mestre cringed back, stumbling away from the sergeant in fear.

The soldier calmly lowered the machine gun, smoke seeping from its barrel. To the alarmed caw of crows, he began to calmly cross the dip to the still body. After taking a few hesitant steps, Mestre came after him.

The soldier prodded Tracksuit with the toe of his boot. He didn't move. He gave him a kick. Another one.

'*Raus!*'

Visibly trembling, Tracksuit began to lift himself up. He rose to his knees, his hands held defensively, or beseechingly, outward.

'Have you seen?' the sergeant boomed, levelling the gun at Tracksuit's crotch. 'Pissed himself.' He raised a boot and pushed it against his chest. Tracksuit tilted backwards to lay flat on his back, his arms raised above his head like a dead man. The sergeant bent over him.

'When I say "*halt*",' he shouted in that same cod German, 'I mean *halt!*'

Chapter 24

'Do I know you?'

'That famous English sense of humour of yours,' said Jacopo.

'Seriously,' I said. 'I genuinely didn't know you had a suit.'

It was Monday and Jacopo was sat behind the Regency-style marble-topped reception desk, an array of three computers ranged in front of him – two of his laptops from the back office, and the larger display Alba used.

'Lending a hand.' He checked one of his laptops. 'I've emailed you the video files from Sunday.'

'Anything else?'

'Nothing special – just to and from the fair. He's on his own.'

'No mamma breaking his balls. So how long are you going to be the public face of Faidate Investigations?'

He frowned. 'Alba had a secretarial agency in reserve, but the Comandante wasn't keen. Dolores mentioned she might have someone who could step in – she's going to find out.'

'A friend of Dolores? And Giovanni's okay with that? Do we know what colour hair she'll have?'

'Not a friend, a cousin, apparently, from the south.'

'Any family's better than none, I suppose.' My phone rang. It was Alessandro. I went through to my office.

'*Ispettore.*'

'You messaged, Daniel.'

'You received the film and photos from the countryside?'

'I did. Unpleasant, but not necessarily illegal, unless the gentleman who was threatened complains. I suppose we could get them on discharging an unlicensed firearm, presuming it is unlicensed. Thin gruel. However, I suspect that is not your purpose.'

'You can ID this soldier, get us the information on the other plate?'

'I can.'

'You will?'

'I'll certainly consider it if you explain.'

I reminded him about Indigo Adler's suspicions about his wife and Mestre, and how Mestre's grandfather had been a former air force general. 'Which got me thinking about the significance of . . .'

'Let me guess,' said the *Ispettore.* 'Ustica. The finale of this lost film? A connection to these deaths?' He let out a long sigh, or perhaps a spume of vape fumes. 'I can understand the attraction, Daniel, but it's more thin gruel.'

'Gruel nonetheless, *Ispettore.* You said you had checked the hospitals for the guy I stabbed in the ribs.'

'And came up with nothing.'

'But those aren't the only hospitals in Bologna, right? The city's a major military base. Aren't there military hospitals?'

Another long sigh. 'There are indeed.'

'So the link between this sergeant and Mestre, Mestre and Elettra Fausto.'

'Yes, yes,' Alessandro said testily. 'You don't need to spell it out: you believe the man who jumped you in the apartment was connected to this fellow, and, I dare say, the pair were involved in the demise of our young love birds.'

'Not professional criminals, but professional killers.'

'I realise you are becoming an Italian,' said the *Ispettore*, 'but possibly in more ways than one? You're becoming infatuated with conspiracy. Where's that pragmatic Anglo-Saxon attitude of yours? Never mind *Love on a Razorblade*, how about Occam's Razor? The most obvious solution is the most likely. You appear to be connecting this with the meanest of threads to events which took place over forty years ago.'

'*But Ustica is still under investigation, Ispettore*. I've been doing some digging. Aren't the families still calling for justice? Didn't the President only just release hundreds of thousands of documents related to the case? I may still be British, but we're not in Britain now – here the truth has a long tail.'

'I'm not so sure it's about the truth, Daniel, more a kind of family obsession – because what is Italy, if not a great extended family? And you're getting sucked in by the familial myth, like the Hardy novel . . .'

'*Tess of the d'Urbervilles*?' I was unsurprised by his learning – most Italians knew more about English lit than the average British undergraduate.

'The farm girl who mistakenly believes she's related to aristocracy and is ruined. Beware, Daniel, not to go too far along that road, else you'll be babbling about it for another forty years.'

'You can't deny it's a lead, though: Mestre's grandfather, Mestre . . .'

'Which is the *d'Urberville* answer to a very simple question – what are Elettra and Mestre up to? I'd bet Signor Occam would say they were screwing.'

I reluctantly pictured Paolo Mestre. One could say he had done his best with what he had – tall, well-built, not especially handsome, but neither was he ugly. He certainly fell outside Anna's 'same kind of beautiful' category, but who was I to say? He and Elettra had grown up together. It was impossible to know what teenage desires Paolo Mestre stirred in Elettra Fausto.

'Be all that as it may,' I said. 'This film was still stolen, the CineBo lovers and Volpatos remain in the morgue, and I've just handed you a possible link to some guys who may be part of a network which goes back as far as Mestre's grandfather, an air force general. Now, I know you're too good a cop not to follow it up.'

Alessandro chuckled. 'Just as I know you haven't discounted the screwing angle. You're still "Bologna's best English detective", after all.'

'And still its only one,' I said.

I was arranging a slot via WhatsApp to visit Alba with Claudio, Rose, Jacopo and the Comandante – the semi-constant hospital vigil being the settled *modus operandi* of most Italian families – when Jacopo appeared at my doorway.

'Director Domori is here.'

He stood with his fingertips beating upon the reception desk and agitatedly chewing gum. As soon as he saw me, he dashed around and grabbed my hand.

'I have news,' he said.

'Come.' I beckoned him through to my office. 'Please, sit down.' He remained standing.

'It's not the film,' he said.

'It's . . . I'm sorry. Dolores!'

'It's not the film,' he repeated.

Dolores appeared in the doorway holding a cup of herbal tea.

'What do you mean,' I said, '"it's not the film"?'

'The negatives you found in the Moviola were not the ones that had been deposited in the archive – namely Toni Fausto's version of *Amore su una lama di rasoio*.'

'Then what were they?' I sucked on my teeth like I might once have drawn on a cigarette.

'Negatives of the classic print.'

'And – we are quite sure these weren't the negatives in the archive all along, that perhaps Mister Adler was mistaken?'

He shook his head. 'I asked myself the same question and had them check the reference numbers on the spools against those in the archive. They don't correspond. I then checked them with the fragments given to us by the police – the numbers match. It's simply not the same film as the one that went missing!'

I didn't feel anywhere near as delighted as the director about this. 'But isn't that just as bad? These negatives being destroyed?'

'Oh no.' He waved his hands. 'Although they are by no means common, the "classic" version of the film was widely distributed in its time – had this gone missing we would have ultimately been able to patch something together through our contacts with archives around the world. No – *the truly unique negatives* were the Toni Fausto ones. They are irreplaceable. And don't you see? They must still exist!'

'Or at least they didn't go up in flames,' I muttered. We finally took our seats around the coffee table. Dolores looked questioningly at me as she blew across the surface of her tea.

Domori eased himself back into the chair, shaking his head in wonderment. 'This Italy,' he said. 'If I had known . . . The screening of *Amore su una lama di rasoio* was meant to be a celebration. My first big event – and it was *my* idea, you know. We didn't *have* to do anything! And it turned into this . . . *nightmare.*'

'So,' I said, choosing my words carefully. 'Do you have any idea why Gianni and Valeria might have had these "classic" negatives?'

'I was wondering the same thing – could it have been that this was just part of a scam? Perhaps Gianni and Valeria didn't steal the negatives at all but had somehow got hold of the classics and were planning to rip us off by pretending they were the missing ones?'

I blinked, momentarily blindsided.

'I suppose anything's possible,' I admitted. 'But I have absolutely no idea why they would do so. And as you said, getting hold of these negatives wouldn't have been easy in the first place.' I thought about the twenty grand in Gianni's mattress – had there been more? Had it paid for these? And if so, where had the money come from? And why?

Dolores was apparently asking herself the same thing. 'Venice?' she said. Domori looked at her questioningly.

'We followed a lead to Lido,' I admitted. 'To the archive of the Film Festival.'

'Hold on.' He looked alarmed. 'This hasn't got anything to do with Volpato and his wife?'

'It's . . . difficult to say.'

'Mio Dio.' He bounced back on the chair. 'My God.' He loosened his tie. 'My wife. My family . . . Am I, are *we* at risk, Signor Leicester?'

'Not as far as I know, director.'

'And . . . *hold on*: what were you doing in Venice? The case was closed. We had stopped paying you.'

'I'm . . . not at liberty to say, I'm afraid. Client confidentiality.' He gave me a hard look as if to intuit who the client was.

'The police are saying the Volpatos died following a burglary gone wrong,' he said. 'But – *the coincidence.* So, if I'm following you correctly, you're saying Colline got hold of these negatives from Venice, and these were the ones that were found destroyed in the car?'

I exchanged a glance with Dolores. 'That seems a strong possibility, yes – we will have to check with whoever has taken over at the Venetian archive.

'But what I would like to know is,' I said, 'presuming Valeria and Gianni originally possessed the Toni Fausto version, which remains the most likely explanation given their track record of stealing from the archive – why would they want this one?'

'And where the hell *is* the Toni Fausto version?' asked Dolores.

Chapter 25

'Clara told me to tell you not to kill this one,' said Anna.

'How is she, after what happened with the Volpatos?' I asked.

'Oh, she's a tough old bird.'

'And you?'

'Me, honey? I'm pretty darn tough, too.' The limousine pulled up at the end of Via Indipendenza.

'I'm sorry, signori,' the driver leaned around, 'the road is closed for the Madonna.'

'You can't go around and drop us somewhere less . . . busy?' I asked.

'I'm sorry, signore, everywhere else would be the same, this is as close as I can get . . .'

The annual procession of the icon of the Virgin Mary to the cathedral clearly took precedence over the requirements of any modern-day icon. I looked through the privacy glass into the busy Bologna evening – the bar seats spread across the closed street were packed full of out-of-towners who had streamed in for the evening. I hesitated.

'Oh, come on,' said Anna, opening the door on her side.

'They won't bite!'

I wasn't convinced. I was conspicuous enough in the evening suit I had hired for the occasion, but I was hardly the main attraction. That would be Ms Anna Bloom who had forgone her usual under-the-radar look and dressed to . . . shock. I was no stranger to attractive women – Lucia had been pretty, Stella beautiful, albeit with her Roman nose and unruly bush of curly black hair not to everyone's taste, but Anna, sitting in the back of the limo in a silver dress, her hair up, face expertly powdered, was instantly recognisable and universally sublime: Aphrodite, Marie Antoinette and, with her long smooth legs crossed towards me, the star of last Christmas's Dior perfume ad. I'd noted the driver checking me out in the mirror as if to ask what kind of man would be worthy of accompanying this vision and when he looked away, I knew I'd inevitably come up short. I was just damn pleased I'd had a shave.

I moved around the car to the pavement where Anna stood waiting. I was already conscious something in the mild evening air had changed; the stream of people emerging from the porticoes running either side of Via Indipendenza was beginning to slow, a hush was rippling outwards from where she was standing to wash across the tables set out in the street.

Anna made an amused smile – I couldn't help thinking, at my discomfort – before linking her arm in mine and propelling us toward a wall of gawping pedestrians gathered at the mouth of the portico.

I felt her nose brush my cheek. 'Isn't this fun?' I looked at her askance. Now she flashed me a smile of some brilliance and the crowd, which a moment before had seemed impenetrable, let out a collective *oooh*, and parted.

We continued along the portico – our objective the Teatro Manzoni, Bologna's second most prestigious music venue after her opera house. I kept my eyes fixed ahead, focused on the prize, while sensing around us the movement of the crowd, which we had apparently not left behind, but had instead chosen to accompany us as a kind of guard of honour, bleeding onto the road and across from the opposite portico, phones held, for the most part, aloft.

I had the strong sensation I was going to appear on the front page of the *Carlino* the following morning, as well as across social media, but there was nothing to do but keep going: I had the sense of being ahead of a tsunami – if we paused for any reason, the exuberance of the mob currently being kept in check by our forward movement, might over-whelm us.

As if to confirm my *Carlino* fears, an apparently professional photographer jumped in front of us and began to snap, bouncing backwards like a demented frog.

'Won't your boyfriend be worried?' I asked Anna.

She frowned. 'What boyfriend?'

'Oh, my daughter said you had one.'

'That was probably something like this.' She squeezed against me and gave a Hollywood smile. The camera rattled away. 'Just for appearances.'

'I see,' I said.

She chuckled. 'What do you see, honey?'

'Um . . . the *teatro*.'

Before we got there, we had to pause to cross a road and I was afraid we'd had it – the crowd began to close around us – but thankfully we made it to the other side. A group of Polizia were present to stem the tide, linking hands and holding them back with indulgent smiles, while our pursuers lost any of their former reticence, employing what English they had to attract her attention – 'Anna! Anna! *Ear* Anna!' – Anna swirled smoothly on her thousand-dollar heels to delighted gasps, graced them with a wave. 'Anna, we love you!' came a forlorn cry. She blew the young woman a kiss, to another thousand snaps.

Waiting outside the *teatro* was a small delegation of nervous RAI executives and local politicians. Naturally, they only had eyes for Anna.

'Welcome, welcome.' A perma-tanned elderly gent with silver hair I recognised as president of the *teatro* and, incidentally, the owner of a luxury leather goods brand, bowed to kiss Anna's hand. He began walking her along the line of mesmerised male functionaries who completely ignored me. I vaguely wondered if Indigo Adler would have received the same treatment, or Anna's personal trainer, for that matter, but I wasn't too fussed. I checked my watch and wondered how long all this would take. In any event: it would be a long night.

Pierluigi Affronto had come a long way since being employed as an assistant sound mixer on the films of Toni Fausto. But beginning at the bottom had also given him a foot up: Fausto, always looking to cut costs, had hired him to write the soundtracks for some of his subsequent films, and Affronto had found further work among his *giallisti* friends, composing some of what were today considered iconic scores to rival the likes of Morricone. And as *gialli* had fallen out of fashion, he had followed a similar course to friend and rival Enzo – churning out tunes for whatever was required, be it telemovies, commercials, or more mainstream cinema – while releasing increasingly respected formal works until he was mentioned in the same breath as Einaudi and Richter.

As the last person to see Toni Fausto alive, and in fact the one who had discovered him dead when he returned to the studio, having gone to the shops to buy some cigarettes, he was a, if not *the*, key witness. The trouble was, he wasn't the easiest person to get hold of. His office had not returned our calls or emails, and as he was actually now based in Rome we couldn't just pop around. I was moaning about this over dinner when Rose piped up: 'Oh yeah, Indigo's trying to get hold of him, too.'

'Really? How did you hear that?'

'Just hanging out with Anna.'

'What do they want him for?'

'The soundtrack. He's not very keen, apparently, too busy. But he's a big fan of Anna's. That's why I know – Indigo called her in to talk to him over the phone.'

'And what did he say?'

'To come and see his concert.'

The auditorium was already full as we walked down the centre aisle to take our seats. Anna's presence had the same 'dampening' effect on the audience as outside, but at least they were too refined to mob us or yell out declarations of love. As we took our seats at the front row, the murmur rose again.

'This must be what royalty feels like,' I whispered.

'But wouldn't it be terrible?' said Anna. 'If you couldn't do something else with your life? If it was *only* about this? I've got *work* – this is just a means to an end. But what if this was the means *and* the end? I've met them, your royals. Not all, but some – nice folks but, *the horror*. No wonder Megs jumped ship.'

'Meghan Markle? You know her?' Anna shook her head.

'I mean, she was just TV, right? I've never done that, although I would certainly consider it, once my looks begin to go.' She covered her mouth. 'Oh my God, doesn't that sound awful? I'm sorry, I'm channelling my agent. What I mean is, honey, in Tinseltown your star is either on the way up or down – and if you're lucky you do TV on the way up like Megs.

'It's not really about artistic choices, I'm sure the studio marketing departments have some kind of fucking *algorithm*. When my agent says we've got this miniseries for you, it's her way of saying "lifeboats!". And you know, it *can* help. I mean – anything can happen, as Bill Goldman said "no one knows anything", right? You can get a telly bounce, some producer or director with real muscle – like Indigo – can insist, but generally speaking that's the rule. So, no, I've never met Megs, she certainly wasn't hanging around your Windsor Castle long enough for me to bump into her, but *goddarn*, I could understand how she felt.'

'And when she was "just TV" she would have never created your kind of stir every time she appeared at something.'

'If she had, poor girl, she might have thought twice before snaring her prince.'

The orchestra began to take the stage, very few avoiding

the opportunity to glance surreptitiously at Anna. As they
were tuning up, a man materialised in front of us and lifted
her hand from her lap, bowing to kiss it.

A bulky, bulldog-faced fellow in late middle age with thinning wisps of grey hair, he was in a black T-shirt, navy jacket
and jeans, while the rest of us men, including the orchestra,
were got up as penguins. Maestro's privilege, I supposed.

'I just wanted to thank you so much for coming.' Pierluigi
Affronto still had hold of her hand. 'I hope we will have time
to speak at the reception.'

'Me too,' said Anna.

'I will look forward to it.' He kissed her hand again before
aiming a curt nod in my direction. He stepped up to the stage
to a round of applause.

'With all these men kissing your hands,' I said, 'I hope you
wash them.' Anna Bloom gave me a sharp elbow in the ribs.

The music was all right, albeit a little like sitting through
a movie with only the soundtrack. And was it me, or was it a
little saccharine? I'd nothing against a tune, but sitting there
I began to muse upon how the Italian obsession with beauty
could smother you with sentimentality. This Affronto symphony was as pretty as a box of chocolates but had me shifting
restlessly in my seat yearning for some meat and potatoes – a
bit of Ludwig van. Indigo Adler's remark came back to me:
Italians buy into the myth of Italy themselves.

Affronto had scored the original *Amore su una lama di
rasoio*, which was probably why Indigo wanted him for the
remake, but back then he had been under the whip hand of
Toni Fausto who, for all his shortcomings, had a touch of

genuine genius and would have been able to bend the eager young student to his will. I doubted Adler would have the same influence over the *maestro* here.

The symphony came to an end and Affronto turned to receive the applause which, rather dutifully, I thought, transformed into a standing ovation. He turned back to the orchestra and applauded them, and they in turn applauded the maestro, the pantomime of appreciation reaching its crescendo when the maestro turned his clapping hands, which must have been aching at this point – I know mine were – toward us, or rather Anna, and beckoned her to join him on at the podium.

'Oh Jesus,' said Anna. 'I was afraid something like this might happen.' She laughingly shook her head. 'Really, no, you're too kind,' she called.

'*Ti prego,*' shouted Affronto, closing his hands together in prayer, a prayer it became clear a goddess was duty-bound to answer.

Before she went, Anna whispered in my ear: '*Italians.*'

All smiles and waves, Anna Bloom made her way to the steps of the stage, where the maestro had descended to meet her, and theatrically bowed to kiss her hand once more. I noticed Anna's smile stiffen as he did so, and she glanced surreptitiously at me before being led up to the stage, where Affronto made a big deal of tapping upon the lectern and silencing the audience before he conducted the orchestra in an 'impromptu' rendition of The Smiths' 'Please, Please Let Me Get What I Want', which Anna had 'played' on the harpsichord in Besson's irreverent reimagining of the French Revolution, and which was probably the most famous scene in the film.

After the orchestra had finished, and Anna had taken a curt-sey, her Hollywood smile now flashing to perhaps a thousand telephones unashamedly held aloft by the supposedly refined audience, instead of being allowed back to her seat, I noticed the maestro whisk her off, stage left. If I was a dog I might have growled. Instead, I remained sitting until the rest of the audience rose to leave. I wasn't exactly overwhelmed with shock, I knew precisely what was going on – the old git, being an *Italian* old git, actually fancied his chances with Anna.

As the auditorium began to empty, I made my own way up to the stage. A couple of orchestra members had returned to recover their sheet music and I asked them, 'The Maestro, where could I find him?' They looked at each other, then shook their heads in unison. A pair of Manzoni staff came up the stairs behind me.

'Excuse me, sir, it's forbidden.'

I turned towards them, a young man and woman. 'I'm Anna Bloom's companion for this evening. She was escorted off-stage by the Maestro. I need to know where they've gone.' The musicians quickly shuffled their papers together and headed off.

'I'm sorry, sir,' said the guy. 'We don't know anything about that. I'll have to ask you to leave by the proper exit . . .' I looked over his shoulder where I could see a couple of security men heading down either side of the auditorium. These kids couldn't stop me, the guys however . . .

I smiled. 'Excuse me.' I went in the direction I had seen Affronto lead Anna. I dove into the wings and all the panoply of backstage – the bustle of the stagehands, the musicians winding down, packing up their stuff, chatting relievedly.

'The Maestro,' I said loudly. 'Where can I find him?' The chatter petered out, all eyes turned on me. 'I'm Anna Bloom's companion.' I could see no one was going to speak up, although plenty were looking at the floor. 'Come on, *ragazzi*, give me a break.' Still no one spoke.

I looked around – there was an entire world back here, of hanging ropes and pulleys, piles of crates and stacked scenery, but no sign of a woman in a shimmering dress and her aged chaperone.

Then it occurred to me: '*Is she still actually here*, in the theatre? *Dai*, you're not telling me he's taken her somewhere?'

If anything, the silence became chillier.

'Come on,' I said. I could hear the security guys crossing the stage. 'Which way did they go?'

Security emerged from behind the curtains.

I grabbed the nearest violin case. The violinist, a brunette in her thirties, shrieked. I flipped the locks and pulled out the violin, held it up by the neck.

'Back off,' I warned the security men. 'Now,' I said. 'You tell me where the old bastard's taken Anna or I break the Strad's neck.'

There was a collective gasp. The musicians held back the security guys. The violinist began sobbing wildly. From the rear, someone said: 'It's not a Stradivarius, it's a Gagliano.'

'Fine.' I raised my arm. The violinist gasped:

'La Porta! He's taken her to La Porta.'

Chapter 26

One of Bologna's smartest restaurants has perhaps its least salubrious setting: over a four-lane carriageway at the beginning of Via Stalingrado. Home of Fausto SpA, yes, but also, further along, immigrant encampments, parading prostitutes, and the Parco Nord which, unless it is hosting fairs or festivals, is not the sort of place you'd want to walk your dog, even during the day.

The posh motorway restaurant vibe continued as I ascended the steps to the whale-like structure straddling the highway. It was a place I had viewed countless times driving in and out of the city, but never felt *la voglia*, or want, to actually visit, despite its Michelin-starred reputation. To a Briton, almost any restaurant meal served up in Bologna was better than you would get at home, not to mention Alba's cooking, so I hardly needed to travel to a glorified service station outside the walls.

Which was a little harsh, perhaps, but I was in a stinking mood as I reached the top of the stairs, pausing before the glass doors to pocket the bow tie, not least because I didn't want to be mistaken for a maître d'. I tried to calm down. I was here for information, not confrontation.

I pushed through the glass doors, momentarily dazzled by what they had managed to do with the space, which appeared like an upscale Mediterranean beach-front restaurant, white, weathered-wood partitions subtly reducing the otherwise cavernous room to a human scale. A harpist was playing in one alcove, while an elderly couple were sitting on a cream sofa opposite. Beyond them, the restaurant proper – a dozen or so square tables set across a hardwood floor at twice the distance you might expect elsewhere. Certainly, there was little more than a burr of conversation above the harp as the diners, mostly two to their tables of four, took their time over carefully curated dishes. All those times I had driven beneath La Porta, I'd been right – this was no place for a barbarian like me.

Pierluigi Affronto and Anna Bloom, however, fitted right in.

In fact, it was entirely possible that they may have contributed to the overall hush, sitting as they were, smack in the centre of the restaurant like the main visual course for diners and staff alike. No one was about to take a selfie, but sharing their evening with Hollywood royalty certainly must have added to the diners' sense of self-satisfaction. And, I thought cynically, whatever else Affronto planned to get out of this, at the very least he would have very publicly demonstrated he was mixing with the stars.

I smiled easily at the pair behind the reception desk – a young woman and older besuited man. 'I'm with Pierluigi and Anna.' I gestured casually in their direction.

'Oh?' The man raised his eyebrows. 'I'm sorry, sir, we only have a reservation for two.'

'Typical.' I began to make my way over. 'Just pull up a

chair and set a place.' Now it was my turn to seize centre stage as I strode across the restaurant to the table where Affronto was mid-way through some decorous story while Anna sat bolt upright, a smile frozen to her lips.

'Darling,' I said, taking her hand and ostentatiously kissing it. I felt a quiver behind me as the pursuing staff froze in confusion, then fell back as Anna let out a laugh, pushed back her chair and gave me a full-on Oklahoma hug.

'*Thank God,*' she whispered. Pierluigi Affronto looked like he had swallowed a spoon, his complexion continuing to redden as the La Porta staff swiftly delivered a chair and set me a place. I smiled at him fondly.

'Daniel Leicester,' I said. 'It's a shame we didn't have the chance to get acquainted.' The waiter came to hover over me. 'Oh, I'll skip the appetiser. Just give me whatever they're having.'

'You speak Italian,' Affronto said to me glumly. 'What are you? French?'

'Well, that's a first,' I replied in English. 'People used to think I was German. I've also been mistaken for Romanian. I'm hoping French is a little closer to Italian, although once a guy told me I was picking up a Bolognese accent. He must have been flattering me. Actually, I'm English, but people never seem to guess that as they can't imagine British people speaking Italian.'

'Oh,' he harrumphed. '*English.*'

'Anyway, I apologise for interrupting your little tête-à-tête.'

'Please,' Anna frowned, resting a hand upon mine, 'don't be.'

'In fact,' I said, 'I really don't need to stay.' Affronto perked up. Anna delivered me a sharp kick beneath the table.

'Signor Affronto,' I persevered. 'Pierluigi. I understand you were the last man to see Toni Fausto alive.'

'I . . .' He looked between us, his jowls quivering. 'I'm sorry, who are you?'

'I'm a private detective.'

'And he's a friend, Pierluigi.' Anna patted my hand.

'We're all friends here,' I said.

'A private detective, you say. Someone's paying you?' He looked at me distastefully. 'Is it Indigo?'

'I'm not at liberty to say, but if you could just share with me what happened on that fateful day . . .'

'Then you'll bugger off?'

'I'd be happy to leave you two lovebirds,' another jab, 'to enjoy your meal.'

'It's quite simple,' said Affronto. 'I popped out to buy a pack of cigarettes, and when I got back, there he was, shot dead. It was the Fascists.' He turned to Anna. 'A terrible thing, they were terrible times.'

'And do you know how the police arrived at that conclusion? That it was Fascists?'

'I've no more idea than anyone else. There was the note sent to the *Carlino*. I seem to recall something about the calibre of the bullets used. When we were looking down at him it must have just happened, because I couldn't have been out for more than twenty minutes, I'd stopped off to get a coffee – my alibi's straight, as I told the police . . .'

'You said "we". I thought you were the first on the scene.'

'I was. I was literally standing there over the body when his brother rang the bell. I don't know how long he had been ringing. I was simply standing there in shock, the smell of gunsmoke still clearly in the air – I knew what it smelled like, I'd only recently completed military service – and finally it registered. I went to open the door . . .'

He swallowed. 'I always felt partially responsible, you know, because that must have been how they got in – I didn't have any keys myself so had left the door on the latch when I'd nipped out. I remember the *commissario* saying it was "very convenient" and I was actually in the frame myself for about as long as they took to establish I had no ties whatsoever with the Fascists.'

'So Alberto Fausto arrived immediately after you had dis-covered his brother. What was he doing there?'

'No idea. It didn't occur to me to ask.'

'How did he react to the scene?'

'How do you think he reacted? His brother was lying on the studio floor with two bullets in his chest. I remember he fell to his knees, let out a whine like a kid, stroking him. "Toni, Toni" . . . It was horrible, truly horrible.'

'And you were mixing the sound . . .'

'I was the sound mixer, that's right. We were actually over-dubbing the vocals. The voice actor for Ron had only just left the studio. That was actually why I had popped out for cigarettes. He refused to have anyone smoking in his vicinity.' He shrugged. 'He always over-dubbed the American stars, thought he was one.'

'This over-dubbing was the technique where you used to get the actors to repeat their lines in the studio, whether they were actually dubbing foreigners or not, right?'

'That's it.' He looked at Anna. 'A peculiarly Italian tech-nique as far as I know. Probably came from ropey sound recording on set, a way to even out the levels, and not waste too much time messing around when you're running to a tight timeline and budget, especially relevant for *gialli*. Was easier to simply re-do the whole thing in the studio where everything was crystal clear, with the added advantage you could import foreigners for a bit of stardust and simply mix the dubbers in with the Italian actors.'

'I know Clint had a blast,' said Anna.

'And what scene were you working on at the time?' I asked.

'Um . . . the bit at the airport, I think. It would have been Ron's part, when he confronts the happy couple. Of course, that was what Alberto ended up cutting.'

'Did he ever say why?'

'No, and I didn't ask. Certainly no one questioned him, he was paying the wages! Well, actually, I remember someone saying the new ending was more of a crowd pleaser, and I couldn't disagree. Toni was always trying to step outside genre, he had all these pretensions, you know. Alberto was the money man – he was only interested in what worked.'

'He had quite a bad reputation, didn't he, Toni Fausto, with the women.'

'I wouldn't say bad . . . perhaps by today's standards.' He winked at Anna, who picked up a fork and stabbed a medallion of chicken.

'So there were no . . . "stories" on set.'

'He'd just tied the knot with Vanessa Tramonte, who was playing Ursula.'

'My part,' said Anna.

'She was certainly enough woman for any man, in fact, two – she had more of a reputation than he did.' He nodded thoughtfully. 'They were a good match. Perhaps both, in fact, had met theirs.'

'And she's . . .'

'Dead. Cancer. Now, I thought you said . . .'

'All right.' I rose to my feet just as a *cameriere* was delivering a huge plate displaying three exquisitely positioned atolls of food. 'I'd ask for a doggy bag, but—'

Anna dabbed her lips with her napkin and pushed back her own chair. 'It was lovely,' she said. 'But I've had enough.'

Affronto spluttered as he realised Anna meant to leave. 'We've another two courses,' he said.

'It was sweet,' said Anna. 'Kidnapping me and all, but I actually don't have to put up with this bullshit anymore.'

'Then why did you stay?'

'Because I was waiting for my knight in shining armour here.' She gave my arm a squeeze. 'He had some questions for you.'

'But Indigo said . . .'

'Honey, I don't give a fuck what Indigo said, although thank you for the concert tickets, your music was really very . . .' She looked at me, then back at him. 'Pretty.'

'Well,' he began to redden again, 'don't think you'll be getting it in your film!'

'You know, hon, I'm not sure it would be right for it, anyway. Now why don't you enjoy the other courses.' She turned to the hovering *cameriere* and manager. 'The food here really is quite exquisite,' she assured them. 'Just the company that sucks.' She took my arm. 'Shall we?'

Walking towards the exit, Rose emerged, out of breath, through the doors.

'Great timing!' said Anna.

'What's she doing here?' I asked.

'I've got your stuff.' Rose handed her a holdall.

'You're a star.' Anna headed for the bathroom.

'She sent me a message once she arrived,' she said. I checked my phone.

'She didn't send me a bloody message. Anyway,' I said, 'this is going above and beyond the call, isn't it? Don't you have work hours?'

She looked at me uncomprehendingly: 'I'm being paid three hundred euros a day.'

'It's not a twenty-four-hour day. You're not a slave, you know.'

'You're working, aren't you?'

'Well,' I said. 'Technically.'

'Anyway, it's not the twentieth century any more, Dad,' she said. 'In case you hadn't noticed.'

Anna performed a remarkably rapid change, although I suppose she had had practice. It took an effort to recognise her, such was the dissonance between before and after. Gone was the shimmering West Coast blonde of Oscar acceptance and audience acclaim, enter the albeit tall casually dressed brunette, her longish auburn hair – a wig, although only to the initiated – tied loosely behind, a pair of anthracite-coloured rectangular glasses balanced upon her nose. She might have been a visiting Danish librarian or a German architect. I recalled her earlier words to Rose about being 'mainly Scandinavian stock'. No kidding.

'Shall we?' said Anna. We followed her outside. 'I'm curious,' she said. 'How did you find me? Pierluigi assured me our location was a "secret", as if I would find it charming, the old scumbag.'

'I threatened to break a neck.'

'Just one?'

'One was all it took. Why didn't you message me?'

'Honey, by then I knew where I was, and where would be the challenge? If I really got into trouble here, I always had your little girl.'

I looked at Rose, standing with the holdall slung over her shoulder, her own auburn hair tied back much like Anna's, albeit real, and almost as tall. I had a wobbly feeling for a moment, as if she was as much Anna's daughter as mine.

'Anyway,' I said, 'I'll call a cab.'

'I'm fine,' said Rose.

'It's late,' I said. 'And it's Via Stalingrado.'

'I've got the Vespa,' she said. It was only now I registered the helmet hanging by the strap of the holdall.

'Jacopo's Vespa?'

'Uncle Jac lets me use it sometimes. It's okay, I know how to.'

'You haven't had any lessons.'

'Uncle Jac has taken me . . .'

'You don't have a licence, Rose.'

'Well, I'll get one!' We looked uncomprehendingly at each other. This felt more than the usual parent-teenager collision, more a fundamental culture gap between the English me and Italian her.

'*We* should take it,' offered Anna. 'It'll be like *Roman Holiday*. You can be my Gregory Peck.'

'But I only brought one helmet,' said Rose.

'Well,' said Anna, 'they didn't have helmets in *Roman Holiday.*'

Now I looked helplessly at them both. 'Rose,' I said. 'All right, take the Vespa straight home. We'll talk about this, with Uncle Jac, later. You and me,' I said to Anna, 'will get a cab.'

'Oh *you*,' said Anna. 'You're no fun. Weren't you about to break necks on my behalf? Now you're not prepared to risk yours to show a gal a good time?'

I wasn't going to rise to this. I called a taxi. As we got in, I said: 'Why is it I feel with you, Ms Bloom—'

'Strictly speaking,' said Anna, 'when I'm in this get-up, you should call me Mandy.'

'Mandy? I'm not sure that quite . . . fits.'

'It was my mom's favourite song, you know, by Barry Manilow. What do you want to call me then?'

'Anna's fine.' I gave the driver the name of her hotel.

'Oh no! I don't want to go home. Driver,' she said in English. 'Take me somewhere cool, you know – *figo*.' He gave me a confused look in the rear mirror.

'*Va be,*' I said. '*Andiamo all'Osteria della Luna.*'

We set off. 'Is this *osteria* cool, then?' asked Anna.

'I'm not sure if you could call it "Hollywood" cool, exactly,' I said. 'But something tells me that's not what you're looking for.'

'We'll see, Daniel Leicester,' she said. 'We shall see.'

Chapter 27

No, I definitely would not have called Osteria della Luna 'Hollywood cool'. 'Dump' would be the first term that sprang to mind, followed swiftly by 'could do with a deep clean', especially the toilet which was accessible via a key kept behind the bar attached to a u-bend of plastic piping, presumably in case someone decided to pocket it, although quite why they felt the need to wire it to a piece of plumbing probably said as much about the possible inebriation of La Luna's clientele as a pun on waterworks.

With its scarred and rickety tables and chairs, framed newspaper clippings and black and white and sepia group photos, sports detritus, bad art, and uneven tile floor, there was really nothing to suggest this was the oldest *osteria*, or pub, really, in the entire city, but the cavernous space that most resembled a wine cellar only without the barrels had been going without interruption for well over five hundred years.

For much of that time it would have been fogged by tobacco smoke, and while it was true some of the spirit of the old Luna had been maintained by converting the tiny courtyard to the side of the bar into, officially, an 'open space', at this time of the evening most smokers, and given that most of the clientele at this hour *were* smokers, preferred to stand out front, there was quite a mob filling the narrow *vicolo* as we approached.

Anna Bloom/Mandy took my hand as we wove through the crowd. I had no idea if it was a good idea to take a celebrity who had only just been applauded by the audience at Manzoni into the grotty heart of Bologna's nightlife, but I had to admit she was pretty good at pulling it off – she had certainly managed on the *traghetto* – and, unless you were paying particular attention, she didn't scream Anna Bloom. These things were all about context, and while Teatro Manzoni, La Porta, or stepping out of a limo in heels and a shimmering designer dress, might seem like appropriate sets for a film star, the Osteria della Luna indubitably did not. In any case, if the shit really hit the fan, I knew a way out the back.

Somewhat to my surprise, I discovered the *osteria* was almost as busy inside as out, its long tables packed with students and their families having picnics, bread, cheese, Prosciutto and salami spread across wrapping paper – despite being called an *osteria*, there was no food on offer at La Luna, but you were welcome to bring your own. Of course – we had reached the time of the year students would be receiving their *laurea*, or degree. It was standing room only in the *osteria*, and pretty packed at that.

'What are you having?' I asked, about to squeeze through to the bar.

'What have they got?'

'Basically, wine or beer.' Anna looked amused.

'I'll have wine, then. But make sure it's their finest.'

I wrestled my way through the press and managed to catch the eye of a *cameriera* who knew me and was reaching for a bottle of Sangiovese even as I plonked five euros on the bar. 'Two,' I said. She slopped the ruby wine into a couple of small glasses, but by the time I had muscled my way back through the pack, liberally spilling the drink over my fingers or other people's shoes, I saw Anna was already being hit on.

'What are you doing leaving a movie star unprotected?' Vesuvio asked in Italian, still holding onto the hand he had been in the process of shaking. Anna gave me a slightly perplexed look.

'Trust you to have spotted,' I said. 'Can't you see she's in disguise?'

'I get that. That's why I knew, see.' He turned to Anna and added in English: 'I'm a celebrity, myself.'

'Oh?' said Anna.

'I have to admit,' I said, 'it's true. Apart from owning this place . . .'

'Oh?'

'Well, a share,' said Vesuvio. 'That's what they say, isn't it?'

'That's what they say. Vesuvio is a, um, rock star. Here in Italy, I mean.'

'*Really?*' She gave him a once over. He certainly looked the part with his long dyed black hair and goatee, SHAM 69 T-shirt, expensive leather jacket, and artfully ripped jeans. Or the ageing bachelor uncle who'd never quite grown up.

'He's the equivalent of . . .' I didn't want to offend him. 'A kind of Italian Bruce Springsteen.'

'Oh?' Now Anna looked impressed.

'Oh yeah,' said Vesuvio, clearly flattered. 'And I'm an *X Factor* judge.' Anna laughed.

'My daughter loves that, the American version, I mean. Have you met Simon? He's the only famous person she's ever asked for an autograph. Maybe I should get yours, just in case?' Vesuvio looked flummoxed.

'I, um, don't have a pen.'

I slapped him on the back. 'She's joking, mate. You are, aren't you?'

Anna waggled her head from side-to-side. 'You never know. I'll have to listen to your music. *Vesuvio*, did you say?'

'After the volcano,' he said. He looked bashful. 'I was young, a bit, how you say? Cocky. I'm from Napoli.'

'Ooh, Naples. I've never been.'

'Come, I'd love to show you around.'

'What do you think, Daniel?' Anna said pointedly. 'Could you take some time out from Bologna to look after me? I hear Naples is pretty dangerous.'

Like Vesuvio, I wasn't completely sure if she was pulling my leg.

'Quite the time for reunions,' Vesuvio said softly in Italian.

'What do you mean?' He nodded up the steps to the area outside the toilet. The crowd standing around the table was about a decade older than the *laurea* party I might have first taken them for, and noticeably more . . . artsy. The men were mostly bearded, handsome and self-consciously smouldering, the women the type that on any other night I might find staffing the bar here at La Luna, supporting their acting, music or painting and why, in fact, it had been so easy for me to get served – because they knew me, because my ex-girlfriend had

been one of them before she left Bologna for Finland to claim
an art prize, because there she now stood, at the head of the
table, pouring a bottle of Prosecco with some blond, bearded
bloke wrapping an arm around her waist.

I was about to turn to Anna and suggest we head out front,
to the courtyard, anywhere would do, when with that spooky
sixth sense you get from being watched, Stella Amore raised
her eyes to meet mine.

There was a roar around the table as the Prosecco over-
flowed the glass and another was swiftly put in its place. Stella
blinked as the bottle was plucked from her hands.

She mouthed: '*Ciao.*'

'*Ciao.*'

She wiped her hands with some kitchen roll and, ignoring
the blond guy gabbling in her ear, made her way down the
steps.

She took my hand and kissed me on both cheeks.

'You're back, then,' I said.

'A visit,' she said. 'I told Rose.'

'You did? Well, you should have known: she's sixteen, it's
illegal for her to tell me anything.'

'We're meeting up tomorrow, her work's really come on.'

'And yours?' I nodded towards the blond guy glaring at
me. 'I see you've had plenty to keep you occupied.'

'Tuomo. He's a curator with Kiasma, Helsinki's modern
art museum. Anyway, *caro*, you're hardly the one to criticise
– I see you've . . . *traded up.*' I had entirely forgotten Anna in
the bubble that enclosed Stella and me, but it seemed Stella
had been paying more attention. Now she turned to Anna.
'Hi,' she said in American-accented English, and I realised

I had never once heard her speak my language. Well, I was about to. 'I'm Stella, Daniel's ex.'

'Wait,' said Anna. 'You're *her*? *The* Stella? Rose is always talking about you. She worships you, you know.'

'I'm sure that's not true,' said Stella. 'Mother figure, probably.' She flashed me a sad smile.

'Are you here long? I'd love to see some of your work.'

Any other artist might have leaped at the thought of Anna Bloom including them in her collection, but Stella seemed typically ambivalent.

'Well, I don't have a studio here anymore . . .'

'No?' I said, disappointedly – I'd been hoping there would be something to bring her back. 'What about Chiara?'

'She sold the Jewish paintings to Israel or something and set up a gallery in Modena. But,' she turned back to Anna, 'Rose can show you my website, and I've also got some stuff in MAMBO . . .'

'Bologna's modern art museum,' I said.

'But obviously, that's not for sale. So, I see Dan's pulling out all the stops to impress you, bringing you here.'

Anna laughed. 'Believe me, it's an improvement on where we've come from.' She glanced up at the group, which had calmed down as it came to realise who Stella was talking to. 'You look like you're having fun. Do you mind if we join you?'

Stella gave me a questioning look as if she didn't want to interrupt anything. 'If you don't mind,' I said, suppressing a vague sense of disappointment she clearly didn't. As we followed her up to the platform and her friends did their best to act too cool for school, I consoled myself with the possibility that her new boyfriend, T'Pau, or whatever he was called, might try to fight me, but somewhat more to my dismay, he turned out not to be an asshole and actually quite convivial, with a Finnish intensity to drinking (abetted by some vodka they had brought with them) that swiftly set the social awkwardness aside and turned the evening into a delirious blur.

By the time Anna was pulling me away, I had put aside my antagonism towards Stella's new lover; I had also, it appeared, experienced 'closure' with Stella, which probably meant I was too drunk to care, and largely forgotten Anna's status as a sort of living monument, as, it appeared, had she – visions of Stella's friends hooting with laughter as they tried on her wig (we all agreed it suited T'Pau best), oblivious to being literally up there on stage for all of La Luna to see.

Fortunately, as we managed to ease our way out, the rest of the bar was either inebriated like us, or we were too drunk to notice they weren't – admittedly, the crowd did part remarkably easily, Anna leading the way, the ponytail of her wig screwed lopsidedly in front of me as we headed outside. We stood swaying in the alleyway, the crowd having thinned and apparently genuinely oblivious to our presence. Anna adjusted her wig.

'Okay?' she said.

'Okay.'

'It's been quite a night.'

'It has.'

'Thanks for coming for me. After the kidnap, I mean.'

'I'm sure you could have handled yourself.'

'But it's the thought that counts. Hey, one more favour.'

'What?'

'Would you mind walking me home? I've gotta admit, I've *no fucking idea* where we are.'

I took her arm. We weren't actually very far from Anna's hotel. I had never got further than the frescoed reception, although naturally Rose had been up to Anna's room, which she had described as 'pretty posh'. Would I make it up now? To be honest, I was too far gone to care, which was probably for the best.

It also led to what I said next – something that had been on my mind since I had caught that reflection of Rose and Anna in the *biglieterria* window and now floated to the surface upon a cushion of alcohol fumes.

'You really told him, Pierluigi.' Anna let out a laugh.

'Silly old letch. Aren't those days supposed to be over? Obviously, Italy didn't get the memo.' She giggled. '*Hashtag: Me too*. Must have been lost in translation.'

'The Italians do kind of pick up on this stuff but, it's difficult to explain: they're a cynical lot. While on the surface they'll make the right noises, it's far harder to get under their skin, to really change people's attitudes. It's a survival strategy, sort of. Speaking of which, did something once happen to you?'

'What do you mean?'

'I saw the way Clara looked at you when she was talking about what went on in movies. I got the sense . . .'

Anna broke away from me, wrapped her arms around herself. Said nothing as she walked, her heels clicking on the paving slabs.

'I'm sorry,' I said, 'to intrude, I'm pissed . . .'

'Angry you mean?' She was looking straight ahead.

'No, I mean . . .'

'I know what you meant, *bozo*.' She grabbed my arm back. 'I speaka the *Eengleesh* Eengleesh. Well, honey, let me put it this way: there wasn't any "me too" when I was trying to make it, it was every girl, and boy, for themselves. Damn it, this thing's going to make my head explode.' She tore off her wig. I looked around, but it was late, there was barely anyone about.

We turned down Via Oberdan, a narrow, pedestrianised street, deserted this time of night. 'I don't know, hon, I'm glad there's more respect and all, but Hollywood was worst in the thirties when times were so uptight a couple couldn't even be shown together in bed – all the abusive shit just went more under the covers, ha!

'You know what all that philosophy taught me?'

'Tell me.'

'*Life's fucking short.*'

'And they say Italians are cynical.'

'A cynic? Moi? Honey, I'm just a *Yokey* from . . .'

She gasped. Up ahead, a man had stepped out of the shadows and into our path. Bulky with a smooth-skulled silhouette, the blood red glow of his cigarette burned like a cinder in the dark.

I steered us sharply towards the other side of the street. The man didn't budge. I looked around, hoping it was nothing, but clocked another useful-looking type approaching fast from behind, clearly focused on us.

I squeezed Anna's arm. 'Get ready to run,' I said. 'And don't look back.'

'But . . .'

'No time,' I said. 'Just do it. Shout for help: "*aiuto*".'

'A-oo-toe?' We were almost level with the first.

I could hear the beat of the man behind me.

'*Go.*' I gave her a shove. Just in time, it seemed. A foot came between my ankles. As I tripped, I saw Anna taking off.

She shot past the other guy, who flicked his cigarette as she tore down Oberdan yelling '*Aiuto!*' at the top of her lungs.

I somehow recovered my footing, and slammed into a wall.

My pursuer was on top of me.

Yet just as through my drunken fug I'd instinctively understood this was trouble, seeing Anna take off without the cigarette guy so much as trying to block her way, I realised this wasn't about the celeb at all.

It was about me.

Time turned elastic.

I was able to parry some blows, even land a couple of punches, while at the same time understand my assailant was stronger, more experienced.

The rock hard fist in the ribs.

Another against the chest.

I was propelled back against the wall, watched a juggernaut blow sweep aside my parry to connect with my jaw.

I felt my knees begin to give. Shunted myself back against the wall to keep upright.

But I knew with stone cold certainty I was beat.

'*Basta*. Hold him.'

A space opened in front of me, but there was no way forward – my assailant had my arm twisted outward, a hand ready to break it at the elbow, as the second man stepped forward. No cigarette now.

A pistol.

He bore down on me with such firm-jawed intent, it barely seemed to matter that I recognised him – the sergeant – as he raised the gun, curling his thick index finger around the trigger.

He was going to switch me off like a light and there was nothing I could do about it.

Chapter 28

'A-oo-toe!'

The flash, the bang.

But I was still blinking. Breathing.

There it was again – even before I heard the pistol clatter to the ground, the sergeant after it.

The grip tightened on my arm and the shock shuddered through me, too, as the sparking machine connected with my other assailant.

We burst apart as if struck by lightning. I fell onto the cobbles, rasping as more explosions illuminated the street.

I was on my hands and knees. I looked up – the sergeant was on his front, outstretched arms twitching, eyes drilling into me. A hand reached down and he was struck by another blue bolt to the neck. He juddered, jaw clenching.

His eyes closed.

A plaintive electric sigh emanated from the hand, a ruby light outlining long fingers.

'Damn it,' said Anna Bloom, straightening up. 'Out of juice. Quick.' She grasped my arm. 'Can you walk? Can you run?'

I was jelly-legged but could stand. I looked at the two

men splayed, apparently unconscious, upon the cobbles, and began to move forward. I stumbled. She caught me, and I clung to her with both hands.

We were crossing a street, we were weaving between traffic, we were climbing some steps. Into a marble reception. Into placid light.

'What happened, signora?' someone asked in English.

'We were attacked,' she said. I slumped onto a sofa. 'Quick, call the police.' She went back to the doors and pulled them closed. Slammed the bolts.

'Signora,' said the night porter. 'Our other guests . . .'

'Well, they can darn well ring the bell, can't they.' She came over to me. 'Are you all right? Daniel?'

Anna's wig had gone, possibly lost somewhere in the street. I noticed she wasn't wearing any shoes, either. Looking up at her, I had the uncanny feeling I was in a film.

I pushed myself up. 'The Carabinieri,' I said. 'Call them.'

'I'm on the line to the Polizia,' said the porter, holding the receiver.

'Fine,' I said wearily. I winced at a twinge in my ribs.

'You're all right?' said Anna.

'I will be.' One of those bastards had landed a punch on an old fracture. They said they were supposed to mend stronger. It didn't feel like it.

'What *was* that, anyway?' I said.

'What do you mean?'

'*That*.' I groggily worked my sore jaw. 'In your hand. Unless you actually *are* a goddess . . .'

'Oh you mean my flashlight?' She sat down beside me and pulled out a black metal tube from her back pocket.

'A hell of a torch.'

'Well, that's what it looks like.' She flicked a switch and a dull light glowed from the front. 'It's more convincing when it's charged. But it works a treat, huh? I take it in my hand luggage. No one ever asks, but it packs one helluva punch. Thirty thousand volts, military standard.'

'A stun gun.'

'You think I'm going *anywhere* unarmed, honey? Back home I have a concealed carry licence. You have any idea how many nutjobs want a piece of me? This is my, um, weapon of last resort, you might say.'

'Right,' I said, rubbing my jaw. 'Thank you for coming back for me.' I squeezed her hand.

'Hey, are you crazy? Honestly, I was pretty *pissed*, as you say, myself. Not thinking clearly. I was half-way down the street by the time I realised it was *you* they were after, not me, and I wasn't about to *bugger off.* Isn't that another thing you Brits say?'

'He had a gun, though. You really could have got killed.'

She smirked. 'All right. Maybe I didn't realise that right away. I mean, it was dark, right? I kicked off my shoes – oh.' She held a hand to her mouth. 'My shoes. Ha. Well, some-one's gonna be lucky. And I figured I would sneak up and . . . *zap* and we'd get the hell out of there. But when I *did* see it, well.' She shrugged. 'Hey, I was committed.'

Anna squeezed my hand back and kept hold, the pair of us sitting there with the night porter hovering around us until finally through the windows I saw blue lights, heard the slam of car doors.

The doorbell rang, a pair of Polizia ambled into the

reception, then were pointed in our direction. Their looks of recognition and frank delight when they saw who was sitting there (and it wasn't me). My imaginary headline in the next day's *Carlino* changing, albeit the photo below of the pair of us approaching the Manzini remained the same.

'Signora,' the cops said in unison. They pulled out their notebooks and it was unclear whether they were going to ask for details or an autograph.

The doorbell rang again, the porter opened it to an elegant figure in a tailored, double-breasted suit. He could very easily have been one of the hotel's guests, but was, in fact, there on business.

Ispettore Alessandro walked up behind the two cops and rested a hand on each of their shoulders.

'Sorry, boys,' he said. 'This is a Special Ops matter. Signora Bloom.' He gave a small bow and I was somehow impressed he didn't kiss her hand. 'Daniel. I see you've had a spot of trouble.' Another first for the evening – hearing the *Ispettore*, too, exercise his English which, like Stella's, was disconcertingly excellent. It did make me wonder why neither of them had ever once felt inclined to help me when I'd struggled to find the right word in Italian. But perhaps they thought they *had* been helping me.

'And you've arrived here how, precisely?' I asked.

'What do you mean?'

'I asked the porter to call you guys but he'd already called the Polizia.'

The *Ispettore* made an amused smile. 'Oh, Polizia, Carabinieri, Daniel, you know it's much the same. Now, tell me what happened.'

***

'And you're sure it was this sergeant you saw with the machine gun?' said Alessandro.

'I'm sure.'

'A colleague was looking into it, I'll chase him up for the name. I was just heading home, as it happens – tomorrow morning, we have a hospital visit. It looks like you could do with one, too.'

When I touched my ribs it felt like they'd been poked with a cattle prod, or Anna's 'flashlight'. I could feel shock setting in, too, a curious cocktail I was sufficiently acquainted with to recognise – prickly, sweat-clammy skin yet an inner, creeping cold. But I wasn't about to wait in casualty at this time of night.

The *Ispettore* raised an eyebrow. 'Would you like me to give you a lift home?'

I looked at Anna. She gave me a wan smile, clearly in the process of coming down herself.

'It might be better if I headed back,' I said. 'I'd like to check on Rose. Will you be all right?'

The *Ispettore* thumbed at the cops still dawdling in the doorway. 'I'm sure our friends will be happy to pass the rest of the shift in the lobby.'

'I've no idea what that was about,' said Anna. 'But I'm pretty sure it wasn't me. You go check on Rose, although I wouldn't worry too much – with those high walls . . .'

'The ancestors knew what they were doing.'

We embraced. Anna leaned into me, resting her warm forehead against mine, rolled down to kiss me lightly on the lips.

'Apart from the attempted murder,' she said, 'it was a lovely evening. And thank you for saving me from my kidnapper.'

'You're welcome. We should try it again, only without the murder part.'

'Or the kidnapping. The ex-girlfriend, well . . .' She looked as if she was considering it. 'I guess we could leave that in – she was a lot of fun. I can see what she saw in you.'

'Don't you mean, you can see what I saw in her?'

'Oh.' Anna let go, turning away and beginning to head for the lifts. 'I know what I meant.'

The *Ispettore*'s limo swept through the dark streets.

'An eventful evening,' said Alessandro. 'I didn't realise there was a kidnap, too.'

'She was joking. But this attempt on my life, *Ispettore*. It's a miracle I'm still alive – those guys meant business.'

'Try not to worry, Daniel – we'll get this sergeant. Unless he spotted you watching him in the woods, he has no reason to believe you can identify him, so should have no reason to flee, and be therefore reasonably easy to apprehend. And by tomorrow we should be able to wrap this up at the hospital.'

'What's this business about the hospital, *Ispettore*?'

'It's thanks to you, Daniel – I think we may have found that fellow you stabbed in the ribs. You were right – a patient was admitted to the military hospital in Via dell'Abbadia. In fact, I was planning to give you a call and see if you'd like to accompany us, but,' he frowned, 'perhaps it would be better if you rested up.'

'Are you kidding?'

The car pulled up outside the Faidate Residence and

both the *Ispettore* and his driver got out with me, the driver scanning the dark pools beneath the portico opposite with a torch, his gun drawn.

'Message me, Daniel, once you are inside and have checked everything is shipshape.' The *Ispettore*'s words belied his usual lackadaisical manner. 'We will pick you up at eight tomorrow. I'll post a car outside, just until we are sure we have this other chap in custody.'

I clicked the fob and the gate swung open.

It seemed peaceful enough in the courtyard, as if the entire family was asleep, as well they should be. Only a light from Alba's house was on, the door ajar, a window partly open. I could hear a baby's cry.

Behind me, the gate began to close on the *Ispettore* puffing on an electronic cigarette. He nodded at me through the vapour.

Through the open window I could see Claudio slumped in an armchair in a vest and tartan boxers, the baby, not yet known as Daniela, cushioned on his big belly. He looked wearily up at me and smiled.

I crossed the courtyard and mounted the stone steps.

The musk of old clay and stucco. Those phantom frescoes, the gentle shadows that met me on each landing as the electric light came on.

I remained on edge in case the sergeant was lurking around a corner ready to put a bullet in my skull, but here in our 'fortress in a city street' I did feel safe. A common error, I supposed, but one that on this occasion fate permitted me: I arrived at our balcony in one piece.

I unlocked the front door and stepped into our apartment, going straight to the kitchen counter and removing a carving knife from the rack – an expensive Japanese one Rose had persuaded me to buy when she was enthusiastic about cooking for about five minutes – weighing it in my hand with the experience borne from my earlier encounter. It would do. I went through the apartment turning on the lights, until there was only my girl's room left. Fortunately, she did me a favour by opening the door herself, bleary-eyed, as I hid the knife behind my back.

'What are you doing? Why's it so bright?'

'Sorry, I was looking for . . . my keys.'

'Your keys?' She looked at me as if I was mad. 'How could you have got in without them?'

'I know – I put them down somewhere and forgot.'

'Are you drunk?'

'Maybe,' I admitted. 'A little.'

'And what happened to your jaw? Is Anna with you? She's got a six o'clock tomorrow.'

'No.' My daughter gave me an appraising look.

'Go to bed, Dad,' she said. 'You can worry about your keys in the morning.'

'All right.' After she went to the bathroom, I returned to the kitchen and replaced the knife.

I sent the *Ispettore* a thumbs up.

Chapter 29

It was a rude awakening – six thirty a.m., when I still had another half hour on the alarm and felt frankly as if I had been put through the spin cycle of a super-size washing machine – but my phone was still ringing and it was Rose.

'What are those uniforms,' she used the trade jargon, I noted, 'doing outside? I asked and they said the *Ispettore* told them.'

'Well, there you have it.'

'Is that why you were creeping around last night? Were you checking the flat?'

'How are you, anyway? How's Anna?'

'Grumpy. She's still faffing about and told me to wait in the lobby. And that's another thing! There's Polizia here, too! They say they're to give her an escort . . .'

'I'm sure that's not necessary.'

'What's going on, Dad? Did you get her into trouble?'

'On the contrary. She sort of got me out of it. I was walking her back to the hotel and someone tried to mug us.'

'*Mug you?* Oh my God! Was she all right?'

'Yeah, fine. Your boss is armed and dangerous. Fought them off with a stun gun.'

'Oh my God. *And that's why you had that bruise on your jaw.* Are *you* all right, then?'

'Fine.' The dog climbed onto the bed and looked at me expectantly. 'You didn't walk Rufus, I suppose.'

'I didn't have the time, I thought you—'

'Fine.' I ended the call, swung my legs off the bed. Rufus jumped down and scampered to the doorway, lingering winningly. 'And where were you when I was creeping around last night?' I said, although actually I knew – sleeping with Rose. 'If it carries on like this, I'll trade you in for a bloody pitbull.'

'There's really no need, you know,' I said to the Carabinieri as they set off with me on foot up Via Paglietta.

'Orders, signore.'

'Orders, okay. But if you could just hang back a bit, make me feel a little less like I'm on a Mafia hit list.'

They looked at each other. 'But you are sort of on a hit list, aren't you, signore?'

I gave Rufus a tug as he loitered at a trashcan. 'I suppose so,' I said, instinctively looking around. 'But let's hope not for long.'

'Let's hope so, signore.'

I waited at the traffic lights to the Viale, cars hurtling either way, with a cop maintaining a polite metre distance on either side.

The guy at the news-stand shot me a questioning look, I mouthed – 'It's nothing'. The cars pulled up at the red lights and I could feel the eyes of their occupants follow me and my straining Lagotto Romagnolo as we were escorted across.

It wasn't until we reached the park of San Michele that the officers gave me a little more space, taking a bench either side while I let Rufus off the leash to have a roam.

The events of the previous night had raised the stakes to a whole new level. I'd come within a heartbeat of being rubbed out and the thought of it brought me out in the proverbial cold sweat. To be honest, I'd been so focused getting to the bottom of the mystery, I'd overlooked the unpleasant side effect – death – that seemed to afflict anyone involved, and there was no reason why I should be the exception to this rule, except, of course, that everyone is an exception to themself.

The cops' phones buzzed simultaneously. They looked at each other and then at me. They got to their feet.

'Signore, we had better go back to the house.'

'Why? What's the problem?'

'It seems the action, it wasn't successful.'

'Wasn't successful?' I called Rufus. 'What does that mean?'

'This soldier they wanted to pick up. He got away.'

Chapter 30

'What the hell happened?'

The *Ispettore* had sent a squad car to pick me up after I had threatened to make my own way over to the military hospital – he would have rather I kicked my heels at *La Residenza*, but I preferred to present a moving target.

'Clearly,' said Alessandro, stepping back from the bar lined with office workers snatching a pre-work *caffè*. 'Our bird had flown.'

'This morning,' I said. He nodded. 'I thought you were going to pick him up last night.'

He rolled his eyes. 'In the event, we weren't able to put the resources in place until the morning shift.'

'Heaven help us if there was a real emergency. Who is he, anyway, this sergeant?'

'*Folgore*. Well, ex . . .'

'That means nothing to me, *Ispettore*.'

'*Folgore* is an elite parachute regiment, a little like your SAS. But he transferred out to avoid early retirement, probably enhance his pension.'

'From the Italian SAS to recruitment fairs, quite a

comedown.'

'He has two ex-wives and seven children, mostly school age. A lot of responsibility, a lot of bills.'

'And his name?'

'Davide Greco.'

'"Greek David". Well, at least now I know the name of the man who wants to kill me.' Alessandro laid a hand on my shoulder.

'Don't worry, Daniel. I won't let that happen.'

'I'm not sure you'll have much say, *Ispettore*.'

The military hospital was one of those buildings that would have probably been the centrepiece of any city outside Italy, but here the former monastery that had been converted into a hospital after the Napoleonic era was just another vast, impractical, rose-pink, porticoed edifice fronted by a cobbled space large enough to parade troops, accessible through a modest arch built to accommodate a horse-drawn carriage which one might pass without a second glance as one hurried along the obscure Via dell'Abbadia.

We crossed the parade ground accompanied by two uniforms.

'The name of the man they admitted?' I asked Alessandro.

'Bruno Mano. A corporal, retired.'

'That old?'

'Fifty.'

'But – retired,' I said. 'Then why the military hospital?'

'Still an auxiliary, apparently, but in truth, someone probably pulled some strings.'

'Why the frown, *Ispettore*?'

'He was one of us – a Carabinieri, with the Tuscania regiment.'

'And they are?'

'Parachutists.'

We entered a lobby far removed from most public hospitals. For a start it was absent of crying kids and ailing old people, shops and vending machines, the general bustle that greeted you on arrival at Maggiore or Sant' Orsola.

On either side of the grandiose, columned entrance were huge oil paintings depicting nineteenth-century battle scenes, while alongside them chiselled stone plaques commemorated the fallen of campaigns from 'Ethiopia, 1895' to 'Russia, 1943', who had presumably made it back to this Bologna hospital, but no further.

The usual duo of the Italian tricolour and EU flag stood behind a massive oak desk where a pair of nurses wearing flat black headpieces with a black veil down the back of their necks like vampiric Emirates air crew, along with starched white uniforms featuring a blood red cross on their chest, were incongruously, given their antique getup, engrossed by whatever was on their computer screens.

They looked up at us only when the *Ispettore* clapped his hands. Startled, they shot to their feet.

'Mano. Bruno. Corporal,' he said, holding up his ID. The nurses bent to check their computers.

'Third floor,' said the first.

'Mario Berti Wing,' said the second. 'It's on the right as you get out of the lifts.'

'Room seventy-three,' said the first. They snapped back to attention.

'As you were,' said the *Ispettore*.

The four of us entered the lift. 'I posted a guard here last night,' he explained. 'Apparently, the corporal suffered a pierced lung and severe internal bleeding.' He nodded at me. 'Whoever stabbed him might very well have killed him.'

'Lucky,' I said.

'For whom?' said the *Ispettore*. 'In any case, he appears to be making a good recovery and is assessed well enough to speak.'

The lift doors opened to a Carabinieri sergeant, who stepped back and saluted.

'What are you doing here?' asked Alessandro.

'I'm sorry, *Ispettore*?' Alessandro stopped the lift door from closing and stepped out.

'Why are you here and not at your post?'

'Because you relieved me.'

'*I* relieved you?'

'Yes, *Ispettore*. You called to say I would be relieved. A Carabiniere has just arrived to take over.'

'This Carabiniere,' said Alessandro, reaching into his jacket and producing his pistol, 'was he from the Tuscania?'

'Now you mention it, he may have been.'

'The room – where is it?'

We took off after the sergeant along the corridor. Alessandro stopped, framed by the entrance of the room, and swore.

Mano had gone.

The *Ispettore* and uniformed Carabinieri bolted off along the corridor.

I found myself alone at the doorway.

In contrast to the antique grandeur of the corridor, the empty room was as modern as in any other hospital.

The click and whirl of the machines beside the bed with the transparent plastic tubes that may have been connected to Bruno Mano. A toppled drip, a crimson-brown drainage sack plopped on top of the sleep-creased sheets like a puddle of poo.

I crouched to peer beneath the bed.

Nothing. I stood up and moved around to the other side, surveying the medical wreckage Mano had left in his wake. He might have been able to talk, but I doubted he was in any shape to move fast or far.

A gentle breath on the back of my neck.

I swung around.

Nothing – just the window.

Wait: a stuttering, shimmering line of liquid crossing the pale green linoleum toward blinds rattling in the breeze.

Yes, the window had been opened. I walked over and parted the blinds.

Tore them aside. They came crashing down.

Behind me, the sound of rushed footsteps, but it didn't matter – I was leaning out of the window, looking down at the corpse of Bruno Mano in his hospital gown, his bare back and arse exposed as it lay on the cobbles.

Chapter 31

'Ruthless,' I said, looking back up at the open window, nurses, auxiliaries, doctors and patients, now gathered at the other windows or in the courtyard beneath the portico while the Carabinieri taped off the crime scene. 'If what your guy is saying is accurate, he only stopped off for a piss before heading to the lift. In which time Greco was able to reach the room, grab Mano, launch him out of the window, and make good his getaway. And bearing in mind that Mano was a trained para himself . . .'

'He may have been taken by surprise,' said the *Ispettore* as if to defend the branch's honour. 'Possibly even sleeping.'

'I doubt it by the time Greco was tipping him out of the window, though. In the end, they would have been better off leaving Mano to "fester and die", as you suggested.'

The *Ispettore* shrugged. 'It's a sign we're winning.'

'Is it? It doesn't feel like it.'

'They're panicking: they can't afford the luxury of keeping people alive.'

'Whoever "they" are. Who are "they" *Ispettore?*'

'I wish I knew.' He took in the scene as if concerned we were being watched. I was wondering the same thing.

'Well, they certainly know you – well enough to imitate your voice.'

'Perhaps it was just this Greco. Perhaps he's a good mimic.'

'And a popular guy, apparently, whose friends like to keep him informed. Did you ever trace that Carabiniere who put the frighteners on Patrizia Bussoni, by the way?'

'I . . .' He shook his head. 'No.'

I crouched beside the corpse. 'Have you got a pen?'

'Don't touch the corpse, Daniel.'

'A pen?'

'Here.' He gave me a pair of latex gloves.

Mano was lying on his front as if he would have had plenty of time to contemplate the ground rushing up to meet him, and his hands were splayed aside at odd angles. This meant that despite his face being flat on the cobbles, his palms were tilting upwards, and on one wrist I had seen something familiar: two small black spades.

'He's been to war, this one,' I said. 'Or are these Mafia kills? I know you use the special forces for that kind of thing down south.'

'Afghanistan,' said the *Ispettore*.

'And Greco?' He nodded.

'When were you going to share this nugget?'

'Things have been moving quickly. I assumed it would come up in our interrogation.'

We watched a navy-blue Carabinieri forensics van emerge through the arch.

'We should get you back home,' said the *Ispettore*. 'I am stepping up your security.'

'Just tell them to be wary about taking any calls from you.'

Alessandro looked grim. 'This is a serious business,' he said. 'Certainly not just cops and robbers. We must all be on our guard.'

He asked the Carabinieri who had been stationed outside to deliver me back to the Faidate Residence. Before I got in the car, I remembered something.

'That captain I met at the Lido.'

'Oh?' The *Ispettore* stood there, three uniforms hovering around him. I shook my head.

'Nothing,' I said. 'He just asked I pass on his regards.' My phone buzzed: a message from Jacopo, the frame of a video featuring Paolo Mestre and Elettra Fausto together in the van.

Just in, it said.

Everyone meet at the Residence, I wrote.

No problem, he replied. *I haven't got up yet.*

'Well,' I said, leaning down from our balcony where the Comandante was having a cigarette and my hands were cupping a mug of tea, 'the *Ispettore* wasn't kidding when he said he'd up security.' Apart from the squad car that was to be stationed on the corner of the street, a pair of Carabinieri had also set themselves up at a folding table inside the gates beside Alba's house, where one was currently cradling the unchristened Daniela, while the other was being talked through Claudio's plans for converting the studios on the ground floor into additional living space for his expanding family, which seemed a little premature seeing as he hadn't yet discussed these plans with the people who actually owned the space. In the meantime, the cops would use one of the former Faidate workshops to shelter if it rained, and during the night. Ominously, they had already unpacked a portable stove and a pair of heaters. It seemed like they were preparing for a long stay.

There was a buzz at the front gate and I was about to go into the kitchen to let them in, but the Comandante said: 'They've disconnected it. People can only enter via them.'

'Great,' I said. 'We're like prisoners.'

'I think you exaggerate,' said the Comandante. 'It could be considerably worse.'

'Christ,' I said. 'Don't even go there.' I knew what he meant: joining the hundreds of Italians in protective custody – usually from organised crime – moved between Carabinieri barracks every few days in a sort of living purgatory.

The Carabiniere had returned the baby to Alba, and the other left Claudio, unharnessing the machine gun slung over his shoulder, while the first went to the pole set a couple of metres back from the gate where you could open it manually. It all seemed a bit over-the-top – our visitor would have already received the once over from the occupants of the *gazzella* parked outside, but uniforms liked to do things by the book, especially if they were on parade.

Dolores wheeled in her bike dressed all in black, with her orange bob looking more Berlin than Bologna. She rested the bicycle against the pole, raising her arms and scowling at the Carabiniere as he tentatively zipped a handheld metal detector up and down. Heaven help him if he had actually attempted to frisk her.

The 'core' team of myself, the Comandante, Jacopo and Dolores now assembled, we sat at the kitchen table and took another look at the video on Jac's laptop.

It was night – 21:22, said the time stamp – parked at Villa Ghigi, Bologna's vast countryside park according to the corresponding map, which would make sense if Mestre had picked up Elettra Fausto near her grandfather's villa in the hills. But it could have been anywhere: only they were visible, bleached by the cabin's light, mirrored in the van's dark glass.

There had been no touching, signs of affection. But there had remained something seedy as they drove: Elettra Fausto with her straight black hair, dark, darting eyes, skinny arms wrapped defensively around herself in a too-big white denim jacket, sitting beside this hulk of a man in his tight khaki T-shirt, muscles bulging with every turn of the steering wheel. Part of me had almost hoped that when they came to a halt the tension would break with a passionate embrace, the only creepy thing the four of us watching from home. But no, it was clear that whatever occurred between them would have an uncomfortably transactional character.

Paolo took a final turn – the thunk and rumble as he came off the road and pulled into the dirt parking area.

Elettra released her seatbelt, wound down the window, shifted to the corner of the cabin to face him, while he visibly tried to compose his features. As Mestre unknowingly looked into the camera, it was still possible to detect a trace of 'Harry Potter' in the mix of fear, hope, and inadequacy that shaded his face before a smile elevated its corners and the would-be tough guy asserted himself. But I wasn't sure it would convince Elettra – she was a professional actor after all, and knew all about masks.

He reached down and produced a rectangular presentation case. 'Please,' he said. 'Open it.'

We saw the black back of the case as she lifted it. 'It's a knife,' she said.

'Not just any knife, it came in this week: a Röhm SS Honour Dagger. Fully authenticated, you don't see them often.'

'That's . . . very nice.' She closed the lid, made to hand it back to him.

'It's for you.'

'I . . .'

'I remembered,' he said, 'when we were kids . . . you were always interested when you came around, used to ask me to take you to the back of the shop where we stored the memorabilia. We used to spend hours back there, just going through it all. You loved the daggers with their death's heads, insisted they were skulls and cross bones, "pirates' swords" you called them, and were convinced there would be a treasure map hidden somewhere, too. Anyway, I thought, well, I thought, I mean – it's worth twelve thousand . . .'

She set the case on her lap. Looked down at her hands laid flat across it. 'Thank you,' she said.

'I just wanted . . .' He dried up. 'Anyway. Have you got it, then?'

She snapped her head up. 'Of course I haven't got it, Paolo. Does it look like I've got it? Or did I leave the cash by the roadside when we drove away?'

'I didn't mean that, what I meant – has he agreed . . .'

Elettra looked ahead.

'Then why . . . *Elettra*, I'm under a lot of pressure.'

'*You're* under a lot of pressure?' Her hands flew up. The intimacy of siblings – or childhood friends. '*How the fuck do you think I feel?*'

He shook his head. 'You don't understand. My associates . . .'

'*Your fucking "associates"*? Traitors, more like, cheap gang-sters . . .'

'Things are getting serious, Elettra . . . Look, *Letti* . . .' He reached out, she drew back. 'You know I've always loved you.'

She shook her head disbelievingly. 'You've "always loved me", you say. What kind of love is this?'

'Look, it's not like that, I swear. I never bothered you, did I, not in all this time. I knew you were famous, you had your life. But *I was always there for you*, ready, and when you called, I came. It's always been like that with our families. That's why you came to me about the film: we stand by each other, all the way. It's the deepest bond.'

'You're wrong, it was never like *this*, never – *there used to be some fucking honour.*'

'No.' Paolo shook his head. 'I mean, yes, of course. There was always honour. But also always a price. You know that – your grandfather knows. It's just the way it is, but it doesn't change how I feel about you, how I've always felt about you.' He glanced back into the camera, sucked at his bottom lip.

'Look – *why not* me?' Elettra closed her eyes. 'I was think-ing . . . we could come to some sort of arrangement . . . I mean, it would be possible – if . . . if we were together.'

'You know I'm married.'

'Oh, that Jew. Don't worry about him.'

Now she looked at him: '*Don't you dare touch Indigo.*'

'*No.* Of course not! That wasn't what I meant. I meant – I could wait.'

Elettra seemed to deflate. She bowed her head, her hair falling across her face, she clutched the case to her tummy.

Paolo's flat profile on the screen like the side of a coin.

She finally looked up, brushing aside her hair. 'What I'm hearing is you've had second thoughts. I mean . . . you're saying you might return the negatives to us, after all?'

'I . . .' Paolo turned to the camera. There it was again: hope's phantom. 'There would be a strong chance . . . I mean, that I could minimise, manage . . . the cost, I mean. Although there would still be my assoc . . . the others.'

'Maybe you could persuade them.'

'That would be harder.'

'You could try?'

He gave her the longest look. 'I could try.'

'Thank you,' she says. He took a deep breath:

'Only it's . . .'

'I admit,' Elettra shook her head as if she really didn't want to, but it was forcing itself out, 'it's true. Since we last spoke I *have* been thinking about what you said. You were right: I asked you for your help because of our connections. Our family . . . history. And it's also true – *I* brought *you* into this, not the other way around. Because we grew up together, because . . . because I thought I could trust you, Paolo.

'Look,' she said gravely. 'Before all this began I didn't see you as more than a friend. I didn't realise *you* saw *me* as anyone other than your "Little Letti". So when you first told me how you felt, it came as a shock because I'd never thought of you like that, but,' she shrugged, 'it's true – you're not that kid I left behind.'

'I'm not! Look, Letti, *Elettra* . . .' He reached out for her, but she raised her hands.

'*Please*, Paoli. I'm . . .' She slapped her forehead. 'God, I'm so fucked up.'

'*Letti . . .*'

'I'm really not what I seem, you know. I think you see me as some . . . I don't know, you put me on a pedestal, but I'm not like that, *not at all.* I'm not worthy . . .'

'But you are!'

'Paoli, I'm not – I'm just an actress. A second-rate actress, playing second fiddle to Anna Bloom.'

'*Fuck her,* you're so much better.'

'It's nice of you to say that.'

'I mean it!'

'The irony is – I really do miss Italy, Bologna. My friends. California can seem so false – I miss people who really know me, you know?'

'*But that's precisely it,*' he said. 'I know you. The *real you* from the store. The beach. This place – sledding in the snow. My God, even the dance classes.'

'I think that's where I got my first taste for the stage. You had two left feet.'

'I only went because of you.'

'No!'

'Of course! And it was you who taught me joined-up writing.'

'No!'

'I couldn't get the hang of it at school and the kids used to laugh, then one day you sat me down and said, "Paoli, we're going to fix this," and we did. *That's* who I see, Elettra, not *Cassandra Sinistra.*'

She sighed. 'But I can't deny, there's a part of me that loves the limelight. I'm not sure I could just let it go. But I've also come to realise,' her voice faltered, 'what I'm saying is . . . Oh God.' She covered her face with her hands.

Mestre reached out to squeeze her shoulder. This time she let him.

Elettra lowered her hands. 'All of this, it's just been such a shock.' She was looking into our camera and I could see those big black eyes brimming with tears. 'Such a terrible shock. But at the same time, you know, the craziest thing is, despite everything, I'm beginning to think perhaps it was exactly what I needed.

'At first, I thought, oh Christ, Italy's dragging me back, but now, it's made me . . . Yeah,' she nodded. 'It's forced me to ask myself what I *really* want, what I'm *really* doing with my life, where I'm *really* going.' She swallowed. 'And in all of this . . . this fucking *quicksand*, I've got to admit – the one thing I've come to appreciate is the importance of the people who are there for you.'

She grabbed his hand. 'Look, Paoli – maybe I'm being crazy, but I promise you this: if you help my family recover the negatives, I'll . . .' Her voice broke, but she nodded as if responding to a silent question. 'I'll seriously consider it.'

Mestre made a sound which may have been a whimper. He sat back and looked at us, almost as if he knew we were there – was willing a spectator for this, his moment. He didn't want to blow it.

Elettra sat watching, unblinking.

He said: 'I'll waive my share, but there's nothing I can do about the others.'

'Five million?' she said. He nodded.

'Thank you,' she said quietly.

Chapter 32

'Wow,' said Dolores, who was watching the video for the first time.

'Wow, indeed,' I said.

'So, five million?'

'Which means they may have actually begun by asking for ten million euros,' I said. 'What the hell is on those negs?'

'Clearly, Mestre and his "associates" believe the Faustos can afford that kind of sum,' said the Comandante.

'Even for a family with that kind of wealth,' I said, 'it's a hell of a lot, which may explain why she wanted to beat him down.'

'Puts a different complexion on Valeria and Gianni,' said Jacopo.

'And the Volpatos. All roads lead back to Toni Fausto's version.'

'With its Ustica ending,' said Dolores.

'Historically,' I said, 'a lot of people have died to cover up that plane crash.'

'Even Toni Fausto himself?' said Dolores. 'But if these negatives *do* contain something incriminating, why not just destroy them? Why extort the Faustos?'

'Perhaps they intend to do both.'

We contemplated this.

'Do you think Mestre really believed her?' said Jacopo. 'I mean – clearly she was playing him, right?' He looked around us. 'Right?'

'A bravura performance,' I said. 'She undersells herself – she's a first-rate actor.'

'If she was,' said Dolores. 'Acting, I mean.'

'Tell me you didn't buy it.'

She thought about it. 'Probably not,' she sighed. 'But there was truth in it too – there was stuff I believed. She was believable.'

'She had to be,' I said. 'It was an improvisation, although I wonder if, given he had obviously gone on about his unrequited love already, she hadn't rehearsed a little, if only in her mind.

'And remember,' I continued. 'We weren't her intended audience. Our disbelief was never willingly suspended. Mestre – "Paoli" – on the other hand, desperately wanted to believe. You're right, Jac, she played him well. She fed his fantasies, and that's what this guy's all about – he's a fantasist. That's what the bodybuilding, Nazi shit is about. Something to pull him through, muse upon while he's sitting in his dusty shop, feed his delusions of grandeur. And there's nothing grander than "Little Letti".'

I got up and wandered out to the balcony, peered over at the Carabinieri sitting at the desk scrolling their phones. I turned to face the kitchen.

'We'll meet with the Faustos,' I said.

'Signor Adler is our client,' the Comandante reminded me.

'At this point,' I said, 'I think our welfare trumps his worries about his wife.'

'It probably wouldn't be smart for them to come here,' said Dolores. 'Even if they agreed. And you can't go to them. Without an escort, I mean.'

'I'm not about to explain to the cops why I'm going to see the Faustos, or have it reported back to the *Ispettore*.' I looked at the Comandante. 'I trust him. It's the chain of command I'm worried about.'

Giovanni, usually the first to jump to the defence of his former employer, nodded grimly. 'Certain elements,' he admitted, 'may be present. But within that context, my boy, perhaps you really would be safer here.'

'Video, then?' said Jacopo.

I could just imagine Alberto Fausto fumbling with a laptop. 'No, I think this requires a more personal touch. As for being safer here, I'm not so sure – if the *Ispettore* knows where I am, probably so does Greco and the rest of his pals in the military. I'd rather not be a sitting duck – I'd prefer to take the battle to the enemy.'

'But how?' said Dolores. I looked again at the Comandante.

'The Residence was built as a kind of fortress,' I said. 'And if there's one feature all castles share, it's another way out.'

'You didn't have to come, you know,' I whispered.

'Are you kidding?' said Dolores.

'Curiosity killed the cat.'

'Maybe so,' she replied as we sneaked down the stairs from the courtyard into the *cantina*. 'But isn't that what cats do?'

The Carabinieri didn't stir, sitting as they were with their backs to us, facing the gates and scrolling their phones.

I closed the door, switched on the light. Unlike many *cantine*, ours was in a pretty good state, not least because we had needed to shore up the foundations of the complex and the builders had thrown in a clean-up for free.

Upstairs, be it the Comandante's rather grand, frescoed apartment on the *piano nobile*, or our own more humble, yet comfortable place above, it was easy to forget the medieval roots of *La Residenza*.

We made our way beneath a series of red-brick arches, our path illuminated by lights draped on a cable running the length of the passage. On either side of us, further passages with crypt-like ceilings disappeared into the gloom. It felt like a labyrinth down here, but the *cantina* had originally been open plan – to store bales of cloth, paper, consignments of metal and wood. Later it had been partitioned to accommodate the Faidate's elevated status as traders of some substance – they had kept silks, ivory, ceramics; spices, tea, coffee, pigment and rare metals; most of all in this centre of learning – books. The successive centuries had seen those traders become printers, publishers, police officers. A theme, if any – adapting to the demands of the city.

And as the requirements of those above changed over the centuries, so had the world below. Today, there was something a little neglected about it: its utilitarian twists and turns led mostly nowhere – empty storage spaces, dead ends. It was a depository for old clothes, Jacopo's defunct electronic equipment, mysterious chunks of ancient machinery, dust-encrusted wicker baskets, empty and full suitcases, stacks of magazines, firewood. There were boxes of Rose's old toys down here and

Lucia's text books. My half-assed attempt at creating a 'wine cellar', the 'strong room' containing the Comandante's legendary black filing cabinet, and, of course, the secret escape route.

'You never mentioned it,' said Dolores. We were standing before a bricked-up arch. I pulled out my keys to unlock the security door. 'When we've come down here before.'

'If I had,' I said, 'it would hardly have been a secret.'

'But the Comandante and Jacopo knew about it.'

I unlocked the door, which opened into what appeared to be just another storage room. I switched on the light. There wasn't much to see – an old oak dining table with some dusty plates stacked on top, a moth-eaten oriental rug below. Against the wall – an antique credenza, empty of crockery. It might have been the remnants of a house clearance or a particularly genteel cell.

'Does Rose?' asked Dolores.

I went to one end of the table, which was on wheels, and pushed. It trundled off the carpet onto the maroon ceramic tiles.

'Rose knows.' I crouched down to begin rolling up the carpet. Dolores stepped off it and watched. 'But then,' I winked, 'she's family.'

The exposed tiles surrounded a metre-square oak hatch, a copper ring at its centre. I slipped my finger through and gave it a tug. I lifted it up and slid the hatch aside. Stone stairs disappeared into the darkness, the definite smell of stagnant water rising to meet us.

'Now you do.' I produced my phone and switched on the torch. 'I guess it means you'll have to marry Jacopo.' Dolores snorted.

I began to descend, steadying myself against the brick walls. I had asked the Comandante if we could get some light and a handrail put in when we had had the rest of the *cantina* fixed up, but he had insisted the existence of the exit remain between us, so nothing had been done since 'Nonno Faidate' – Giovanni's father – had been involved in various nefarious activities during the Second World War. Dolores began to follow. 'Should I pull the top closed?' she asked.

'God, no, it's claustrophobic enough as it is.' I was standing in a puddle at the bottom of the stairs, which seemed ominous. I hadn't counted on having to wade my way out. I pondered turning back, but Dolores was close behind and already shining her light over my shoulder.

'Fuck! Is that an *iron* door? Was it some kind of air raid shelter?'

'I've no idea,' I said. 'Possibly.' It looked more like the kind of bulkhead you found in navy ships and submarines with a central wheel used to secure the surrounding bolts. I gave it a go. The wet certainly hadn't helped, but I finally got it to turn in a spray of rust. 'Early version of a security door.' I pushed. The door grumbled open. I stepped into the brick passageway, blood red with moisture and potted with puddles. In the dark, my light picked out another door. Dolores laughed.

'You're kidding me.'

'You know the Faidate,' I said. 'Belt and braces.'

In fact, this one wasn't a big deal – tarred oak, it simply required an old-fashioned key, and unlocked easily.

'Oh,' said Dolores, as it opened into yet more tunnel.

'You were expecting a canal.' I meant the vast network that ran beneath the city streets. 'Can you smell them? They're near, but no.' I raised my light and continued on, vermin scattering out of our path. 'These connect the *palazzi* along Via Solferino. They were service tunnels, used by servants to come and go, and provide an exit for the owners in the event the city was overrun. If you think of the canals as arteries,' I arrived at a fork and took the passage to the left, 'then these are like Bologna's veins. They were used as air raid shelters during the war. Now,' I pointed upwards at the black plastic tubes supported by brackets above our heads, 'it's the internet.'

We arrived at an alcove where a set of black steps led upwards, as age-worn as those that had led us down. Climbing up, we came to a modern security door set in an iron frame. It opened into a room not so different from the one we had left in the Residence, with whitewashed walls and a ceramic tile floor, only absolutely bare, apart from a wall light and humidifier, which hummed into life as we stepped inside. There was an identical security door set opposite. We closed the first behind us and I opened the second onto a gloomy corridor. Spiralling above, a stone staircase. Ahead, a front door, a set of post boxes upon the wall beside it. I checked the mail – just a few circulars. I wouldn't have expected anything more as the box was labelled 'Bianco' – a false name for a false address.

I opened the door onto the portico of Via Solferino. As I closed it behind us, Dolores noted the plaque on the wall.

'*Fondazione Domenico Caro*, 1656. Who's Domenico Caro? What's the foundation?'

'I've honestly no idea,' I said. 'All I know is that our family has had an "apartment" here for a very long time.'

'Since 1656?'

'It wouldn't surprise me.'

The Comandante's limo stopped in the street below. We stepped down from the portico. I joined Giovanni in the back, while Dolores climbed beside Jac at the wheel. We set off for Fausto SpA.

Chapter 33

By the time the video had ended, Alberto Fausto seemed all of his eighty-plus years, and more – as if the life force had been sucked from him and despite his natty clothes, or perhaps because of them, he was in his funeral best in his coffin rather than propped up by a high-backed leather chair.

And Elettra was looking at him not so much as a granddaughter as a mourner, clutching his hand as if she never wanted to let go, oblivious to the tears drawing dark lines down her face, outlining her jaw before dripping onto the table. In fact, Alberto Fausto looked so dead, I was vaguely surprised when he spoke: 'I am glad you took this to us, Giovanni.'

'How did you get it?' asked Elettra. 'Who? Why? What . . .' Now Alberto laid a hand on the hand that was laid upon his.

'Shush, Eli. Don't worry.'

'I mean, *nonno*.' She looked fiercely at me. 'What the hell?'

I played dumb – this was the old men's round.

'As you can see,' continued Alberto, 'we appear to have gotten ourselves into a bit of a pickle.' The Comandante nodded as if they were discussing a bad burraco run.

'This figure,' he sniffed. 'If your granddaughter's efforts garner results,' he gave her the encouraging smile one might a six-year-old ballerina, 'five million—'

'Not a catastrophic sum.'

'And the original . . .'

'We would have had to have sold up.' The Comandante nodded, reached into his side pocket for his cigarettes. He opened the box, proffered it to Alberto, who smiled thinly and took one. Dolores censoriously slid a huge crystal ashtray between them.

'It sticks in the craw, though,' said the Comandante. 'Extortion.'

'And the pocket,' agreed Alberto.

'And furthermore,' the Comandante let out a regretful plume of smoke, 'it seems that my family has also been pulled into its orbit.'

'How so?' said Alberto.

'Yes!' added Elettra. 'How?'

'Oh,' the Comandante vaguely waved his cigarette, 'the details aren't important, my dear, although I do understand your distress.'

'You can't begin to understand.'

'But there was an attempt on the life of my son-in-law, Daniel here, by one of Signor Mestre's "associates" – a military man, a special forces sergeant.' He looked pointedly at Elettra. 'Are you acquainted?'

She pulled her hands away from Alberto and sat back in the chair with everything crossed.

'Perhaps it is better you aren't. He appears to have left a trail of corpses in his wake, beginning with those two young people, followed by an elderly couple in Venice, and latterly one of his former colleagues at the military hospital in Bologna. In between, he made an attempt on Daniel's life.' He looked at Alberto. 'So I'm afraid, from our perspective, old friend, this has gone beyond a private matter between yourselves and *Famiglia Mestre.*' He glanced at me. 'And then there is this mysterious *association* with Ustica,' he drew on his cigarette, 'which is troubling. It appears to poison whatever it touches.'

'Once we get the negatives back,' said Alberto, 'I can assure you everything will be resolved.'

The Comandante nodded. 'I don't doubt you believe that.' He looked at Elettra. 'The pair of you. But, here's the thing – didn't you also believe that when you had Mestre and his men take them in the first place?'

Alberto rested the remains of his cigarette in the ashtray and sat back, closing his eyes as if he had returned to the grave. Now Elettra plucked it up and took a drag. She looked angrily at him, then across at us.

'*Basta*,' she said. 'Enough with these games. It's like this: that bitch at CineBo and her boyfriend discovered it was Uncle Toni's version when they "borrowed" the negatives – all these film buffs are mad for him – to view in private. Which was when they found . . .'

Alberto, despite his still-closed eyes, gave her a small nod. 'The negatives contained . . . *material* implicating *nonno* in the clean-up around that plane crash. So the shits decided to blackmail him. Apparently, they wanted the money to make some stupid film. They said they'd replace Uncle Toni's version with the "classic". Of course, that was when we all still thought we were the only ones who knew it was Uncle Toni's version in the archive – before Indigo came bounding in with news about his fucking "discovery".'

'So – what then?' I asked. 'Why not just pay up and take the Toni Fausto version with its incriminating "material"?' Elettra scowled.

'These shitheads had blackmailed us. Why should we trust them?'

'So you decided to have them killed?'

'No! But . . . I wanted to teach them a lesson. To teach them they couldn't fuck with us.'

'That certainly sounds like Cassandra Sinistra,' I said. 'So that's how you got involved with Mestre?'

'I remembered he had always boasted about how his family still had the old connections. He told me he would make the problem go away. Only instead of giving us back the negatives, they decided to squeeze us for much, much more.' She looked at me with all the conviction of a witness in a courtroom drama.

'Paolo Mestre claimed to still be associated with the network that your *nonno* collaborated with over Ustica – he helped bankroll the cover-up, right?'

She glanced at Alberto, then back at me. Nodded.

'Which his brother Toni suspected, hence the reference at the end and . . . he slipped in something else?' Now I got the poker face, from them both.

'Alberto,' I said. 'Paolo Mestre's grandfather Ettore was involved with you in the cover-up – so I guess you could say it was a role handed from grandfather to grandson. Grandfather to granddaughter?'

He gave me a sour look. He said to the Comandante: 'I don't see where any of this talk is getting us.'

'Because we believe we know where the Toni Fausto version is,' said Giovanni, 'and how to get hold of it. And that is what we are going to do.'

'But . . . you won't go to the police?'

'I think you appreciate, Alberto,' said the Comandante, 'if we were going to inform the authorities, we would have done so already. Had we not been brushed by this poison ourselves, frankly, we might consider doing so, but for now I think this business is better kept among ourselves. For one thing, we have no idea how far the toxin has spread. We honestly don't know who we can trust within the police.'

'Then why not just let us pay Mestre and his cronies?'

'I have a question for you, Alberto,' said the Comandante. 'In your dealings with General Mestre all those years ago, did the group you were working with strike you as one given to blackmailing its collaborators?'

'Certainly not. We were doing our duty – what we could to protect the interests of the state.'

'Whether it was in its interests or not,' I said.

'Yet apparently,' the Comandante continued, 'its successors have no such qualms.' He shook his head. 'These people might very well belong to the same group, but they are not behaving like them. I find it very difficult to believe this activity is "sanctioned" from above. If, at some future point, the truth was to come out, I suspect its perpetrators would be treated with the very same ruthlessness with which they have dealt with everyone else.'

'What he's saying,' I said, 'is once they've got what they want from you, they'll shut you up, too.'

Chapter 34

'If we are to believe Elettra Fausto,' I said as we drove back along Stalingrado, 'her intention was to just scare these kids, maybe rough them up a bit before grabbing the negatives. But if this secret is so explosive, and she knew what these people were capable of . . .'

'You mean you doubt Signora Fausto was telling the whole truth, Daniel?' The Comandante smiled bleakly. 'Well, we are where we are.'

'And where we are, apparently,' I said, 'is that we "know where the Toni Fausto version is and are going to get it". That's actually news to me.'

'Me, too,' said Dolores. 'Did you know?' she asked Jacopo, behind the wheel.

'Maybe a little.' He shrugged.

'And you didn't think to mention it?' Another shrug.

'*Stronzo*,' Dolores said under her breath. I might have to put the engagement party plans on hold.

'Oh, I have not been idle, Daniel,' said the Comandante. 'While you have been off gallivanting with actresses.'

'I would hardly call it gallivanting,' I said. 'I was working.'

'As was I. The level of security at the Mestre shop sparked my interest. It seemed a very expensive system for a bookshop, so I asked our consultants to make some enquiries.'

'By "our consultants" you mean the Nonnies?'

'He asked them to case the joint,' Jacopo piped up.

'They sent around a pair of their operatives,' said the Comandante. 'Ostensibly to investigate the report of a gas leak. They waited until Paolo Mestre had left and were shown, rather reluctantly, apparently, by Signora Mestre—'

'The mother,' I said.

'To the rear of the store, where there is a barred strong room apparently full of boxes and cases we must assume comprise the military memorabilia Mestre sells online. In the corner of this room is a substantial safe.

'There is also the numerical touchpad for the alarm. While one of the men distracted the mother, the other examined it more closely and discovered the code on a sticker upon the inside of the case, which I said seemed most remiss of them, but Nonno Salvatore assured me was actually very common.

'Apparently with this kind of alarm one usually employs an electronic fob, which one clicks before entering, thereby dispensing with the need to type in the code. Otherwise, you have to punch in the code within thirty seconds of entering. The case, which is apparently triggered if tampered with, should have been closed, but,' the Comandante gave me a meaningful look, 'was open. Further observation of the store indicated that Mestre's mother has been opening and closing the Libreria of late and does not appear to possess, or use, the fob, which probably explains this.'

'You say the case is tamper proof.'

'It triggers an alarm if tampered with. However, Salvatore assures me this can be dealt with. In any event, we are hoping the mother leaves the door open, for her convenience.'

'A strong possibility,' I admitted. 'If she has to make it to the touchpad in half a minute. But more to the point – what makes you so convinced that the negatives are actually there?'

'If one considers Occam's Razor . . .'

'That again? The simplest answer is the most likely? Do they teach this at Carabinieri school?'

'Actually, Daniel, yes, they do, but I'm afraid yours is a fallacious *simplification* of a highly applicable law of parsimony. It is a problem-solving principle: that each accepted explanation of a phenomenon can be challenged by a potentially infinite number of more complex alternatives, and since failing explanations can always be provided with *ad hoc* hypotheses to prevent them being falsified, simpler theories should therefore be prioritised over more complex ones because they tend to be more *testable*. It should form the founding pillar of any investigation and, frankly,' he sighed, 'is why I so often despair at the wild theories of some of our prosecuting magistrates.'

'What you mean,' I said, 'is that all things being equal, because Mestre is the point man, has the secure lock-up, safe, and a sophisticated alarm system, the most testable hypothesis is that the negatives are there.'

'*Precisely*. If he turns out not to have it, then . . .'

'It's back to the drawing board. The way you put it, Comandante, makes it sound rather more of a gamble than a sure thing.'

'But a gamble with favourable odds, Daniel.'

'Now you're really making me nervous, Giovanni.'
'Oh? Why?'
'You're not a gambling man.'

Chapter 35

We set out the following evening after I had undertaken the usual manoeuvre through the tunnels. Without Dolores, this time, who would take the wheel of the Alfa and be waiting in Solferino, with the Comandante beside her.

I had never actually visited the Nonnies at home but always imagined Salvatore and Miranda, the aged patriarch and matriarch of our preferred crime outfit, living in a spacious bungalow full of knick-knacks along a quiet, tree-lined street in Casalecchio, Bologna's outer, affluent suburb of families and new builds. Perhaps they would even have a swimming pool for when the grandkids visited. But I had, as usual, got it wrong – for a start, they were in Casalecchio by name only, actually at the end of a dirt road in the countryside.

Once we had cut through a clump of woods, and the spiked iron gates monitored by surveillance cameras had automatically opened to the sound of dogs barking, we drove into a sprawling complex consisting of a huge farmhouse, a couple of barns, and a number of almost certainly *'abusivo'* – without planning permission – buildings including a garage, workshops, a modern storage facility, and yes, a large swimming pool, with a clubhouse constructed beside it, along with a small playground.

There must have been a dozen people at work or wandering between the buildings; a couple of women were taking in the washing, toddlers running around them. Getting out of the Alfa, I had the uncanny sense the Faidate Residence must have once been a little like this, albeit to a medieval scale.

I spotted Nonna Miranda sitting in the vestibule of the farmhouse, a plastic tub on her lap. She called out and a younger woman came to help her up. She supported her on one side while Nonna propelled herself forward with the help of a gnarled wooden walking stick. We met them half-way.

'You're still breathing, then,' she said to the Comandante. 'Your son-in-law hasn't decided to "help you down the stairs" yet?'

'Speak for your own family,' I said, smiling at the harassed-looking woman beside her.

'On the contrary, Englishman! My girl here knows me and Salvi are the only thing keeping this lot together – a nest of vipers!' She seemed quite proud. 'And who are you with the orange hair?'

'Dolores, signora.'

She scowled. 'You're not one of them, then?' Dolores knew what she meant. She shook her head. 'You're from the south, *vero*?' Dolores nodded. 'Yes, yes, I see it,' she said. 'A Neapolitan *puttana*.' Even the Comandante was shocked, but Dolores laughed:

'I'll take that as a compliment,' she said. 'Coming from the most famous whore in the history of Bologna.'

'You should, deary,' said Miranda. 'There's none more formidable than an honest whore.'

I nodded to the warehouse. 'I'd be careful what I said about our friends from the south in front of your friends from the south.' I knew the only reason why independent outfits like the Nonnies were permitted to survive was because they served as a useful conduit for mob money.

'I've no idea what you're talking about, Englishman,' Miranda said with a malevolent glint. 'Anyway, presuming you're looking for Salvatore, he's over there with your crew.' She waved her stick at the open garage. 'In the meantime, I'll finish sorting your mushrooms. Couldn't see you depart empty-handed.'

'Picking out, or putting in the poison ones?'

'I'll leave that for you to discover, *caro*.'

We headed towards the garage. 'Always a pleasure,' I said to the Comandante.

'And long may it last, Daniel. When they've gone, well . . .'

'We'll just have to deal with whoever takes over.'

'It won't be as simple as that, I'm afraid. Their "friends from the south," as you put it, will decide who that will be, after which . . .'

'I get it – we'll be compromised. But aren't we already, Comandante? We're dealing with criminals, after all.'

'In a limited sense, yes, but, as you know, Daniel – the Nonnies and I go far back, before any of us were, indeed, "nonnies". There's a bond . . .'

'You convicted Salvatore for bank robbery, Giovanni.'

'But we understand each other. Times, however,' he looked around, 'are clearly changing. It's true, we may be "compromised" but we are currently *compartmentalised*.' He waved at Salvatore, standing at the open back of white van. 'No,' he said. 'When they go, we do, too.'

We trailed the van back along the dirt road in our headlights.

My phone rang. 'Hi,' I said. 'How's it going?'

'It's gone, here, Daniel Leicester,' said Anna Bloom. 'We're all wrapped up for the day, I think I may have *finally* slipped the watchful gaze of your daughter, and was wondering if you'd like to show me a more grown-up time tonight.'

I laughed: 'You mean you want to go back to La Luna? They're probably still talking about the last time.'

'There's that,' said Anna. 'I hear there's also a Paul McCartney concert.'

'I read the tickets were sold out in the first ten minutes.'

'Well, what do you know, I might have some connections. Might even be able to see if I could wrangle us a backstage pass . . . or two.'

'I . . . ' I looked at the van ahead, turning onto the main road. 'I'd truly love to, Anna, but I'm afraid I'm tied up with work.'

'Really?'

'Believe me,' I said. 'Honestly, otherwise . . .'

'No, no. I'm . . . you know, just at a loose end. Oookay. Well, call me.'

'I will, I'm sorry . . .'

'Don't be.' The line went dead. I looked at the screen – *Anna Bloom, call ended* – before switching the phone off.

'Your actress?' asked the Comandante.

'She had a backstage pass to the Paul McCartney concert,' I said hollowly.

'You should have said!' said Dolores. 'I'd have gone!' I glanced at her, she seemed dead serious.

'Nice "work",' said the Comandante, 'if you can get it.'

I was standing on my own in Strada Maggiore under the portico opposite Libreria Mestre, although we would be going in through the back, which the Nonnies reckoned was the weakest point.

The gates were operated automatically, but that didn't appear to be a concern – they had some box, a little like an old-style car radio, that would run through the signals until it found the right one.

And there they went: the doors opening, an amber light flashing, while one, two, three men, who moments before might have been walking casually along the portico, a pair with large holdalls, another with a backpack, melted into the shadows. I took the steps down onto the road but was held up by an oncoming bus. I made it across, up the other side, and through the opening, just as the gates began to close.

I followed those shadows around the back. Keep against the walls, that was the instruction. The car park at the rear of Libreria Mestre was a rectangle of asphalt occupied by a dozen cars, half of which were sheltered beneath a flimsy corrugated plastic shelter abutting a stone wall, beyond which sprouted the palm tree of an adjacent garden. The wall continued around the back, ending at a continuation of a *palazzo* on the next street, which meant the parking space was overlooked on three sides.

Either way, no one seemed to be looking out, and the garage door of Mestre's shop was cloaked by shadows. The 'gas men' had established that the garage opened onto a bay, which was not alarmed. Beyond that, up three steps, was the rear of the shop proper, which was secured by a standard door with a medium-secure lock, that would take an experienced locksmith no more than a minute to pick. We would then have thirty seconds to switch off the alarm.

The Nonnies in question were two whip-thin Calabrian burglars, covered in tattoos, and the safe cracker: a six-foot-plus local guy in his fifties with sideburns, a black shirt open half-way down a hairy chest showing off a chunky gold cross, and an Elvis Presley quiff, who introduced himself as Sandro (the Calabrians hadn't said a word to me and spoke only in dialect among themselves). Sandro, on the other hand, was a typically sociable Bolognese, and seemed intent on providing a hushed commentary, hand resting laconically upon my shoulder, as the Calabrians went to work.

'First they'll do the lock . . . I mean, really, did you even see that? Any fool can break that. Ooh, on your marks.' The Calabrians, one crouched at either end of the garage door, lifted it almost soundlessly by around a metre and we slipped beneath, the door descending softly behind us.

A light came on – a halogen one of them had produced from their holdall.

'And here we are,' said Sandro. Here we were indeed – Mestre's white van dominated the garage, but the bay was still large enough for there to be plenty of room around it. Up some steps – the rear of the store. 'Now this will be a keener test,' said Sandro. As they examined the lock between them, one of the burglars glanced back at the pair of us and said something to his pal, who hissed. 'You know,' confided Sandro, 'I'm not sure they like me.'

'It's not a fucking soccer match,' said the one who had looked at us.

'My mistake,' Sandro said easily. '*Forza Crotone.*' As the burglar turned back, he whispered to me, 'Pressure.'

Squatting by the door, the first Calabrese requested a series of tools from the second, who passed them upwards. Sandro, meanwhile, ostentatiously inspected his watch – a Rolex submariner.

'*Pronti?*' the first asked the second. He nodded, and went to stand above him and took hold of the door handle.

'Here we go,' Sandro whispered. 'If it all turns to shit,' he nodded at the garage door, 'leg it.'

Gripping hold of some kind of drill with one hand, while pinching a tweezer-like instrument with the other, the first Calabrian pulled the trigger. There was a metallic grinding as he fiddled furiously with the tweezers. Suddenly, a shudder and a click, and the door opened. The second Neapolitan bounded around him into the room as the alarm began beeping furiously.

There was a shout: '*Cazzo!*'

Now the first sprang into the room. I followed on behind while Sandro headed in the other direction. He furiously gestured me to join him by the door, but I wanted to see what was wrong.

The bleeps were gaining urgency while the first Neapolitan was furiously trying to pick the closed box. So much for the old lady leaving it open.

'English!' Sandro stage whispered. The second Calabrian dug into the holdall and produced another box-like device, this like a car battery charger, and flicked a switch, which glowed red.

The bleeps were forming an almost constant whine.

'*Vai,*' said the second. The first was ready with a crowbar. The cover of the box flew off. He hastily punched in the keys. The sound stopped.

'*Ma, vafanculo!*' The first punched the air, the pair hugged. Crotone might have scored. I looked back at Sandro, who was straightening himself up from his position by the garage door. His black bushy eyebrows arched like a pair of caterpillars. He rubbed his long-fingered hands.

'All right, then,' he said. 'To work.'

The Calabrians regarded him haughtily as he unburdened himself of his hefty backpack and laid it open on the floor by the strong room, which was like a cage, with criss-crossed iron mesh and a hefty-looking metal door secured by a formidable-looking lock.

'Okay, u-hum, I see.' Sandro picked up a selection of shining metal tools that might have been designed for dental surgery on a hippo, and went to work.

I turned to the Calabrians. 'What happened with the cover? How did you stop the alarm?'

They turned their disdainful gazes upon me. 'Jammed the wireless,' said the second. 'Stopped the signal.'

'As simple as that?' The first made a contemptuous smirk.

'Yes, Englishman,' said the second. 'As simple as that, if you've got ten thousand to spend on a jammer.'

There was a clunk and a clatter. The lock seemed to have literally disintegrated in Sandro's hands. He opened the door. The Calabrians looked disappointed. 'Now,' he went inside, 'for the main course.'

The safe sat beneath a shelf filled with presentation boxes of various sizes and shapes. While Sandro set out his stuff beside it, I opened one – inside, an Iron Cross, the accompanying card read: Authenticated: presented to Oberfeldwebel Wilhem Streng of the Panzergrenadier Division Großdeutschland, 1943. I turned the card over. Est. 6000.

I looked down at Sandro on his knees, running his hands gently across the black metal safe as if it were a living thing.

'Well?' I said.

'Well, indeed,' said Sandro. 'Well, well, well . . .' The safe was about as high as he was on his knees, around half as wide and half as deep. In other words, it was a big bugger, with an old-style circular combination lock set square in the centre of the door.

'I haven't seen one of these in years,' he said. 'He probably bought it from a jeweller's. Too small for a bank, too big for a lawyer's.' He looked up at me. 'If I had a little time, I could crack the combination but . . .' He took in the scene. 'While I could put the lock back together, our flush is busted with that broken alarm case.' One of the Calabrians made a gesture I didn't recognise but could easily interpret. 'And as much as I respect this beauty, I'm not going to put my liberty on the line for her. No.' He picked up a drill. 'We'll go nasty.'

I stood back as he went in, goggles on, sparks flying. Even with some special kind of cushion wrapped around the wheel of the drill, it made a hell of a noise. I looked at the Calabrians who stared blankly back at me. Apart from the fact that they had all their stuff packed up and were clearly ready to run, they seemed relaxed, and ice-cool. I thought about what the Comandante had said, and realised he was right – once the old people had gone to the great penitentiary in the sky, there would be no doing business with these people. Sandro, on the other hand, seemed all right. I would have to remember to get his contact details. I would also, I thought, have to get our security systems overhauled. The ease with which we had gained entry to Libreria Mestre, from the front gates to the locks, had shattered my illusions we were in any way secure at home.

'There.' Sandro withdrew the drill in a cascade of metal filings. 'I'm sorry, darling, but it had to be done.' The door opened with the whiff of hot metal. He peered inside, rocked back. 'See what you're looking for?'

More presentation cases stacked the shelves. Some files. A Luger in an open box, accompanying it, a box of bullets.

Filling the bottom shelf – a black canvas bag. I pulled it out, opened it up: packed with flat grey boxes marked in black felt-tip: *Amore su una lama di rasoio.*

Chapter 36

I walked back along porticoes bathed night orange, the holdall slung over my shoulder. There could have been anything inside – my clothes, except the bulging shapes were clearly angular; books, then, except that few could carry that amount of books on their back. No, it was a cargo altogether more explosive, I thought, something that many had died for, and some might still.

I finally arrived in Via Solferino, the *Fondazione*, at the far end, when I laid the bag down. There was a bar still open on the corner, and instead of carrying on, I went there, ordered a beer and sat outside, the holdall at my feet.

Were we really just going to surrender these to the Faustos without knowing what they contained? Sure, we would have removed the gang's leverage – we could even begin to make it known through certain channels what had transpired and place them on the back foot. *But could we actually trust the Faustos?* The Comandante had his filing cabinet for a reason.

If information was power, I was about to surrender ours.

I finished my beer, swung the holdall back over my shoulder, and headed back the other way.

***

Keeping a wary eye on any light that might escape from beneath the old lady's door, it didn't take me long to open the lock using my pick set. Slitting the red and white police tape, I opened Gianni Colline's front door.

The apartment still had that mouldy stink but by now I was almost beginning to find its sheer familiarity strangely comforting.

I went into the bedroom, set the bag down, checked my phone.

A barrage of messages I didn't pay heed to except Rose: *Nonno told me you were out 'on a job'. Whatever it is, take care and let me know when it's over!*

Out safely, I replied, *Home soon.*

But not just yet. The time had come to finally understand what we were dealing with. I laid the holdall upon the slashed mattress and began to go through the boxes until I found the ones I was looking for.

I unboxed the negatives and slotted them into the canisters on either side of the viewfinder. It took a while of fiddling with the mechanism to thread them through, but finally everything appeared ready to go. Pulling up a stool to the viewfinder, I flicked the switch.

The private eye was sitting at an outside bar table, an empty cup of coffee in front of him, smoking. A ray of sun bleached his skin, he put on a pair of sunglasses. The door of the *palazzo* opened and Ursula emerged with a pair of suitcases. CUT to the snoop. He stubbed his cigarette, began to rise as a cab pulled up at the kerbside and the driver got out. INTERIOR, CAB Against the clearly projected backdrop of the car travelling through Bologna's porticoed streets, Franco, or George Malouf, passionately kissed Ursula while the driver eyed them in the rear-view mirror. CLOSE UP The pair had parted, but their faces were in profile.

'In the end, I didn't think you would,' the voice of George Malouf dubbed in Italian.

'In the end,' said Ursula, presumably in her own dubbed voice, 'nor did I. But then, I did.'

'Franco' kissed her again as the back-projected streets of eighties Bologna zipped by.

EXTERIOR Bologna Marconi Airport, the low-rise red-brick terminal building, not looking so very different from today. A sunny, busy afternoon. CUT to the couple getting out of the cab at Departures while the driver opened the boot to lift out their luggage. They went inside. WHITE. The rattle of the spools running out.

I dug out another pair, my hands trembling with the tension, and a dreadful sickening feeling – was I about to watch Toni Fausto's ending and *still* not understand?

INTERIOR, PI's car. The PI was in the driving seat, Vittorio – Ron Manchester – sat pale beside him with the eclipse of a blackened eye, and a plaster beside his ear. They were stuck in traffic.

'Dammit.' Ron Manchester, dubbed in Italian, smashed the dashboard with his palm. The PI, visibly sweating, hammered the horn. CUT to the airport, where Ursula and Franco were checking in. They were given their tickets and we followed them, Ursula glancing a little plaintively back toward the entrance, as Franco led her towards the gates. EXTERIOR Marconi. The PI's car pulled up at departures. Ron

Manchester got out, dashed inside. INTERIOR Departure Gate. George Malouf and Vanessa Tramonte sat somewhat stiffly side by side, hand-in-hand. CUT to Ron Manchester arguing with a uniformed official. Finally, he pushed past, the official hurrying after him. CUT to George Malouf and Vanessa Tramonte at the gate. Ursula's last, wistful look over her shoulder turning to shock as she saw Vittorio approaching. She froze. Now Franco saw his brother and tried to move her on. CLOSE UP of Ron Manchester, the official's hand on his shoulder. CLOSE UP of Vanessa Tramonte. Manchester, dubbed in Italian, spoke, but it was not to Vanessa.

'Brother,' he said.

CLOSE UP of George Malouf, who began to reply, but it was not his dubbed voice we hear, but Alberto Fausto.

'You pig.'

'Brother,' said an unfamiliar voice.

'What kind of monster are you?'

'Really, Alberto, are you drunk? What are you talking about?'

'You always were an animal. I told Mother, but she wouldn't listen, you were always her little boy.'

'Now what the hell is this? Can't you see I'm busy? If you want to break my balls again about being Mamma's favourite, then can't it wait until a family reunion? That's the usual style, no?'

'Isabella.'

SILENCE. Meanwhile, the dialogue in the film had ended, Ron Manchester was watching the couple disappear along the departure gate. Slowly, ever so slowly, the frame drew back to show us the flight: ITAVIA 870. Destination: Ustica.

'No, *come on*, Alberto. *No.* You've got this all wrong, it was nothing! It never happened . . . Look, Alberto, *look.* All right – I didn't want to say, but it was *her*, okay? The silly little bitch wouldn't leave me alone.'

A gunshot. Another.

EXTERIOR: the couple climbed the stairs to the plane. INTERIOR: Ron Manchester watched them from the lounge.

The screen went white. This ending had never been credited.

'Was it worth it, Englishman?' I looked around. Sergeant Davide Greco stood by the mattress, holding a silenced pistol. I glanced toward the doorway but knew I didn't stand a chance.

'I guessed you wouldn't be able to resist. Can't say I blame you. Quite the climax, eh?'

'From what I can make out,' I said, my mouth dry, 'there was no secret at all. About Ustica, I mean.'

'Apart from that commie director's snivelling "comment" at the airport, you mean? Oh no, not at all. It was all a little more personal than that, as you have seen.'

'Alberto killed his brother for . . . sleeping with someone?' Greco nodded. 'Who is this "Isabella"?'

'Oh,' Greco shrugged. 'Family.'

'*Nothing to do with Ustica.*'

'Well,' Greco shrugged, 'I wouldn't entirely say that – it is, after all, the reason we got involved. If it hadn't been for the clean-up all those years ago, well . . .'

'People keep calling it a "clean-up". Like ethnic cleansing, it's a sanitised word for murder.'

He shrugged. 'Call it what you like.'

'So it continued to exist, then. After Ustica, this group.'

'Why would it go away? But I wouldn't call it a group, exactly. I mean, we don't get a cap badge! Let's just say individuals within various ... organisations have historically been ready to ... take certain measures in the interests of the nation, at various times, for various reasons. Trusted men, you might say. Not all in the military. A sort of informal patriotic network, with deep roots.'

'That go back as far as this General Mestre.'

'Further, almost certainly, into the mists of time! Old ties, connections, a common purpose.'

'Which Alberto Fausto and Ettore Mestre shared.'

'Apparently.'

'And when Alberto murdered his brother, the first people he called were . . .'

'He scratched our back, we scratched his,' said Greco. 'Now, flash forward thirty years. There's a damsel in distress . . .'

'Elettra Fausto.'

'Who doesn't want poor *nonno* to go to gaol. Who can she rely on?'

'You.'

'That's it. Only, you know what?' He shook his head. 'It's actually not like the old days.'

'It's the twenty-first century,' I said dryly.

'Something like that.'

'You mean your "patriotic network" is not what it was?'

'Is anything what it was, Englishman? Mestre's fucked – I mean, there's not much money in old books and Nazi nostalgia.'

'He seemed to be doing all right to me.'

'Not enough to stop the building from crumbling down around his ears, apparently. And as for the rest of us foot soldiers, what future do we have? Shitty pensions. Crappy holidays. Nothing to pass onto the kids, grandkids. Meanwhile, well, *they've* got it all – we thought we were serving the interests of the state, it turns out that we were actually only serving them.'

'So you wanted to take what was owed.'

'That's about it. Anyway.' He levelled the gun at my belly. 'Enough chitchat. Pack up this stuff.'

I did as I was told, desperately searching for a way out. Was there anything I could say, do, that was going to save me?

'You killed the kids because that was part of the plan,' I said. He gestured for me to continue. 'Your buddy because he would give the game away.' Nothing. 'And the Volpatos?'

'Ah.' This seemed to spark his interest. 'You mean that couple in Venice? I read about them.' He waggled the long gun from side to side. 'We had nothing to do with that.'

'Come on, I saw the Carabiniere with that killer tattoo of yours.'

'Be that as it may – no. Actually, I wondered about them myself. My guess is it's down to you.'

'*Me?* How?'

'All your questions. The guy stole from his own archive for a pay-off. Figured he'd been found out. Offed himself out of the shame. It happens, you know.'

I thought of the old lady smothered in her bed. The way Volpato had died. Yes, from shame – with a suitably sardonic touch.

I realised I had run out of words.

I packed the bag and held it out.

'Place it on the floor. Step back.' He crouched to pick it up. 'Well,' he said, as if we were parting at a railway station, 'I'll be off, then.'

He smiled, rather cruelly. He knew precisely what I was expecting.

'Now you know how things stand,' he said. 'I've decided you'll be more useful alive: you can make this work for us, and the Faustos. They will deliver the cash tomorrow, and you will be there to make sure it goes without a hitch. Alternatively, you can spend the remainder of your short life looking over your shoulder.'

I nodded.

He began to back out. 'Cheer up, pal. You've been granted a second chance. Don't blow it.'

Chapter 37

I didn't leave straight away. I went to sit back on the stool, stare sightlessly at the Moviola. I'd thought I'd had it. I might still have: my bet was this was less a reprieve than a stay of execution.

Still, the Comandante had been right – we and the Faustos may have fallen foul of the Ustica network but, as Greco himself had confirmed, this operation was rogue. It had nothing to do with the shady figures in the government and security apparatus – our problem was solely the sergeant and what remained of his gang.

I let out a long, long breath.

My phone buzzed a call: ANNA BLOOM. I wasn't precisely sure what I had been thinking about myself and Anna, but whatever it was, it now seemed as distant as watching her on the big screen or reading about her in the news. I let it ring out. Instead, I called the Comandante.

'Daniel?'

'It's me.'

'I tried to call.'

'I wanted to do something first.'

'Daniel – are you all right? Are you hurt?'
'No, all in one piece.'
'But something has happened – tell me.'
I told him.
'Come home,' he said. 'We need to talk.'

Everyone had left – Jacopo across the landing to his own apartment, the Comandante below, to his. I stepped onto the terrace. The automatic gates, whose vulnerabilities were earlier the main thing on my mind, closed behind Dolores, pedalling off into the darkness. Thankfully, Rose had long since gone to bed by the time I had arrived home, and in any case, I suspected my message would have sufficed. She had a head full of her own things – she only required the basics from me.

There was a glow from the laptops of the Carabinieri in the workshops below, while across the courtyard the rather relentless, but reassuringly spirited, wailing of the baby whose name now hardly seemed to matter, was keeping at least one parent awake.

The streets were empty, porticoes quiet. Bologna had hunkered down, dreaming sweet and foul – there was no lack of incident in her long history. And tomorrow I would add to it.

I went back inside, pressed my ear to my daughter's bedroom door. I could hear nothing. I moved on.

Chapter 38

There was an uncommon breeze the next morning, one of the few weather phenomena one did not often encounter in Bologna, 'inside the walls', at any rate. But then I was waiting outside, on the forecourt of the petrol station where the walls would have once stood, while the traffic whizzed around the four-lane Viale, sweat dripping down my flanks as a result of the ballistic vest strapped beneath my black jumper and brown sports jacket.

A grey Audi limousine with tinted glass windows pulled up. The front passenger door opened. The Faustos. I ducked my head in – there was Alberto, and Elettra, in black jeans and a matching jacket, a baseball cap on her head with her hair tied back *alla* Anna Bloom.

I got in. 'The cash?'

'In the boot,' replied Alberto. I checked out the driver – an elderly guy in a suit and tie.

'Our usual chauffeur,' said Alberto. 'They warned us – no surprises.'

'I'm sure they did.'

The car pulled out and we began to glide along the Viale.

The instructions were simple – keep going until Alberto received a message on his phone, which he had set upon the armrest between himself and his granddaughter.

'How are you doing?' I asked her.

She looked grave. 'How do you think?'

'But do you think you'll be able to go through with it?'

Now she looked offended. 'Of course! A relief to get these pieces of shit off our backs once and for all.'

'You settled on five million, right? But won't Mestre be expecting something in return?'

Elettra gave an impatient shake of the head. 'Don't worry about Paolo. I'll deal with him.' She looked out the window, clenching and unclenching her fists.

I glanced again at the driver, then turned to Alberto. 'He . . .'

'Roderico has been with me since the beginning.'

'So – Isabella?'

Alberto's face turned a paler shade of stone.

'My mother,' said Elettra, not looking away from the window. 'The fucker raped my mother.' She reached out and squeezed Alberto's hand. 'His daughter-in-law.'

The limo ate up the Viale, glided between sets of traffic lights. Pulled up to shuffle forward in the inevitable queues.

Without looking at my phone to check the dates, I made a crude calculation. As we accelerated from another set of lights, I said: 'So . . .'

'Yes,' Elettra said coldly. 'I am.'

We had circled the old city for another thirty minutes when the message finally arrived. Before Alberto reached the phone, Elettra had picked it up and was showing it to Roderico.

'But it's just here.' He braked, swung the limo over to the side. I looked around – a Vesper swerved around us, then zipped in front. We followed it into a small parking bay beside some traffic lights.

'This is it?' I asked.

'That's what it says, signore.'

In front of us, the rider had got off and given a thumbs up, although his visor remained down. It was an unlikely place for a handover, I thought – by the ruins of one of the city gates, with traffic streaming around the roundabout before continuing along the Viale or heading north along a major road out of the city. *Va be'* – in a sense, I found the normality reassuring.

Elettra and I got out. The others had been instructed to stay inside the car.

The boot popped open. Inside, a pair of silver metal brief-cases. I took them out. They were certainly hefty, but it didn't feel like five mil. Elettra apparently read my mind: 'It's all there,' she said. 'Five hundred euro notes. They don't make them anymore but, lucky us, they're still legal tender.'

'Lucky us.'

We went around the front of the limo where the guy stood. He gestured us to follow him toward a green iron gate set in an old red-brick wall. He undid the padlock and stepped aside to let us in.

Then it became clear.

Chapter 39

Because apart from its porticoes and food, its cars and computing and packaging, Bologna has always been an armed camp. Positioned as it is in the centre of the industrial north, the city has been Italy's railway hub and the main base for its military ever since the railway network had figured in any general's plan of attack.

It should have come as no surprise Greco would choose one of these places for the handover – barracks were dotted along the Viale, precisely so the army could get to those railways. Only most of them were now abandoned. After Italy had dispensed with military service, the facilities had been mostly left to rot. Anywhere else they would have been sold off, maybe converted into much-needed housing, but – this was Italy.

So there we were, barbed-wire crested wall to our backs, looking at a deserted military base, still in surprisingly good nick despite the grass sprouting through the tarmac of the road that we began to walk down behind our helmeted chum, passing between deserted brick buildings with mostly unbroken windows. My previous sense of relief had now dissipated.

Despite being almost literally a stone's throw from ordinary
life – we could still hear the traffic churning beyond the walls
– I felt queasy. We might as well have been on the Moon. We
were certainly on Sergeant Greco's turf.

The place was all squares and rectangles – the vast,
grass-pitted space of the parade ground, row upon row of
single-storey residential and office blocks. Ahead, the single
building that looked as if it pre-dated 1960 – a kind of
military monolith crossing the T of the entire site, a portico
running its length, squared columns and arches supporting
three storeys of regimented, rectangular windows.

That portico was interrupted at the main entrance, set
in the centre like an open robot mouth. Parked in front – a
navy-blue SUV I recognised as Greco's, although I noted the
number plate had been changed.

The double doors were jammed open. We followed the
man into a dim, fusty-smelling entrance. Dingy stone staircases swept upwards on either side, while matching lifts
were sealed off with hazard tape. But we continued onward,
through another set of double doors, where things brightened
up.

In fact, we were back outside, or at least that was how it felt
– a vast, roofless space that may have once been an auditorium
but appeared to have become a receptacle for dumped office
equipment, while three storeys above, great, rust-coloured
iron girders criss-crossed the cloud-patched sky.

'They sold the roof.' It was Greco, sitting upon the side
of what appeared to have once been a filing cabinet but had
been swallowed up by the weeds and creepers that had taken
over this place. 'Or maybe someone took it, who knows.' He

nodded amiably at Elettra – 'Hello again, princess' – before levelling the machine gun I'd seen him with in the woods at me.

Paolo Mestre, who had risen from his own perch as we entered, approached us looking at once terrified and love struck.

'Elettra.' He stood before her but kept his arms pinned to his sides. She gave him the merest of smiles and didn't move an inch.

'Over there.' Greco gestured to me with the gun.

I carried the cases to a folding table that appeared to have been brought especially for the occasion, and set them down. 'Step back. Aldo.' The motorcyclist came up behind me and forced my arms upwards to frisk me.

'He's wearing a vest,' he said. Greco nodded at me with, perhaps, what may have been a little respect.

'Over there.' He gestured to a desk turned upon its side hung with ivy. 'Aldo' produced a gun and prodded it in my back. When I reached the desk, I turned around to face him and was somehow dismayed to see he had lifted his visor. It did not, apparently, matter if I was able to identify him. Beyond the barrel of the gun, which demands the attention of anyone being held at the wrong end of one, I saw disinterested blue eyes.

The click of latches. Even from ten or so metres away – the metallic whiff of five million euros. Greco, machine gun slung over his shoulder, checked the contents as Paolo and Elettra looked on.

'Well,' Greco said finally, failing to keep an edge of relief from his voice, 'it's all there.'

'Of course it is,' Elettra said flatly.

'Letti.' Paolo could no longer restrain himself. He took her, limply, in his large arms. 'I promise you, you won't regret this.'

'The negatives, Paolo,' I heard her say.

'Of course!' He let her go and walked over to the upturned cabinet from behind which he produced the canvas bag. He brought it over to her. 'We could keep them if you like – just you and I.' She took the bag and crouched to go through it. He squatted opposite. 'I mean, now we have them, we don't actually have to destroy them, we could keep them in the family, now they're safe . . .'

Had it been anyone else, Paolo Mestre might have instinctively raised an arm in his defence, but precisely because it was Elettra Fausto, the love of his life, apparently reaching out to embrace him over that great bridge of time, he welcomed her with open arms, of course he did.

Blood drove down the blade, flowed over Elettra's fingers.

Mestre's eyes bulged, hands flapped around her arm as she dug the dagger deep into his neck.

Raising her other hand to close around the quivering handle, with an effortful grunt she drew the knife sideways.

It was only now Sergeant Greco, busy admiring the money, took notice – the eruption of blood may have splashed his cash.

He unharnessed the machine gun, swinging it toward the pair. He pulled the trigger. The bolt snapped but nothing happened.

'*Fuck.*'

Aldo looked around. I was about to go for his gun, but wasn't quick enough: '*Shoot him,*' Greco shouted.

I lurched sideways as he pulled the trigger.

The shot holed the desk, but before he could get off another, a shot ripped through the air and his helmet exploded.

Aldo staggered backwards, a third of his helmet gone in a smoking mash of carbon, plastic and brain. He dropped the gun and fell flat on his back.

I scrambled toward him, grabbed the pistol, but Greco was already making for the exit. As he ran, there was another deafening shot and a clump of creeper, that may have once been a chair, disintegrated in his wake.

I picked myself up and went after him, pushing through the swing doors into the reception. He was already outside, digging into his pocket in front of the SUV, the useless machine gun flung to the ground, a silver briefcase set upon the car roof.

'Stop.'

He hesitated for a moment, but then carried on, as if in slow motion, without looking around. He finally produced his key fob and clicked. There was a clunk as the doors unlocked.

'What I'm going to do, Englishman,' he reached for the handle, 'is get in the car.' He began to open the door. 'Take my money.' He lifted the case off the roof. 'Well, part of it, anyway.' He flung it inside. 'And get out of your life. Don't worry – you won't see me again.'

'Stop.'

He didn't stop.

I pulled the trigger.

Greco sank to his knees, still holding onto the open door.

He let go, flopped forward, face down onto the driver's seat.

***

Sergeant Davide Greco remained like that, as did I, gun pointed at his inert body, until the *Ispettore* arrived, rifle slung over his shoulder.

He went over to the car and checked Greco, shook his head and came to me.

'He won't be any more trouble.' The *Ispettore* gently eased the gun from my grip. 'Shall we see how the lady is getting along?'

He led me back into the auditorium.

Elettra Fausto knelt trembling beside the corpse of her childhood friend.

Discarded nearby, sauced with gore – a double-edged dagger with a silver swastika embossed upon its ebony handle.

Chapter 40

Dolores came to pick me up and was canny enough to keep quiet. The Comandante and Jacopo were waiting in the courtyard when we pulled in and, sure, we embraced long and hard, but again with barely a word.

I went upstairs to the apartment. Rose was nowhere to be seen, her bedroom door open as it had been that morning – she had left before I got up so I had never had a chance to kiss her goodbye. Perhaps that hadn't been a bad thing.

I closed the bathroom door, stripped and loaded my cordite- and blood-stinking clothes into the washing machine.

I stepped into the shower, standing with my hands flat against the tiles as the water washed over me. Slid down into a squat to finally sit with my back against the wall and my knees pressed against my chest.

Stayed like that until finally, after many, many gallons, even the boiler said *basta* and the water ran cold.

Chapter 41

'Oh, hey, Dan.' Dino's paddle hand engulfed mine. The flash of that spade tattoo beneath his sleeve line.

I surveyed the film set – the usual chaos. 'Have you seen Rose?'

He frowned. 'I think so, at the refreshments trailer earlier. Can I buy you a coffee?'

'That's kind, but I'm in a bit of a hurry. I'd just like a word with my daughter.'

'Sure, boss. No problem. I'll take you over.'

I followed Dino through the alleyways of trailers. Truth be told, I also hoped to apologise to Anna for ignoring her calls, as she was now apparently ignoring mine.

Dino left me at the door to Anna's trailer. I knocked. No answer. As I tried again, the door fell open.

'Hello?' I peered in.

Rose was on her knees among half packed tubs.

'What's going on?'

She burst into tears.

'She's gone, Dad. She's left.'

'What?'

'Apparently there was this part in a western and they needed her immediately. There was a clause in her contract or something . . . whatever, anyway, she's gone. Indigo says most of the location stuff was done in any case and he only needed her for the scenes in the US.'

'Just like that?'

'Oh, Dad.'

I held her. 'Gone,' she said into my shoulder. 'Just like Stella. They've both gone, while I'm stuck here.'

'There, there.' I stroked her head. 'You'll be gone soon, too.'

'Not soon enough.'

'It'll always be too soon for me.'

'Oh, Dad,' Rose sat back, wiped her eyes. 'You know I don't mean *you*, don't you?'

I laughed. 'Oh, I know.' She got up and grabbed some tissues.

'Hey,' she said, blowing her nose. 'News – Alba's daughter finally has a name.'

'So, she's finally decided on Daniela?'

'No,' said Rose, suddenly serious. 'She calling her Lucia, after Mum.'

Chapter 42

INTERIOR cab. Ursula, played by Anna Bloom, slams the door. She takes the face of her lover, Franco, played by Italian actor Riccardo Lenzi, in her hands and the pair indulge in a full-tongued kiss, the driver glancing at them in the rear-view mirror as he sets off through the back-projected streets of Boston in a clear homage to the style of Toni Fausto, who was in turn copying the playful artifice of Alfred Hitchcock.

Franco pulls back: 'You're sure about this?'

'I've never been so sure about anything in my life,' says Ursula.

CUT to a spacious office in the business district. Guiseppe, played by another Italian legend, Ghigo Ercolani, takes the call. He looks out over the city as the private eye reports back. It is only now his fear is confirmed – that his American wife is having an affair – and not with his handsome young assistant as he suspected, but his own brother, who had arrived a week ago ostensibly to see how they were settling in.

Ercolani is a master at conveying emotion, and as he thanks the PI, it is the very stillness of his face that communicates his grief – the betrayal by a brother he has always indulged and who has repaid him by running off with his wife. He believed he and Ursula had resolved their differences the previous evening, which had ended with a round of passionate lovemaking, but no – she had fallen for the gaudy charm of his shallow sibling, and was simply buying time.

Vittorio presses the intercom.

'Call me a cab.'

INTERIOR airport. Again, Indigo Adler has switched the emphasis: Ursula is leading Franco through the terminal building, not the other way around. You have the sense that Franco knows this time he had gone too far – that he enjoyed the excitement of their summer fling but this is altogether too real for him. He is getting cold feet, but is equally too weak to pull out now. And Ursula? What of Ursula? Adler has given his Ursula more agency in keeping with the times, but he has refused to place her on a pedestal. Certainly, Vittorio is far from blameless – his withholding nature drove his wife into the arms of his brother – but Ursula is no saint. Adler respects the character too much for that: she is not, as she tells a friend, prepared to 'make do'. And it is this duty she feels to herself which detonates the relationship between the two flawed brothers or, as Anna Bloom pithily put it to me, invoking another philosopher: 'Hell is other people, hon.'

INTERIOR Departure gate. Flight 143 to Los Angeles is ready to board. Ursula and Franco rise with the rest to join the queue. CUT to Vittorio as he makes his way through the airport. CUT to the couple showing their tickets and stepping past the desk. Ursula spots Vittorio and hesitates. She moves on, but it is enough to alert Franco, who stops, stands staring at his brother as his brother stares at him.

Finally, Vittorio gives the smallest nod. Franco, tears flowing freely, returns the acknowledgement, then follows Ursula down the tunnel. EXTREME CLOSE UP: Vittorio watches them go. If it wasn't extreme, you perhaps wouldn't notice the subtlest crinkle at the corners of his mouth, the edges of his eyes.

Of a smile.

WIDE SHOT behind Vittorio as the gate empties, the United Airlines flight number and destination clearly visible on the departure board, but there is nothing significant about it that I can see. Adler has correctly judged an American audience would not stomach a reference to their own collective Ustica – 9/11. Instead, his twist is conveyed by the subtlest of expressions – the sense that only at that final moment does Vittorio realise he is not mourning the loss of an unfaithful wife, but celebrating liberty from a degenerate sibling.

I ask myself: did Elettra Fausto confess all to her husband? Picturing her sitting like a crow in a puddle of blood, I find it hard to believe. Instead, I think of Indigo Adler's steady gaze behind that puppyish smile – neither cuckold nor slavish fan, he saw altogether more than he was letting on.

The credits float upwards in white script as Vittorio stands there, the noise of the airport carrying on around him. Finally, there she is: Assistant to Ms Bloom, Bologna *Rose Maria Faidate*.

The CineBo lights came on.

'What did you think?' I asked Rose. She nodded, cleared her throat.

'Yeah,' she said. 'It was cool.'

Later that evening I wrote to Anna to let her know we had seen the movie and how good she was. Although I could see that she had opened my message, she didn't reply.

Author's Note

While the movie *Love on a Razorblade* and Toni Fausto are of course fictional, the controversy surrounding the fate of the Itavia Flight 870 is sadly all too true. As I was working on *Italian Rules* in June 2021, President of the Republic Sergio Mattarella marked the 41st anniversary of the incident with a call 'for a more complete reconstruction of the facts'.

President of the Chamber of Deputies Roberto Fico added: 'Some pieces are now acquired, and contribute to the definition of a judicial and historical truth. Each institution must now work to ensure that the other pieces emerge and are placed in the right order. Because . . . there has been deception, omissions, complicity and conspiracy, also on the part of some deviant sectors of the state apparatus.'

Museo per la Memoria di Ustica is in Via di Saliceto, 3/22, 40128, Bologna.